Bubble World

Bubble World

Carol Snow

Henry Holt and Company
New York

Henry Holt and Company, LLC
Publishers since 1866
175 Fifth Avenue
New York, New York 10010
macteenbooks.com

Henry Holt® is a registered trademark of Henry Holt and
Company, LLC.

Library of Congress Cataloging-in-Publication Data
Snow, Carol.
Bubble world / Carol Snow.—1st ed.
p.   cm.
Summary: After sixteen-year-old Freesia learns—and tells her friends—that
their perfect life on a luxurious tropical island is not real, she is banished
from her virtual world to the "mainland," where people are ugly,
school is hard, and families are dysfunctional.
ISBN 978-0-8050-9571-5 (hardcover)—ISBN 978-0-8050-9809-9 (e-book)
[1. Virtual reality—Fiction.   2. Interpersonal relations—Fiction.   3. Family
life—Fiction.   4. Science fiction.]   I. Title.
PZ7.S6807Bub 2013   [Fic]—dc23   2012028168

First Edition—2013 / Designed by Ashley Halsey
Printed in the United States of America

1 3 5 7 9 10 8 6 4 2

For the Snow cousins,

Tom and Bob Snow; Annie Zurheide;

and Meghan, Connor, Michael, and Kiley Sullivan—

you're all perfect just the way you are.

1

The signs were all there, but Freesia chose to ignore them. She didn't question the power surges. The electrical blackouts. The sudden departures that bordered on disappearances. Had she been paying attention, Freesia would have noticed that things on the island had fallen a little bit out of sync. No, more than a little bit: a lot a bit. Nothing so terrible that you'd cry malfunction, but still.

But Freesia never looked for, considered, or even noticed much of anything, good or bad, until she'd had her first cup of frothy coffee, and this morning, for the first time in her admittedly short memory, no coffee smells tickled her nose when she sat up among her fuzzy pink and orange pillows and stretched her toned, tanned arms toward the cloud mural overhead.

The missing coffee? Yes, it was a sign—the second on that day alone—that something in Freesia's world had gone very, very wrong.

The first sign had come a few minutes earlier, when the

two peacocks, Ashley and Jennifer (both of whom were boys), failed to wake Freesia with the latest Chase Bennett song. Instead they just kind of screeched and screamed, which would have flipped Freesia out if she hadn't been so utterly tired from staying so utterly late at Ricky Leisure's pool party. When Freesia was tired, she didn't flip out. She just got really, really cranky.

"Shut it!" she told Ashley and Jennifer as they began their second round of screeching.

Just like that, the peacocks changed their tune. Rather, they started their tune—Chase Bennett's latest, to be exact.

It's another day.
On the island we say, Hey,
Hey, oh. Hey, oh. Hey, oh.
Don't wanna see you frown,
Girl, turn it upside down.
Hey, oh. Yeah, turn it upside down.
Girl.
Hey.

Chase Bennett? Was an artistic genius.

Freesia shooed the peacocks back out to the balcony. The rising sun cast a pink glow on the glassy ocean that lay beyond the island's crystal sand. Graceful waterbirds dove for silver fish, and twenty kinds of flowers released their perfume into the still, cool morning air.

But Freesia didn't notice any of this, because it looked

perfect and pretty and peaceful like this every morning, and besides, *she still hadn't had her coffee.*

"Mummeeeeee!"

Freesia's mother appeared at the door, almost as if she'd been waiting. She looked mom-perfect, as always: nice and trim with shiny brown hair, shiny tanned skin, shiny pink nails. She looked a lot like Freesia, only older. And shinier.

"Sweetie?"

Freesia pointed to her white night table, empty except for her bubble, a solid silver ball cradled in a trumpet-shaped charger.

"Peacocks. Loud. Coffee. No coffee." The very effort of speaking exhausted her.

"Sweetie!" Just like that, Freesia's mother hurried out the door. Just like that, she returned, bearing Freesia's favorite chunky mug, filled to the brim with steaming, frothy coffee.

"It's Tracey's Famous Coffee!" she told Freesia. "Nothing like a coffee cloud to start your day the Tracey way!"

Freesia forced a smile. She adored her mother, but did she have to say the same thing every time she served coffee? And what about that coffee cloud business? It was frothy, sure, but a cloud?

"Would you like an omelet, oatmeal, or pancakes for brunch?" her mother asked.

"Pancakes."

"In here or in the kitchen?"

"Here."

"Should I stay, or should I go?"

"Go."

Her mother turned to leave.

"Wait."

Her mother turned back.

"I love you, mummy of mine."

"I love you too, sweet Freesia." Mummy's skin sparkled with affection.

Freesia blew a kiss. Her mother pretended to snatch it from the coffee-and-flower-scented air and slip it into the pocket of her peach satin robe before heading downstairs to make breakfast.

Alone now (except for the peacocks), Freesia took her coffee, her silver bubble, and a plush pink blanket out to the balcony, where she settled onto a pillowy lounge. Ashley watched her from the corner while Jennifer jumped on the railing and fanned out his magnificent tail.

Freesia's house looked like a fancy cake built into a hillside full of other fancy-cake houses. In the half-moon harbor below, kayakers dipped paddles into glassy water, navigating around quiet white boats and lolling blue buoys.

When she'd gulped enough coffee to clear her cloudy head, Freesia settled her chunky mug on a glass side table and cupped her bubble, which was now a tangerine-sized silver ball, in both of her hands. Soon, the bubble began to emit a greenish light, and her hands grew warm. As she drew her hands apart, the bubble grew larger, first to the size of an orange, then a grapefruit, then . . . something larger than a citrus fruit. Like a honeydew melon, maybe. Deciding that honeydew-melon-sized was perfect, Freesia balanced the silver bubble on her knees and reached for her mug.

"Enemy check," she commanded, sipping her cooling brew.

The bubble's green light changed to blue. Soon names emerged on the screen, followed by messages.

CHAI COTILLION . . . NOT TRANSMITTING

TASER LUCAS . . . NOT TRANSMITTING

DARE FIESTA . . . NOT TRANSMITTING

Dash it. Freesia only had three enemies, and as many times as she had tried to catch them at weak or ugly moments, they only used their public bubble settings when they were being especially luminous or triumphant.

"Fine. Friendlies check, then."

A long list of names appeared on the orb. Freesia tapped the edge of her pink-polished fingernail onto **RICKY LEISURE**. Just like that, Ricky, curled up in a yellow blow-up raft and still wearing his swim trunks from last night's pool party, came into focus. The raft was out of the water, lying in a patch of sun near the pool cave entrance, just down from the steps that led up to one of two waterslides.

"Ricky? Ricky, wake up!"

After a few more *Rickys*, he lifted his head up and rubbed sleep out of his eyes. If Ricky had any enemies, they might enjoy seeing his blue eyes all puffy, his golden hair sticking up at strange angles. But everyone liked Ricky, and besides, even at his worst, he looked utterly de-vicious.

Ricky groped around the raft until he found his own bubble, which he didn't bother enlarging from its original size. Now Freesia could choose between two views: the panoramic she'd started with or face-to-face. Ricky wasn't wearing a shirt. She chose panoramic.

"Freesia! Where is everybody?"

Freesia laughed. "Party's over, Ricardo."

"What time?"

"Dunno. I left around two, but a few people were still there. Cabo, Ferdinand . . . Chai."

She checked Ricky's face for a reaction to Chai's name. Nothing. If Ricky and Chai ever linked, she'd just—ugh.

Not that Freesia wanted to link with Ricky herself or anything. She liked him too much. And everyone knew that if you linked with someone and it didn't work out—it never worked out—you wound up on their enemy list, whether you found each other noxious or not. After Jelissa Moon, Ricky was her best friend. Freesia couldn't risk losing him.

"You going to cultural immersion?" Freesia asked.

"Dunno. What's the language today?"

"Korean."

"Too hard. And I don't like kimchee."

"Well, you better come tomorrow for Spanglish. We can share nachos."

A maid in a white uniform, one of Ricky's many serfs, appeared at the edge of Freesia's bubble and handed Ricky a glass of pale green liquid.

"Kiwi mocktail?" Freesia asked.

Ricky shook his head. "Happy juice. If you come over, I'll share."

Freesia laughed. "I had enough happy juice last night. And anyway, some of us get into trouble if we miss class."

Freesia's parents added shells to her personal bubble account every time she went to class. If she skipped, she got shells taken out. Freesia needed shells for clothes, coffees, conch burgers—everything, really. For her, more shells equaled more fun: simple. But Ricky was lucky. His parents lived on the mainland and kept his account full no matter what he did or didn't do.

"Bubble me later?" Freesia said.

"Come see me," Ricky said. "After class. I'll be dressed by then."

"Don't get dressed for me." Just because they were just friendlies didn't mean Freesia couldn't appreciate his sinewy brown arms and his rippled abdomen. Ricky rarely did anything but lounge around drinking happy juice, yet he was all muscle.

She said, "After immersion, I'm going shopping with Jelissa. I want something new for the dance. And then I've got music class."

"What's the dance theme this week?" Ricky asked. Every Saturday night, there was a dance in the Rotunda's grand ballroom. Students from the Advanced Event Planning class chose the theme and dress code, plus they took care of the decorations, the music, and the food.

"Sweet Seventeen. The girls are to wear girlie dresses. The boys have to dress all in white or all in black."

"Come over tonight, then," Ricky said. "I'll throw another party."

"All righty." Freesia blew Ricky a kiss and then tapped her bubble three times. Immediately, it turned back to silver and shrank to its original size.

Another party at Ricky's house. That was something fun to look forward to. Freesia liked looking forward to things.

● ● ●

With only two and a half hours to get ready for her one o'clock cultural immersion class, Freesia finished her coffee and ate her pancakes, which her mother had wheeled in on a white-cloth-covered table. Then it was time to pick out clothes.

Freesia's closet was a giant square room with a skylight, a pink chenille love seat, and a gold mini fridge filled with sips and nibbles. Along the walls, racks and shelves held jeans (skinny, loose, cropped, flared), dresses (frilly, slinky, tight, lacy), tops (blouses, tees, tanks), sweaters (long, cropped, silky, chunky), purses (huge, tiny), and shoes. Lots and lots of shoes. Wheeled ladders helped her reach the higher shelves, where she kept her costumes and holiday clothes. At the closet's far end, a floor-to-ceiling mirror offered lighting options for daytime, evening, or disco.

Freesia tossed her bubble onto the love seat, retrieved a lemon sipper from the mini fridge, and surveyed her options. Skinny jeans with a billowy blue blouse? No. Orange sundress with tan wedge heels? No. White miniskirt with . . . anything? No, no, no.

"I have nothing to wear," Freesia said out loud. And then she laughed, because of course she could go a year without repeating an ensemble.

She retrieved her bubble from the love seat. As soon as she touched the silver orb, it turned green. She held it in her palm and pointed toward the mirror.

"Attire assistance," she commanded.

The mirror went dark, and then it lit with a lifelike reflection of Freesia wearing thigh-high boots and a black tube dress she'd forgotten she owned. Cute, but . . . not quite.

"Daytime," she told the mirror.

Black tights and flats replaced bare legs and boots. A hot-pink cardigan went over the dress. Better. But not exactly what she had in mind.

"Another," she said. The mirror went dark and then she was back, the lifelike image of Freesia, this time in faded jeans, strappy tan sandals, and a short-sleeved floral blouse.

"Better," she said. "But another."

Again the mirror went dark for an instant before projecting another outfit. This was going to be the one. Freesia could feel it.

What? No! The Freesia in the mirror wore a floor-length, one-shouldered gold-sequined gown that she'd bought for . . . she couldn't even remember. A Sweet Fifteen, maybe. She'd never really liked it, and anyway, she'd said daytime, not evening, not formal, not dance.

"Daytime!" she told the mirror.

In the instant before the picture changed, Freesia realized something awful. The girl in the mirror, the one in the gold gown, wasn't her. She'd been so distracted by the outfit's inappropriateness that she hadn't even noticed, especially since the girl looked a little bit like her. Only the girl was shorter. Fatter. With frizzy dun hair, bushy eyebrows, and bumpy skin.

Freesia had never seen someone so ugly.

Why did she look so familiar?

And then she was gone.

The next outfit was up: knee-length jean shorts, a white eyelet shirt, long coral beads, tan espadrilles. Perfect. It was perfect!

Okay, truth: it wasn't perfect. But it was good enough. And this time the girl in the mirror was Freesia, no doubt about it. There were her long limbs, her flat tummy, her gentle curves. Her thick hair, brown with a touch of copper, shone under the skylight. Dense black lashes rimmed enormous green eyes. No bumps marred her flawless skin, which was creamy beige with a touch of pink. If Freesia were able to choose her appearance, she'd look precisely the way she did.

Hands shaking, Freesia busied herself retrieving the knee-length shorts, the eyelet blouse. She couldn't find the coral necklace, so she chose a turquoise one instead.

Who was that girl?

A bubble upgrade. That's all it was. Every once in a while, the bubbles got funny while improvements were being loaded. Usually they just ran a little slow. Or maybe the picture flickered. Nothing like this. But that didn't mean it was anything to wonder or worry about.

Freesia didn't like to worry—she wasn't real big on wondering, either—which is why she didn't realize that, yes, the mirror's error was yet another sign that something in her world had gone very, very wrong.

But who had time to think about signs! Freesia had only an hour and forty-five minutes to get ready for immersion. Here's how it broke down:

Shower and steam room: 35 minutes

After her palatial closet and ocean-view balcony, the shower and steam room was Freesia's favorite thing about her suite. The entire room was tiled in blue and green glass. Two showerheads meant she could be drenched on both sides at once. And the sound system? Was wicked: all Chase Bennett, all the time. She could have listened to someone else if she wanted to, but why would she?

Clothes: 12 minutes

She'd already chosen her outfit, of course—or, rather, her bubble had chosen it for her. But after all that steamy shower time, it took a while for her to dry off, moisturize, and get dressed.

Hair: 23 minutes

For special occasions, she called in a stylist, but for a day of class and shopping, she curled or straightened her thick, coppery locks herself. Today she curled her hair. Quite nicely. And then she sprayed it with a custom spritz scented with—what else?—freesia.

Makeup: 19 minutes

Twenty minutes would have been better, but she was on a schedule. Gloss, bronzer, eyeliner, mascara . . . she looked de-vicious.

Accessory check: 8 minutes

Since she'd already decided that her necklace was fine, she used the extra time to see if any of her enemies were transmitting from their bubbles. Bingo. Chai Cotillion, wearing too much makeup as usual, was already on her way to immersion class . . . and wearing a purple-and-black leopard-print minidress!

What was Chai thinking?

The dress was hideosity itself.

It was going to be a good day.

Outfit registry: 2 minutes

Freesia returned to her closet and once again pointed her bubble in the direction of the mirror. "Outfit registry," she commanded. The bubble flashed. Her picture would be automatically filed by time and date, and the bubble would alert her if she inadvertently repeated an outfit within a time frame of her choosing (currently four months, though she was thinking of upping it to six).

Gathering of supplies: 4 minutes

She pulled her soft tan bag off a hook outside the closet and filled it with her bubble, a brush, two tubes of lip gloss, and sunglasses.

Plan check with Jelissa: 1 minute, 35 seconds

"We still on for shopping after immersion?"

"Of course!"

"Dresses?"

"And shoes!"

"I just saw Chai on the bubble."

"Me too."

"Her dress . . ."

"Hideosity!"

"Love you oodles!"

"Love you more!"

Bond with family: 25 seconds

"Good-bye, Mummy and Daddy. I'll be home late."

"Have fun, sweetie. We'll make sure your room is clean and your mini fridge is full!"

"You look beautiful, as always," her little sister, Angel, told her. "When I get older, I want to be just like you!"

"Love you all!" Freesia blew a kiss, and then she was out the door and on her way to class.

$\mathcal{2}$

The Summers family—Freesia, Angel, and their parents—lived on the island of Agalinas, a hidden Pacific paradise somewhere off the coast of California. Northern California or Southern? Freesia didn't know. Or care. Geography was boring. Not as borrifying as world history or classic literature, but still pretty dull.

Freesia had been on the island for as long as she could remember, and the one time she'd asked her parents if they could visit the mainland, they said, "There's no reason to go there. It's nicer here."

It would be almost impossible to reach the mainland, anyway. Barges brought island residents everything they needed—food, happy juice, clothing, surfboards, building supplies, makeup, and jewels—but there was no passenger ferry or airport.

No matter. Her parents were right. Why would anyone want to leave? The island's one real town, Avalon, sloped up a lush hillside around a wide, calm harbor filled with pleasure boats, pedal boats, surf runners, and kayaks. The town beach had soft, clean sand. A long green pier had a smoothie bar and a fish-'n'-chip shop. Quaint pastel-colored buildings faced the water from behind the cobblestoned front street. That's where Freesia and her friends went for clothing stores, coffee shops, taco stops, street festivals, and impromptu concerts.

Beyond the harbor on one side, colorful fish, pink kelp, and spinner dolphins made the warm turquoise cove a snorkeler's playground. At the harbor's other side, an enormous white, red-roofed rotunda, cleverly dubbed the Rotunda, jutted into the blue sea like an enormous wedding cake. That's where Freesia went for movies—a new one every month!—and the Saturday-night dances.

Beyond the Rotunda, the Island Beach Club had pink sand and curtained cabanas. Behind that, under a grove of palm trees, a cluster of bright yellow buildings housed Agalinas Learning World.

It was a long walk from Freesia's house to the learning center. Some days she drove her pink itty car. Other times, like today, she took the zipline that ran from the end of her street over the harbor, depositing her on a platform between the beach club and the learning center.

When Freesia arrived at class, her cheeks pink from the wind, her Korean language and cultural immersion class teacher, Mr. Lee, waited at the door wearing pressed khakis, a blue button-down shirt, and a floral print tie.

"*Ahn-nyong-ha-se-yo,*" he greeted her.

"*Ahn-nyong-ha-se-yo,*" Freesia replied, her accent flawless.

Next, he asked whether she'd like coffee or tea: "*Cophe ane myun cha dushil lae yo?*"

"*Cophe.*"

So far, so good. But when Mr. Lee kept on speaking Korean ("*Terrasu e' eum ryo su ga, joon be he su yo*"), Freesia's brain started to hurt.

"English, please."

"Refreshments are on the patio," he translated.

"We having barbecue today?"

Mr. Lee shook his head. "Bibimbop. Rice with fried egg, vegetables, and meat. And kimchee too, of course. Did you do your home assignments?"

"No," Freesia said. "They were too boring. And anyway, I had a party to go to."

"Good work," Mr. Lee said.

Jelissa Moon, her red hair brilliant in the dappled sunlight, was on the patio already, trapped in conversation with Chai Cotillion. Freesia helped herself to a cup of sweet, mellow Korean coffee before winding through clusters of students to rescue her friend.

Boys thought Chai was pretty, but to Freesia, she just looked puffy. Puffy lips. Puffy cheeks. Puffy chest. Puffy bottom. *Puffy.* How was that a good thing? She wore thick black eyeliner and about ten coats of mascara, shiny red lipstick, and a perfume that reeked of night bloomers. Her white-blond hair fell just below her shoulders. The color had to be fake, though to Freesia's never-ending frustration, she never had roots. Either Chai's hair grew really slowly or she dyed it weekly.

As for Chai's hard, whiny voice, no one, male or female, could find it anything but annoying.

". . . dress came from Paris and the shoes from Milan," Chai was saying to poor Jelissa, naming two cities that sounded vaguely familiar from the week Freesia had spent in World Geography last year before transferring into Advanced Eye Makeup. If Chai's purple leopard-print dress and white platform sandals came from those places, Freesia didn't need to know anything more about them.

"Freesia!" Chai bared her teeth in something that didn't even vaguely resemble a smile. "Dare and I were just talking about you earlier."

"Is he here?" Freesia scanned the patio beyond Jelissa and Chai for Dare Fiesta, number three on her enemy list.

Chai shook her head. "He gave me a ride in his itty car, but I didn't want Korean coffee. So he said he'd pop back to town and pick me up a wackaccino. He is so sweet. But I guess you know that."

Everyone knew that Freesia and Dare Fiesta had been linked last year, but everyone but Chai knew better than to bring it up.

"What were you and Dare saying about me?" Freesia asked.

Chai examined her fingernails, which were super long, slightly pointy, and painted purple. "Just, you know. That it must have been hard, first having Dare de-link you, and then Taser."

Freesia tensed. "Taser did not de-link me. It was mutual."

Taser had utterly dinked her, but she didn't really care, and anyway, it was none of Chai's business. Taser spent all his shells on arcade games and day passes to the island's interior, where he raced motorbikes and played zap wars. He wasn't ready to have a girl-link.

"Think I'll get some coffee before class starts," Jelissa chirped. "Come with me, Free?"

They practically bolted across the patio, equally enraged by their encounter with Chai.

"Wackaccino," Freesia muttered.

"She's a sea slug," Jelissa said.

"A sea snake."

"I abhor her."

"I abhor the bore more."

Jelissa and Freesia burst out laughing. They'd had this conversation a hundred times before.

Jelissa helped herself to the sweet coffee. "Did you see her at Ricky's party last night? Acting all fizzy with Cabo?"

"I saw her fizzing with Ricky early in the evening." Freesia poked Jelissa's arm, which was the teeniest bit plump, but in a good way. "I thought Cabo only fizzed with you."

"Hush!" Jelissa, already rosy, turned a deeper pink. "Cabo is an utter Garibaldi, but he and I are just friendlies, at least for now. But we were standing by the waterslide, having an utterly nice, utterly *friendly* chat, when she"— Jelissa paused to glare at Chai—"*bounced* over, *grabbed* his hand, and said, *Take me down the waterslide?* And off they went."

"No."

"Yes."

"The pool slide or the ocean slide?"

"Ocean."

Freesia shuddered with fury. "Sea serpent."

"Sea sow."

Freesia said, "And now she's got Dare running around after her. Can't she leave any of the boys alone?" Freesia stole a look at her puffy blond nemesis, who stood alone in the middle of the patio. "Where's Bitsy today?"

Bitsy Trip was Chai's best friend. Also her only friend. Bitsy was sweet and quiet, a perfectly okay person except for her odious taste in friends.

"Dunno," Jelissa said. "I haven't seen her for a couple of days. Maybe she found a new friend."

"Or maybe she can't compete with Dare for Chai's attention," Freesia snarled, annoyed at herself for being jealous.

Mr. Lee came around the building and said something in Korean.

"English, please," several students said at once.

"Would you like to meet inside or outdoors?"

"Inside," a few students called.

"Outdoors," chimed some others.

"Good!" Mr. Lee said. "Glad we agree! If you want to go inside, go inside. If you want to stay out here, stay out here."

Assorted students refilled their coffee and tea mugs and shuffled into the yellow building, followed by Mr. Lee. Freesia and Jelissa claimed a patio table . . . only to have Chai cross the pink patio stones and—oh, no—point to one of two vacant chairs.

"This seat free, Free?"

Freesia was stunned into silence. If Chai was on her enemy list, she was on Chai's. They were *not* supposed to sit together. Finally, she swallowed hard and said, "As far as I know."

Chai dropped her handbag on the chair nearest Freesia and plopped herself next to Jelissa. She gestured to the handbag-marked chair. "For Dare."

What? Two enemies at Freesia's table? This was too, too much.

Jelissa made a desperate stab to rescue her. "What about Bitsy?" she asked Chai. "There isn't enough room for her at this table, so maybe you should—"

"Bitsy's gone."

"From the class?"

Chai waved her hand. "From here. From everywhere. The island. Poof."

"She never said good-bye," Freesia said.

"Why should she?" Chai snapped. "Were you friendlies?"

"Where'd she go?" Jelissa asked.

"The mainland. Of course." Chai rolled her eyes.

Just then, Dare Fiesta, carrying a large cardboard cup, hurried onto the patio, and Freesia forgot all about Bitsy. (Which was too bad, because Bitsy's disappearance was, of course, yet another sign.)

Dare placed the cup in front of Chai. "Big wackaccino, extra creamy."

Dare wore khaki shorts, boat shoes, and a rumpled, untucked white oxford shirt, its sleeves rolled up to reveal strong brown forearms. His dark brown hair fell in a perfect wave across his forehead. A fresh sunburn warmed his straight nose and chiseled cheekbones. If only Dare were ugly, Freesia would have gotten over him long ago, but Dare was the biggest Garibaldi around.

Chai picked up her wackaccino. "Oooh, Dare, you're magical." She fluttered her goopy eyelashes.

Without meaning to, Freesia let out a teeny tiny retching noise, and Dare finally noticed her.

"Freesia," Dare said. "Hi."

"Dare," Freesia said. "Hi."

"Awk," Jelissa said.

"Very." Dare grinned at Jelissa and then at Freesia, who felt her face go hot. Then he took the seat next to Freesia and—was it possible?—scooted several inches in her direction, away from Chai.

Freesia wished she'd worn the black tube dress and thigh-high boots. And then she hated herself for wishing she'd worn anything that might appeal to Dare. And then she went back to hating Chai, which felt so much better.

Mr. Lee, smiling, came out of the yellow building. "*Taehwa!*"

Honestly. Would he never learn?

The class shared a communal sigh and chanted, as one, "English, please."

"Conversation time!" he said. "Pair off and talk to your friend in Korean for the rest of the class. The serfs will serve you bibimbop and kimchee. Enjoy your immersion experience!"

He scurried back into the yellow building.

Freesia was about to catch Jelissa's eye and bolt for

another table when her best friend popped up and turned to Chai. "Let's pair off."

"But . . ." Chai looked at Jelissa. Then at Dare. Then back at Jelissa. She did not look happy.

Jelissa said, "We never got a chance to finish our conversation from earlier. About your . . . couture? I am utterly eager to hear more about your vicious clothes. And where you bought them. And how much they cost."

Chai looked stunned. "But—"

"It's getting hot out here in the sun," Jelissa continued. "Let's snag that table in the shade—the one way over there— before someone else takes it." Jelissa grabbed Chai's wrist and hauled her across the patio, away from Freesia, away from Dare.

Freesia gnawed on her lip to keep from laughing. Jelissa? Was the best friend anyone could ever have.

Dare grinned at Freesia. "Guess that leaves you and me."

"Guess it does."

Dare gazed across the patio. "That was nice of Chai."

"Huh?"

"To change tables for Jelissa, even though I got the feeling she'd rather sit in the sun."

Boys? Were doltoids.

Freesia tossed her hair and tried (failed) to sound casual. "I didn't even know you and Chai were linked. It didn't show up on my bubble report."

Dare blinked with surprise. "Chai and me? Oh, no. We're just friendlies."

"*Really?*" She sounded too happy.

"Sounds like you don't believe me."

"Of course I believe you."

Ha! Dare lied as easily as he breathed. At least that's what Freesia had told herself after he dinked her by saying, "My feelings for you are so strong that they scare me."

"It's just nice to have someone to talk to," Dare said. "Chai's a really good listener. But it's not the same as . . ."

"What?"

"You know."

"What?"

"Not the same."

"Not the same *as what*?"

"You know."

"No! I don't know! For Todd's sake, Dare, just say it!"

Dare's brown eyes grew soft. Wide. And really cute. "It's just not the same as you," he whispered.

Freesia trembled. She had dreamed of re-linking with Dare ever since . . . well before Chai came into the picture, that's for sure. But could you re-link in the middle of Korean immersion class? Was that even allowed?

"Will you go out with me tonight?" he asked, almost as if reading her thoughts. "For a walk in the moonlight? Or a meal? Or a black ocean snorkel?"

"Yes!" she said. And then, "No! I mean—I told Ricky . . . Ricky is having another pool party tonight. And I told him I'd go. Come with me? As my . . . person who comes with me?"

"I will be your date."

"That will be excellent." As thrilled as she was, she squirmed at the thought of walking in with Dare: all the glances and whispers and rumors. What if they didn't re-link, after all? The giggles would never cease.

"Meet me there," she told Dare. "At Ricky's house. Ten o'clock?"

"I'll be there at nine fifty-nine," he told her.

3

"**I**f they aren't linked, why is he getting her coffee and driving her around?" Freesia, climbing into Jelissa's bright green itty car after class, tried—failed—not to stare at Dare and Chai, two parking spots away.

"Laugh," Jelissa commanded, pushing the ignition button. The little car sputtered to life.

"What? Why?"

"Just laugh." Jelissa began backing out. She looked retro-fabu, as always, wearing huge white sunglasses to protect her eyes from the ocean's glare and a lime green scarf to keep her red hair in place. She wore her bubble on a chain like a pendant.

Like all itty cars, Jelissa's was open air with a canopy top. Unlike most canopies, hers was patterned with daisies.

"Ha. Ha. Ha ha ha!" Freesia inhaled too hard and coughed on the itty car's vanilla-scented exhaust.

Jelissa hooted. "That was loopy." She put the car into gear and chugged away from Agalinas Learning World.

This time, Freesia laughed for real—and somehow managed to resist the urge to turn around for a final look.

"You can't let them see that you care," Jelissa admonished her.

"I don't care."

"You don't fake things very well."

Freesia sighed. "Well, I don't want to care, anyway."

The day had warmed up. Freesia was glad she wasn't walking, though a pleasant breeze from the sea brought tangy smells of salt and seaweed, while the wind from the itty car—which went fifteen miles per hour at top speed—blew her hair and kept her cool.

In movies, Freesia had seen bigger, faster cars: guzzling glass-and-metal boxes that would explode upon impact. In the movies, there was always some kind of impact: with walls, trees, other cars, or people. Only itty cars were allowed on the island of Agalinas. That was okay with Freesia. In Agalinas, the distances were short, the weather was always lovely, and, really, who'd want to be shut up in a big metal box?

Jelissa parked the itty car in a small lot at the edge of Front Street. No need to lock it: the car only responded to Jelissa's bubble. Freesia and Jelissa strolled along the cobblestone street. The town beach was on one side, pretty pastel shops on the other. They passed the ice cream parlor, the juice shop, the music center, and the explosives depot before reaching the Dressy Dress Shoppe.

Around Front Street, there were no parents and no children

younger than eight. Freesia only saw parents and little kids in her friends' homes. The only adults she saw in public were teachers, shopkeepers, serfs, and sports instructors. She didn't find that strange, though. It had always been that way.

Inside the dress shop, two petite girls with matching black bobs and matching black-and-white striped T-shirts straightened circular racks organized by dress color.

"Welcome!" said one.

"Can we help you?" asked the other.

"We're okay on our own," Freesia said. She came in this shop at least once a week, sometimes more, but the shop girls never seemed to remember her.

Freesia dug into the pink rack, Jelissa into the green. When they'd hit a few more racks and their arms were full, they trudged to the dressing room at the back of the store. The matching salesgirls pulled back the heavy flowered drapes that separated the cramped store from the huge dressing room.

"You first." Jelissa dropped her dresses onto one of two overstuffed couches and made her way to the mocktini bar, where she poured a pink drink for Freesia and a green one for herself, topping each with a shiny red cherry and a paper umbrella.

An enormous three-way mirror dominated the room's back wall. From her pile of dresses, Freesia chose a short, sleeveless hot-pink number and hung it on a hook next to the mirror. Then she took her bubble out of her bag. The warmth of her hands turned the bubble green. She pointed the bubble at the dress and then the mirror. The mirror flashed as if a camera bulb had gone off and then showed Freesia in the hot pink dress.

Jelissa handed Freesia the pink mocktini. Freesia sipped it. So did the Freesia in the mirror. Freesia turned to the left, and then to the right. So did the girl in the mirror.

"Too short?" she asked Jelissa.

Jelissa shrugged. "The dress fits you well, but then, everything does. I think you can find something a little more vicious."

Freesia put down her drink and chose another dress to hang on the hook. Once again, she pointed her bubble toward the dress and then at the mirror, until a projection of her appeared. She did this several more times until she made her final selection, a shell-pink tea dress with a tulle skirt and rosettes around the collar.

"Now *that's* vicious," Jelissa said.

Satisfied, Freesia settled down with a second mocktini (which tasted of watermelon), while Jelissa hung her own dresses next to the mirror, considering a couple of green taffeta gowns before settling on a cherry-patterned dress with netting underlay.

"Cabo will like that one," Freesia teased her.

Jelissa tossed her gorgeous red hair. "I don't dress for Cabo. I dress for myself."

"Smart girl."

"Besides, we're just friendlies." She blushed.

"Mm-hm," Freesia said.

When they left the dressing room, the salesgirls were once again fiddling with the round racks.

"Can we help you?" one asked.

Freesia held up her pink dress. "We're ready to check out."

"But of course!" The salesgirl crossed the store to a tall silver counter. Only now did Freesia check the price tag: ninety shells. Ouch. The hot pink dress had been half that.

"It's awfully expensive," she said to Jelissa. "And I still need to get shoes. And jewelry. Plus I'll want to bring in a stylist—"

"It makes you look like a fairy ballerina," Jelissa said.

"But shoes—"

"You can wear an old pair of shoes. Or borrow some of mine. The dress is perfect. You have to have it."

"You're right." Freesia placed the dress on the counter, reached into her bag for her bubble, and—

Everything went black.

And silent.

Another power outage. Third time this week. But why would it be dark in the store when the front window opened up to the daylight?

Freesia was *this close* to flipping out when the lights came back up. She stood in the middle of the store, still holding the pink dress. But . . . hadn't she placed it on the counter already?

"It makes you look like a fairy ballerina," Jelissa said.

"But . . ." Freesia blinked at her friend.

"You can wear an old pair of shoes," Jelissa said. "Or borrow some of mine. The dress is perfect. You have to have it."

"You just said that," Freesia said.

"Because it's true."

"Oh. Right. Of course."

Freesia crossed to the counter, where the salesgirl waited, smiling. Hands trembling, she placed the dress on the counter.

"You get a lot of power outages?" Freesia asked.

The salesgirl smiled. "All the time. I hardly even notice them anymore."

She rang up the dress. Freesia handed over her bubble, no longer caring how much she spent.

Out on the street, she said, "I don't mean to get flippy, but didn't you think that blackout was a little . . . off?"

"What do you mean?" Jelissa said.

"You did notice the blackout, didn't you?"

"Of course. But you got me thinking about Cabo, and . . ." Jelissa laughed. "Let's buy shoes!"

"Of course," Freesia said.

Just as they turned to stroll to the shoe store beyond the dress shop, Taser Lucas came out of the explosives retailer. His streaky light brown hair needed a cut, and his sunburned face needed a shave. Or not. Taser knew how to work the rugged look. He always looked like he had just come back from adventuring through the island's interior.

Frozen on the sidewalk, they stared at each other.

Jelissa wiggled her fingers to break the spell. "Hi, Taser. What've you been up to?"

He blinked at her. "I, um, just got back from adventuring through the island's interior."

Jelissa nodded. "Sounds . . . sweaty."

Taser went back to staring at Freesia, his mouth twitching as if he had something to say.

Jelissa pointed to the pale green shoe shop next door. "'Kay, Free. I'll be in there."

"'Kay," Freesia said. She looked at Jelissa, then back at Taser, then at the ground. "This is a hundred kinds of awk."

"Did you see the blackout just now?" he blurted.

Freesia stiffened—and then laughed with relief. "Yeah. This may sound crazy, but for a minute there, I thought I'd imagined it."

"Because everyone else acted like nothing else had happened?"

"Yes." She felt somewhat less relieved.

"Sit with me." Without waiting for her to say yes, he crossed the cobblestones and sat on a green bench facing the harbor. She followed, of course, not because she wanted to talk to him, necessarily, but because she looked forward to repeating the conversation to Jelissa.

Farther down the sand, a steel drum band played island tunes. On the beach in front of them, some children, nine or ten years old, dug holes and splashed at the water's edge. Two boys and a girl crafted a sand sculpture: a dolphin, or maybe a shark.

Freesia hummed along to the band and waited for Taser to say whatever it was that he found more important than shopping for shoes.

The best he could do was this: "Do you ever wonder if . . . maybe you're the only one who's real? Like the world around you is all make-believe?"

Had this been three months ago, while their linkage was unraveling, she would have felt compelled to comment on his egomania. Instead, she kept her answer short.

"No."

He scratched his scruffy chin. "I thought everyone thought that sometimes."

Freesia inhaled. She exhaled. She counted to four before speaking. She might have counted to ten, but she could be shopping right now, and she wasn't willing to waste six seconds.

"Taser. If that were true, then *I* wouldn't be real. So why would you care what I thought?"

"Excellent point." He smiled. Taser had a nice smile—she had to give him that much. It made his eyes crinkle and his cheeks dimple. And then he stopped smiling.

"What happened?" she asked.

He stopped smiling. "Upgrades have been run on all my favorite zap war games. *Flaming Trenches. Navy Squadron.* Even *Nuclear Assault: Canada.*"

"And that's a problem?"

"Yes! No. Sort of. I was playing Canadian Nukes yesterday, and for the first time ever in a game, I was scared. The mushroom cloud, the Mounties . . . it was intense. For the first time ever, it all seemed completely real! I felt the heat of the explosion, smelled the sweat of the horses—"

"Of course it felt real. It's supposed to. That's how you know you're getting your shells' worth." Not bothering to hide her exasperation, Freesia crossed her arms and looked at the kids making the sand sculpture. It was a dolphin. Definitely.

"But if *that* wasn't real, then how do we know that this—" He gestured at the beach, the children, the steel drum band. "How do we know that all this isn't imaginary, too?"

She said, "Maybe you should take a break from zap wars."

A chirping sound came from Freesia's bag. She pulled out her glowing bubble and tapped it twice to read Jelissa's message: **YOU NEED TO HELP ME MAKE A VERY IMPORTANT SHOE DECISION!!! (NOT REALLY BUT YOU CAN TELL HIM THAT.)**

Freesia stood up. "I can see why you're distressed. But I've got to go help Jelissa pick out shoes. Taser, you should refresh your life. Drink some happy juice, lie on the beach . . . and stay out of the explosives shop."

"In the shoe shop." Jelissa held up a white platform sandal with ankle-tie ribbons. "How's Taser?"

"Paranoid and delusional."

"So—same as always." Jelissa put down the sandal and picked up a tall red pump.

"Some things never change," Freesia said. "Except . . ."

"What?"

"Haven't things on the island seemed a little flippy lately? I mean, all the power outages. And people leaving without saying good-bye."

Jelissa shrugged. "Stuff like that has always happened. It's no big deal."

"You're right." Freesia sighed with relief. She wasn't very observant. That's why she hadn't noticed life's out-of-whackness until now. She remembered the ugly girl she'd seen in her closet mirror this morning. Nothing like that had ever happened before, but—

Jelissa held up the two shoes. "White or red?"

"Red," Freesia said. "Definitely."

4

An hour later, they were back at Agalinas Learning World. Mr. Coda, the music teacher, wearing his usual round wire glasses and tropical print shirt, stood outside the door of the yellow music building, which had curved walls and a dome-shaped ceiling for optimal acoustics. Mr. Coda taught voice, instruments, and music appreciation.

"Welcome to music class!" he greeted Freesia and Jelissa. "Today we will be studying the music of Wolfgang Amadeus Mozart."

"Know what would be really vicious?" Freesia said. "Listening to Chase Bennett tunes instead."

"And maybe doing some karaoke," Jelissa added.

Mr. Coda clapped his hands. "Chase Bennett and karaoke it is! Refreshments are on the patio."

Freesia and Jelissa got lime sippers and sat at a shady outside table to listen to the advanced music students. Purple butterflies, known as ballad flies due to their note-shaped wings, danced in the air, while harmonizing hummingbirds hovered around a potted pink bush.

One student, soaked with sweat, pounded an enormous drum set. Others strummed ukuleles, slammed electric guitars, blew into trumpets, or sawed electric violas. Individually, each sounded magical, their endless hours of practice evident in every note. Jumbled together, they produced a chaotic cacophony that hurt the girls' ears.

"Inside?" Freesia asked.

"Please." Jelissa tossed back the remainder of her lime sipper, and they scurried into the building.

Inside, on the round center stage, a string quartet performed something boring but inoffensive, probably by that Mozart guy Mr. Coda had mentioned. Along the curved outer walls, interactive music stations offered virtual guitar, virtual drums, virtual piano, virtual conductor, and a virtual polka band. There was always a line for the virtual polka band.

"Too bad they don't have a virtual Chase Bennett," Freesia said.

"Forget virtual. I'd like to see the real thing!"

When Mr. Coda entered the room, the students arranged themselves in chairs around the center stage. Cabo was in this class, along with Ferdinand, another friendly. Both boys were of average height, with powerful shoulders and square chins. They looked so much alike that they could pass for brothers if not for their opposite coloring. Cabo had black hair, black eyes, and cappuccino-colored skin, while Ferdinand was white blond and fair.

Jelissa slipped into the chair next to Cabo. Freesia pinched her friend's arm. Jelissa swatted her away and held in a giggle.

Onstage, the string quartet, two women in long black dresses and two men in tuxedos, finished their performance, stood up, and bowed.

"So now you know about Mozart," Mr. Coda said as the quartet walked offstage.

The students nodded.

"Let's move on to Chase Bennett. How many of you did your homework?"

Hands shot up. Homework was never mandatory, but everyone was happy to do fun assignments. This week, they'd been asked to listen to at least three Chase Bennett songs.

"Extra credit?"

About half the students, Freesia and Jelissa included, raised their hands to indicate that they had found Ten Interesting Things About Chase Bennett.

"Excellent! Let's see what you learned. Starting with . . . you." Mr. Coda pointed to a girl in the second row.

She stood up. "Chase Bennett was born in Texas but moved to Hawaii when he was six months old."

"Correct! Someone else?"

"When Chase Bennett was five years old, his mother bubblecast him singing a reggae-infused take on 'Happy Birthday.' That bubblecast has been viewed over ten million times."

"Also correct. Next?"

Jelissa popped up. "Although Chase Bennett is most

famous for his mastery of the ukulele, he also plays the guitar, banjo, harp, and piano."

Mr. Coda complimented Jelissa and quickly collected six more interesting facts about Chase Bennett:

- Chase Bennett's favorite food is spaghetti, and his favorite candy is gummy worms.
- Chase Bennett loves to surf.
- His hair just naturally grows that way.
- His eyes are turquoise colored, not green, as some have claimed.
- He has two dogs (a Chihuahua named Squirt and a German shepherd/golden retriever mix named Buster), a white cat (Cottonball), a lop-eared rabbit (Penelope), and three hamsters (Curly, Mo, and Bill). Rumors of Cottonball eating Mo are utterly untrue.
- Now that he's eighteen, Chase Bennett appears to have outgrown his peanut allergy.

Mr. Coda called on Freesia to relate a final interesting fact.

She stood up and cleared her throat. "Several bubble reports have recently linked Chase Bennett with twenty-year-old singing sensation Felicity Flufferhaus."

All the girls (and some of the boys) gasped.

Freesia smiled. "Chase Bennett denies these reports. He says he barely knows Felicity and that when he falls in love, he will be the first to tell the world."

The girls sighed in unified relief. But news of Chase Bennett's continuing availability wasn't even the best news of the day.

"Excellent work!" Mr. Coda said, clapping his hands. "But as it turns out, I have one more interesting—utterly interesting, I'd say—fact about Chase Bennett."

The entire class, even the boys, leaned forward.

"When asked, just this morning, about his summer plans, Chase Bennett said that he is planning to sail his yacht to . . . Agalinas!"

The crowd went wild, with giggling, squealing, hugging, and, yes, even a tear or two. When the immediate hysteria died down, a boy raised his hand.

"Mr. Coda? When is summer?"

Mr. Coda blinked several times and tilted his head to one side. "I'm not exactly sure. Soon, I think."

5

Mummy was in the kitchen, stirring something in a pot.

Daddy was at the table, reading a newspaper.

Angel played with fashion dolls on the floor.

"Good afternoon, Freesia," Mummy said. "I'm making spaghetti, your favorite!"

Daddy smiled over his paper. "Did you learn a lot in school today?"

Angel scrambled off the tiles. "Oooh, Freesia, what pretty things did you buy? Let me see, let me see!"

What if Taser was right? What if her sweet family wasn't real? The thought made her heart hurt and her legs wobble.

"Todd dammit!" Mummy yelled.

Daddy threw down his paper. "What happened?"

"I was draining the pasta, and I scalded myself. Stupid, stupid!"

Freesia smiled (even though she felt bad for her mother,

who seemed to be in a fair amount of pain). Imaginary people don't burn themselves.

"Well?" Angel asked, hands on narrow hips.

"Well what?" Freesia said, mirroring her sister.

"Aren't you going to show me what you bought?"

Freesia pulled out the pretty pink dress. Angel, who loved anything to do with ballerinas, oohed and aahed and fussed over the rosette neckline. Then Freesia opened her box of pointy silver shoes (on sale for only fifteen shells—no need to wear an old pair after all) and let Angel teeter around the kitchen.

"Soon your feet will be as big as mine!" Freesia said, realizing she'd said that lots of times before and that somehow Angel never seemed to catch up. "Angel, how old are you?" she blurted.

Her sister's mouth dropped open. "You don't know?"

"Of course I do. You're . . . fourteen."

"Almost fourteen and a half," Angel said.

"It just seems funny that—" Freesia stopped.

"What?" Angel's big blue eyes filled with innocence. Angel would be beautiful someday. She was beautiful now, but in a little-girl way: fairy blond hair, cherry cheeks, slim hips, and coltish legs.

"Someday you'll be as big as me," Freesia said. "It's just funny to think about that."

Angel was a late bloomer, that was all. So what if she still played with dolls and barely even looked at her bubble. So what if she looked closer to eleven than fourteen. Angel loved Freesia, and Freesia loved her. That was as real as it got.

"Dinner's ready!" Mummy chirped, having apparently re-covered from her scalding. She filled four plates, and they took them out to the sunny deck off the kitchen, where they could watch the boats toodle around the harbor and the waterbirds dive for fish. Freesia loved this time of day, sitting with her family, eating Mummy's tasty food, thinking about her glorious today, looking forward to her glorious tomorrow.

"We are lucky to live here," Daddy said. And everyone agreed.

Freesia didn't need to ask her bubble for attire assistance before heading out to Ricky's pool party. Last night she had worn her favorite swimsuit, so today she'd wear her second favorite. And tomorrow . . . tomorrow she'd wear her blue polka-dot dress with her white go-go boots. No need to ask for attire assistance then, either.

"Bye, Mummy and Daddy. I'm going to a party."

"Will you be home tonight?"

"Probably. But not till early morning. So don't wait up."

"Okay, then, have a happy time!"

A party was just what she needed, Freesia thought, start-ing up her pale pink itty car. When she was alone, she tended to think, and that was never, ever good. She didn't want to think about the ugly girl she'd seen in her mirror. She didn't want to think about what Taser had said. She just wanted to drink happy juice and dance and laugh and fizz with Dare. And maybe Ricky. But mostly Dare because he was already on her enemy list so she didn't have anything to lose.

Ricky lived in the island's biggest house. High on a cliff just beyond the Rotunda, it had views of the harbor and the beach club, and even peeks of the interior. Torches illuminated a vast rooftop patio, which had sofas and hammocks and a jet tub big enough to hold twenty people. A rope bridge led to Ricky's two waterslides, one of which emptied into the swimming pool in Ricky's lower yard, the other into the ocean.

Freesia parked her itty car on the curb right outside Ricky's house. Oh, no. Judging by the empty road, she was the first one at the party: never good. But then, this was Ricky. Why not enjoy a little twosey time with her second-best friendly?

She pulled her silver bubble out of her tote. It turned green, then blue. "Friendlies check."

RICKY LEISURE: TRANSMITTING

He was by the pool, but the raft was gone. And he was dressed. In real clothes, not his swim trunks. Nothing fancy— just white shorts and a navy blue T-shirt—but still. It looked like he had showered and shaved and maybe even combed his hair.

Truth? She liked Ricky better when he was rumpled.

She spoke into her bubble. "Ricky? Did I get the time wrong?"

He didn't answer, just hurried to the front door, where he greeted her with a glass of happy fizz. The lights in his house were dim, the music—Chase Bennett's greatest hits—turned down low.

"What's the occasion?" she asked, taking a sip of the

fizz. It tickled her tongue, warmed her throat, and instantly made her feel . . . not happy, exactly, but relaxed. Ready for happiness.

"You're here. That's the occasion. Let's go up to the roof."

The night was dark and clear. The air smelled of salt and flowers. From the rooftop patio, Freesia could see the Big and Little Dipper, Orion's Belt, and the Eye of Todd. Far below, phosphorescence turned the black ocean neon green as it licked the shore.

"I'm surprised no one else is here yet," Freesia said.

"I didn't invite anyone else." Ricky kept his eyes on the glass, on the bottle, on his shoes. He drained his happy fizz. He refilled his glass and topped off Freesia's, and then he threw the empty bottle over the edge of the patio, toward the ocean. It shattered on the rocks below, the sound like a jingle. The ocean would soften and churn the shards until they came back to shore, sea glass that sparkled like jewels.

Freesia was about to tell Ricky that she liked him so much but thought they should just be friendlies, blah, blah, blah. But blame it on the stars, blame it on the happy fizz, or just blame it on what she really wanted: Freesia leaned in for a face-link.

Their noses touched, and her whole face grew warm and glowy. She'd have thought that face-linking with Ricky would be better than with Taser, though maybe not quite as good as with Dare, but face-linking always provided the same kind of warm, pleasant numbness.

After maybe ten seconds, a cool breeze crossed her face, marking the face-link's end.

"I've been thinking about doing that for a long time," Ricky said.

"Me too, but—"

"*Hello? Anyone here?*"

At the sound of Dare Fiesta's voice, Freesia took a big step backward.

"Oh my Todd," she muttered to Ricky. "I told Dare you were having a party tonight. Because . . . I thought you were."

Ricky held up a hand. "*Hola, amigo!*" Spanglish was the only class Ricky attended regularly. He really loved nachos.

"Am I . . . early?" Dare wore swim trunks, a towel draped around his neck.

"I got the time wrong," Freesia said. "I thought the party started at ten, but actually—"

"It starts at two," Ricky said.

Dare gawked. "In the morning?"

Ricky shrugged. "Guess that's too late, because hardly anyone said they were coming. Want some happy fizz? I was just about to open another bottle."

"No, thanks." He patted his perfect abdomen. "I'm in training."

"For . . . ?"

"Paddleboard racing. Championship is coming up."

Ricky shrugged. "Well, I'm not in training." He crossed to his rooftop fridge and pulled out a bottle.

"Care to go for a ride down the waterslide, Freesia?" Dare asked. "Pool or ocean—your pick."

And then everything went black.

6

hree steps forward, and she hit a wall. Three steps to either side, same thing. One step back, and she knocked into something. A chair? Three steps diagonally, and she hit another wall. It was warm and just a little bit sticky.

"Ricky? Are you there? Dare? Can you hear me?"

Don't panic, don't panic, don't panic. . . . It was just like this at the Dressy Dress Shoppe. Well, except for the walls and the chair. Or whatever it was. Any second now, the town lights would come back on, and the stars . . . Why would the stars go out in a blackout?

Back at the wall, she groped along the surface, searching for an opening, a handhold—something. Her breathing came fast and ragged. Her heart pumped so hard it made her chest hurt.

"Ricky? Dare? Somebody help me!"

"*What the—oh, crud!*"

Someone was on the other side of the wall. A girl. Her voice sounded like someone Freesia knew. But who?

"Mom? Mom! Get in here! Now! It's freaking out! Moooooom . . ."

Angel. The voice sounded like Angel, only . . . older. And—

"Make it stop! I hate that thing!"

Meaner.

"I told you I didn't want that thing next to my bedroom. It's always laughing and singing, and my friends don't even want to come over anymore because they're all, like, You've got a freak living in your house."

Another voice, also familiar. "Oh. My. God. Did her medication run out? Or did the program crash? I knew we should have bought the extended warranty. I told your father—"

It sounded like . . .

"Mummy?"

"It's looking at me!"

"Mummy!"

"Get your father, Angel. Tell him to call tech support."

"MUMMY!"

She could see now. The wall was clear and round, like . . . a bubble. A great big, hard bubble. Mummy was on the other side of the wall with Angel, only Mummy didn't look shiny and happy like usual. She looked tired and pale and messy as if she'd been sleeping—but also like she looked tired and pale and messy all the time. And Angel: Angel had blossomed. She was taller than Mummy, taller than Freesia, probably, and just as beautiful as Freesia always thought she would be, even though black eye makeup had smeared under her light eyes, lending a ghoulish air.

"It's okay, Francine," Mummy said from the other side of the transparent wall. "Calm down."

Freesia started to cry. "Mummy! I'm so frightened!"

"Enough, Francine. Chill out! Close your eyes or something. We'll give you your meds and get tech support on the phone and—"

She was back. On the roof. Ricky had passed out on a lounge chair. Dare gazed up at the sky.

"Freesia, what's wrong?" Dare took her in his arms, but just in a friendly way.

"A bad dream. Or—a blackout? Was there a blackout?"

Dare shook his head. "It's dark, but . . ."

"The happy fizz," Freesia said. "I shouldn't have had so much."

7

The signs were all there, and Freesia couldn't help but see them. Ashley and Jennifer, the male peacocks, screeched and screamed her awake until she yelled, "Shut it," at which point they launched into Chase Bennett's timeless lyrics.

It's another day.
On the island we say, Hey . . .

Another day on the island. Wasn't it a little odd the way things never changed? Not the weather, not the routine, not even her sister? What would happen when she finished school? No one ever talked about it.

And, oh my Todd, not again: the one thing she didn't want to change. *Where was her coffee?*

"Mummy?"

Her mother appeared right away, happy and shiny as always.

"Sweetie?"

"Um . . . would you mind getting me some coffee?"

"Sweetie!" Mummy hurried out and came back with her chunky mug filled to the brim with frothy coffee.

"Thanks," Freesia said.

"It's Tracey's Famous Coffee! Nothing like a coffee cloud to start your day the Tracey way!"

"You don't have to say that every time." Freesia took the mug.

Mummy smiled. "Would you like an omelet, oatmeal, or pancakes for brunch?"

Freesia hesitated. "Oatmeal."

"In here or in the kitchen?"

She hesitated again. "Kitchen."

"Should I stay, or should I go?"

"Stay."

Mummy stood there, smiling.

"Actually, you can go," Freesia told her.

Once her mother left, Freesia took her coffee and her bubble out to the balcony. It was another beautiful day. Of course it was. Every day on Agalinas was clear and warm: something to do with its position in the Pacific Ocean and the jet streams from . . . somewhere warm.

Maybe she should have paid attention in Geography.

Nah. Geography was borrifying.

Freesia settled on her pillowy lounge on the balcony. She held her bubble till it turned warm and grew to grapefruit size before she decided that, no, she did not need to check on her friendlies and her enemies. She did that every day. Maybe the island of Agalinas wasn't in a rut. Maybe it was just her.

"I'm going to walk down to the beach," she informed Ashley and Jennifer, who didn't even pretend to care.

"I'll eat my oatmeal later," she told her shiny mother before heading out the back door and down the hill.

The steel drum band she'd seen yesterday was setting up on the sand. She nodded hello and then strolled onto the green pier, past the smoothie stand and up to the boat rental kiosk. The same trim, weathered blond man had been there forever. Well, not forever, just as long as Freesia could remember, which wasn't so long at all, really. She gave him ten shells for a half hour on a pedal boat.

Being out on the water calmed Freesia. Agalinas's water was so clear she could see straight to the sandy bottom. Schools of pink and blue and orange fish swam over sand dollars and starfish, while sea horses bobbed among pink kelp and silver bubbles.

As she pedaled away from shore, small pleasure craft and tiny sailboats gave way to big sleeper boats. She rounded the back of the largest boat and read the name:

FREEDOM
NEWPORT BEACH, CA

On the boat's back deck, a silver-haired man sat in a white vinyl chair, sipping something steamy from a silver cup.

When Freesia drew near, he held up a hand. "Greetings."

Freesia stopped pedaling. "Greetings to you, too. Are you visiting from the mainland?"

"Sure am."

"What's it like there?"

The man smiled. "Crowded and dirty."

"But what does it look like?"

"Flat," he said. "And brown. And the buildings are close together, and the air smells bad."

"Why do people stay there, then?"

"You don't get to choose the place you call home. You're lucky to live in Agalinas."

He stood up, waved, and disappeared into the boat's cabin.

Freesia just managed to pedal beyond the harbor to the edge of Snorkelers' Cove before she had to turn around to return the boat to the man on the green pier.

At home, she hurried to get ready for class. No need for attire assistance today: she'd already picked out the polka-dot dress. Nor did she have time to confirm her plans for the day with Jelissa. Wait. What were her plans for the day? Maybe she'd go back to the cove. She could go snorkeling. Take a ride on a spinner dolphin. Maybe Ricky could go with her . . . if they were still friendlies after last night's face-link. Funny: she'd been so preoccupied with her bad dream that she'd all but forgotten about it.

She and Ricky face-linked! Wait till Jelissa heard about that.

Freesia dashed into her closet and grabbed a bikini to put under her dress. Snorkeling later: yes, definitely.

Since she normally rode the zipline to school, today Freesia drove instead, parking her pink itty car next to Jelissa's green one.

Mr. Lee, her Korean immersion teacher, wearing his usual pressed khakis and blue button-down shirt, waited outside the door of the bright yellow building.

"*Ahn-nyong-ha-se-yo*," he said.

"English, please."

"Good morning. Would you like coffee or tea?"

"I thought today was Spanglish immersion."

He shook his head. "Tomorrow. Today you learn about the Korean language and culture. For lunch we will eat bibimbop. Rice with fried egg, vegetables, and meat. And kimchee too, of course. Did you do your home assignments?"

"But, Mr. Lee . . . we had Korean immersion yesterday," she said.

"Refreshments are on the patio."

Freesia didn't want refreshments. She wanted the world to make sense. Or she wanted to *not think* about whether the world made sense.

She retreated to the parking lot, where she sat in her itty car's front seat and took long, deep breaths.

Everything would be okay.

She needed to stop staying out so late.

She needed to stay away from happy juice, happy fizz, and any other happy beverage that Ricky offered.

Next time Taser wanted to talk, she would say no. She didn't need him putting loopy ideas in her head.

Inside her bag, her bubble chirped. A message from Jelissa waited. **YOU COMING?**

"Message reply," Freesia whispered to her bubble. "I'm in the parking lot. Come see me."

Jelissa would make her feel better. She always did.

Less than a minute later, Jelissa climbed onto the seat next to her. "What's wrong?"

Freesia opened her mouth to tell Jelissa about her conversation with Taser, the blackout at Ricky's, the repeating Korean immersion class. And then she realized: it was all crazy talk! And crazy talk is borrifying!

"Ricky and I face-linked last night," she blurted out.

"No!" Jelissa's eyes, already wide, grew huge.

"I didn't mean for it to happen. And I don't think it means we're linked or anything. But I get the feeling that Ricky feels something for me. That he's not just fizzing."

The more Freesia talked about Ricky, the less she thought about the blackout. She said, "I've always liked Ricky."

"I know you have!" Jelissa said. "Who wouldn't? He's devicious!"

"But I don't want to risk our friendship. And once an ex-link—"

"Speak of the devil," Jelissa said.

Just like that, Dare Fiesta pulled up in his white itty car. He parked, climbed out, reached toward his drink holder, and—oh, no.

Dare had stopped for coffee two days in a row.

Mr. Lee was teaching Korean immersion two days in a row.

Jelissa—how had she not noticed this before?—was wearing her yellow dress. Jelissa would never wear the same thing two days in a row.

Maybe there weren't two days after all.

"Refreshments are on the patio," Jelissa told Dare.

He held up the paper cup. "This is for Chai."

"Wackaccino?" Freesia said, her voice thick.

"How'd you know?"

"Just a guess." Her knees were feeling wobbly again, and her stomach: not good. She would definitely avoid the kimchee.

Freesia and Jelissa followed Dare toward the yellow building.

"I was so glad when you bubbled me," Jelissa whispered. "Chai had me cornered, bragging about where she got her stupid clothes."

"Paris and Milan?" Freesia asked, hoping Jelissa would say no—even as she noticed that Dare had on the same button-up white shirt and khaki shorts as before. There was no denying it: today was yesterday, and yesterday was today. Freesia felt sick.

"Paris and Milan—yes! How'd you know?"

"Happy guess."

"Forget about Chai," Jelissa said. "I can't wait to hear about Ricky. I can't believe you face-linked in the middle of that big party and no one even saw you! We still on for dress shopping later?"

Freesia nodded. It was all she could do. Walking onto the

patio, she shouldn't have been surprised to see Chai wearing the purple leopard dress, but she couldn't help but stare. After that, she was prepared, more or less, for Chai and Dare to sit with them. For Jelissa to pull Chai away during conversation time so she could be alone with Dare.

Little things were different. Chai didn't save a seat for Dare, because he was already on the patio . . . though the same table was empty, as if it were waiting for them, as if they were somehow fated to sit there. And Freesia didn't drink the Korean coffee, choosing lukewarm tea instead. ("Really?" Jelissa asked. "I thought you loved Korean coffee.")

But as soon as they were alone, Dare fell right into his script. "That was nice of Chai."

"You mean to change tables for Jelissa, even though she'd rather sit in the sun?" Freesia asked.

"Exactly!"

"But you and Chai are just friendlies," she said.

"It's just nice to have someone to talk to," Dare said. "Chai's a really good listener. But it's not the same as—"

"As me."

"As you." His brown eyes grew soft.

Freesia had to get out of there. Now.

"I'm not going out with you tonight," she said, pushing back her chair and standing up. "Just so you know."

"Of course you are."

"No, I'm not. But thanks for asking."

She abandoned Dare and her lukewarm tea and fled from Agalinas Learning World.

8

*S*he waited on the bench, down from the steel drum band and behind the kids sculpting something out of sand, until he came out of the explosives retailer. Right on time. And just as she'd remembered him: streaky hair, sunburn, stubble.

She strolled across the cobblestones, right into his path.

She said, "You're about to tell me that you just got back from the interior. And then you'll ask if I saw the blackout just now. Except . . . there wasn't a blackout this time. Maybe because I didn't go into the dress shop or—I don't know. And then we'll go sit on the bench over there." She pointed toward the sand. "The next song coming up is 'Tide Is High,' by the way—and you'll tell me about your latest zap wars."

Taser stared at her some more. "You too?"

All of a sudden, Freesia felt so much better. Less alone. Not quite so loopy.

"Let's walk to the end of the pier," she suggested. She couldn't bear to hear the steel drum band play the exact same songs as yesterday or watch the sand sculpture evolve from vague fish to definite dolphin. It was worse than flippy. It was creepy.

At the end of the pier, she told him everything: about the ugly girl in her closet mirror, the blackout in the Dressy Dress Shoppe, and, most frightening, the little room with the clear walls.

Boats bobbed in the harbor. A kayaker passed them and waved.

"I wasn't sure," Taser said, "if we really were repeating yesterday or if I just . . . if there's something wrong with my brain. Last night, when it happened—I was asleep. And when I woke up, it was too dark to see anything, but I was lying on this recliner. I just lay there, breathing hard and shaking. I kept my eyes closed and then . . . I was back."

"Do you think there are others like us?" Freesia asked.

Taser was quiet for a long time. "I'm not even sure that you're real," he said, finally.

Freesia had never felt so offended. She slapped him. Hard.

He gasped and covered his cheek with a sunburned hand.

"Was that real enough for you?"

"I can't believe you did that," he said.

"You love nothing more than pretending to kill people in your zap wars, but you can't bear a little slap? Stop acting all dark and tortured. We need to figure out what we're going to do."

"In that case, I need to show you something." He led her back down the pier and along the shoreline, which jutted out to a rocky point before scooping back in at the little cove where she'd planned to spend the afternoon snorkeling. That seemed like such a long time ago.

In the bushes near the far end of the cove, he'd hidden a small, scuffed silver skiff. The boat had bench seats and a tiny motor.

Freesia hesitated. "Why not just rent a boat from the guy on the pier?" Taser's boat didn't look very steady. Or clean.

"I don't want to waste my shells. Plus, I like knowing this skiff is here. I like knowing it's mine."

He hauled the boat to the edge of the sand and into the warm turquoise water. Freesia took off her shoes. Once the water reached her knees, she climbed onto the little vessel, staying low so she wouldn't tip it over. In the cove below, a spiny pufferfish and a miniature sea horse danced among the bubbles.

Taser scrambled in behind her, shoving off from the sandy bottom before pulling out a paddle and silently gliding along the shoreline.

"Why not just use the motor?" Freesia asked.

"Don't want anyone to hear us." He kept his voice low, even though there was no one in sight.

"But, Taser. If what you say is true, that no one else is real, what does it matter whether or not anyone knows what we're doing?"

"Shh!" He kept paddling.

Exasperated, she crossed her arms over her chest. Fine. Let him paddle. Let him sweat. She'd just sit there while he got them to wherever they were going. It wasn't like she had anything better to do. Like—oh my Todd!

"My dress!"

"What?" They had reached the end of the cove. Two dolphins that had been tailing them leapt up and spun in the air, dove to the sea bottom, and swam away.

Freesia said, "If today is yesterday's do-over and I never went back to the Dressy Dress Shoppe, then I never bought my dress for the dance. And I didn't get my silver shoes, either! What if someone else buys them? What will I wear?"

"You're not really thinking about dance clothes at a time like this."

"At a time like what? Taser, I'm flipping out here, but that doesn't mean I've forgotten my priorities."

They had just rounded the corner of the cove. Immediately, the water turned dark and choppy. Instead of sparkly sand, ragged bushes hugged the rocky coastline. Taser pulled a cord, and the boat's motor roared. Under power, the skiff lurched over the waves, landing time and again with a thud and a splash. Boat excursions almost always went in the other direction, past the beach club. Everyone knew the surf on this end of the island was wild and cruel.

Soon, the shoreline loomed tall and green and rocky, the island of Agalinas looking like a jagged mountain dipped in moss and dropped in the sea. Waves smashed along the cliffs. There was no place to land the boat, no way to scale the cliffs even if they did.

"We should go back," Freesia shouted into the wind, just

as Taser turned toward shore. A wave scooped the boat up like a surfboard and hurled it toward a jumble of rocks.

This was even more terrifying than being in the room with clear walls. Freesia grabbed the bench seat, closed her eyes, and screamed.

She would never see Mummy, Daddy, or Angel again. She would never shop with Jelissa, flirt with Dare, or face-link with Ricky. In a flash, she realized something: She loved her family. She loved her friends. She even loved her noisy peacocks. That was as real as it got.

She was still screaming when the boat landed in churning water. Taser had turned off the motor and was back to paddling. Around the boat, white foam accessorized a lime green pool. A natural stone dock lay ahead of them.

"I found this place by accident one day," Taser told her.

"We could have been killed," she said.

"Maybe. It would have been kind of interesting, though, don't you think? To see if we'd be brought back to life like in a zap war?"

"This isn't a zap war," Freesia said. "Nobody ever said those were real."

The boat bumped against the rock. Taser climbed out and tied the bowline to some thick vines. In a rare show of chivalry, he reached down for Freesia's hand and helped her out. Fright turned her legs wobbly. They were safe for now, but sooner or later, they'd have to journey back over the waves.

A black cloud passed over the sun.

"Does it rain here?" Freesia asked.

"Yeah. Every day at about . . . now."

At that, water fell from the sky. It was nothing like the gentle, sweet-smelling sprinkles they got right before sunset each day in Avalon. This was a dense, violent, angry downpour.

"This way." Taser motioned to a cave entrance dripping with flowering vines. The cave was warmer than she expected. Still, she shivered in her wet clothes. She followed Taser through a stone room to an alcove that held a small, teardrop-shaped pool. Steam rose from the glowing, jade-colored water and thickened the air.

"Phosphorescent hot springs," Taser told her.

Freesia rubbed her arms. "If I had a towel, I'd go in," she said. "I'm wearing my swimsuit."

"I can get you a towel from the supply room."

"From the . . . what?"

"I've been coming to this cave for about four months. Maybe six. I lose track of time. Each visit I bring something new. So I'll be ready when . . ."

"When what?"

"I'll get you the towel."

"But . . ."

Taser took off into a deeper part of the cave. Freesia had about ten questions she wanted to ask him, but they would have to wait. She was so cold, and the little pool looked so warm. She peeled off her soggy dress, revealing a ruffled pink bikini, and hung her clothes from a piece of quartzite that stuck out from the cave wall like a natural hanger. Another quartzite hanger jutted off to one side; she hung her bag on it.

She dipped a toe into the silky warm water. Crouching down, she felt for the bottom with her foot, only to discover a natural bench running along the sides. Her motion set off the water's phosphorescence and made it glitter and glow with greater intensity. She settled onto the bench and let the warmth envelop and relax her.

Before long, Taser returned with a fluffy white towel. "There's a bigger swimming pool farther back," he told her. "And a firefly garden and . . ." His voice trailed off.

"What?"

"It's a surprise. You'll see."

A big pool. A firefly garden. And a surprise. Todd almighty, was Taser trying to get romantic?

"Taser. We are not re-linking."

He gawked. "What? You think I brought you here to—"

She glared at him. "You don't have to say it like it's so odious."

"It's not odious. At least not *so* odious. It's just . . . superfluous. We don't have time for intrigue. Not when there's so much we have to do."

"Like?"

"Like recruit forces, plan strategy, stockpile more supplies. We need to fortify the arms and explosives cache—"

"*You have weapons in here?*"

"Of course. That's the surprise."

"*Of course?* You say that like it's normal. Like *you're* normal. Like this entire cave is not in danger of blowing up at any moment!"

She scrambled out of the jade pool and reached for the towel. It didn't matter that her swimsuit was so tiny. He wouldn't notice, wouldn't care. All Taser ever thought about was war, war, war. How could she have let him suck her in like this?"

"You know what I think?" she said.

He tilted up his chin, which he probably thought made him look superior but in fact just gave her an unwanted view up his nostrils. "Obviously not, since you haven't told me. But frankly, it doesn't matter what you think because the reality is that—"

"The reality, Taser, is that you are completely disconnected from reality! You have spent so much time playing zap wars and bubble games that you can't even tell the difference between what's real and what's make-believe. Speaking of bubbles, I need to tell my mother I'm going to be late so she'll keep my dinner warm."

She took her bag off the quartzite hook and pulled out her silver bubble, held it between her hands and . . . nothing.

"Argh!" She stamped her foot on the stone floor. "It must have gotten wet."

"Bubbles don't work here."

"But what if you need to ask your parents something? What if you feel like sharing a friendly giggle? Or maybe you're bored and you want to see what everyone is wearing today, what then?"

"None of that matters. Don't you get it? If you can't see them, they can't see you. We're safe here. You hungry? I've got beans."

She chucked the white towel on the ground and reached for her clammy dress. "Beans are odious. You are odious. And this cave? Odious." She yanked the clammy dress over her head.

"This cave is not odious." He sounded hurt.

She snorted. "You'll defend the cave but not yourself. Take me home."

He dropped his head and nodded. That was the weird thing about Taser. Well, one of the weird things. He acted all tough and aggressive, but as soon as anyone fought back, he crumpled. Maybe that was why he was so much happier in his imaginary worlds with his imaginary friends. They were easier to control.

They climbed back into the skiff, and he pulled the cord to start the engine. The surf had calmed a bit. They took one stinging wave while getting past the break; otherwise, the ride went smoothly. Neither spoke until Taser steered the boat up to the sandy beach at the far end of the cove.

"How do you explain the repeating day, then?" Taser asked as she climbed over the side and into the warm, calf-deep water. A school of tiny purple fish tickled her ankles.

She said, "It was just a blip. A burp. A malfunction. There are some things in life that we just can't understand."

Four strides, and she was on the sand. The sun, low in the sky, illuminated wisps of pink fog and made Agalinas glow like a mirage.

Taser turned the boat around and walked it to deeper water before climbing back in.

"Where are you going?" Freesia asked.

"Where do you think?" He dipped his paddle in the water and headed back to the open ocean and his secret cave.

Freesia shook her head in disgust. How could she have thought, for one moment, that Taser could help her understand? True, peculiar things had been happening, but there had to be a rational explanation.

Taser's skiff disappeared around the end of the cove. Freesia settled on a fallen tree and pulled her bubble out of her bag. Immediately, it turned green. She enlarged it to grapefruit size. "Enemy check."

Taser was not transmitting, of course, and neither was Dare, but Chai's signal was strong. Freesia tapped a pink fingernail on her name.

Chai was lounging in a beach club cabana. A bright yellow bikini exposed all her puffy bits. Freesia changed the view to panoramic. As the view widened, she saw Chai's leg, draped over . . . *What? It couldn't be!*

But it was. Chai had a leg draped over Dare's leg. And a hand on Dare's arm. And then she leaned over and—*no!*

Just like that, Chai and Dare face-linked for all to see. Unable to look away, Freesia held her breath and counted: one-wackaccino, two-wackaccino, three-wackaccino . . . The face-link lasted fourteen excruciating wackaccinos.

"That should make you forget about Freesia," Chai said.

"I might need some more help forgetting," Dare replied.

Freesia couldn't bear any more. She tapped her finger twice on the bubble, ending the transmission.

Why would Dare want to forget her? Just yesterday he had confessed that he still had feelings for her, and—ugh! When he'd asked her out today, she'd turned him down and run away. How could she let Taser get to her? She'd lost sight of the things that really matter in life.

Like boys. And clothes. And dances.

She had to talk to Jelissa.

"Friendlies check."

Freesia was just about to tap a pink fingernail on her best friend's name when the bubble disappeared, along with the entire world around it.

9

" I was supposed to be at the mall like twenty minutes ago." The girl's voice, slightly muffled, filtered through the darkness.

"It's not my fault, so lose the attitude. The updates were supposed to be done by now." A woman this time. "Did you call tech support again, Darren? *Darren?* Are you listening?"

"What?" A man, distracted. "Oh. Yeah. They said they were having trouble locating her signal."

"That's ridiculous." The woman again. "She's been here the whole time. Where's she going to go?" A laugh: hoarse and not really amused.

"I need money for the mall," the girl said.

"Call them again, Darren," the woman said. "Darren? Darren! *Would you put down your phone and listen to me for five minutes of your life?*"

From the man, a hiss of irritation, and then, "You tell me to call tech support. And then you tell me to put down my phone. How'm I supposed to call tech support without the phone?"

"It's waking up!" the girl shrieked.

Freesia's vision was clearing, the space around her growing from black to gray. She was in the room with the clear walls again, not-Mummy, not-Daddy, and not-Angel gaping at her from the other side.

She was sitting in a black recliner and holding on to a ball, also black and surprisingly warm, about the size of a tangerine. Oh my Todd, was that her bubble? Even though it was the wrong color? She cupped the black sphere in both hands and waited for it to turn green or blue or to grow larger.

"Call Jelissa," she commanded, hands shaking. Nothing.

"Call Mummy." Nothing.

"Friendlies check."

Frustrated, Freesia chucked the not-bubble to the ground.

"Don't do that!" not-Mummy shouted. "Do you know how much a control ball costs?"

"Tech support said she might be disoriented," not-Daddy said. "Said we should talk to her in soothing voices."

"*You need to drive me to the mall.*"

Trembling, Freesia got out of the recliner and crossed to the transparent wall nearest her not-family. "Where am I?"

Not-Daddy exhaled.

Not-Mummy said, "Francine, you're not in Agalinas anymore."

Not-Angel, looking agitated, tapped at a small rectangular thing. She wore short black shorts, bulky black boots, and a raspberry tank top cut so low it showed the edge of her bright green bra. Not-Angel needed attire assistance in the worst possible way.

Beyond the clear walls were other walls: white, flat, square. Her giant bubble was a room within a room outside the bubble, a narrow bed lay under a window covered with heavy black curtains.

There was no room for any other furniture. Her space within the clear walls—her giant bubble—was bigger than she'd realized. In front, black rubber flooring covered a half-moon of open space. The black recliner sat in the center, an extendable metal arm holding a tray with a tall metal cup and plate, both empty. In the back, a shower and toilet stood on white tile.

Freesia asked, "So is this . . . the mainland?"

Not-Mummy and not-Daddy exchanged a look.

"It is."

"But how did I get here? And who's Francine?"

"I told you the choose-your-own-name feature was a bad idea," not-Mummy grumbled to the man.

"Well, you're the one who pushed Bubble World in the first place."

Not-Mummy and not-Daddy put their heads together. Freesia heard him say, "Tech support said that as long as she's down for less than three hours and we administer the STM blocker, she won't remember a thing."

Not-Angel burst into tears. "You said you'd take me to the mall! You're going back on your word! You don't pay any attention to me!"

"Fine," not-Mummy said. "Let's all go to the mall."

● ● ●

Freesia didn't know what to expect when, legs wobbly, she followed her not-parents out of the room with the plain white walls. Would she encounter a cave? A rooftop deck? A sparkly banquet room with a long table laden with sips and nibbles?

But no: beyond the wall with the white walls were . . . more white walls, dotted here and there with framed pictures of ugly people. An open doorway revealed a clunky brown desk with a glowing box on top.

"My office," not-Mummy explained without being asked.

They passed a few more doors, all white, all closed, and then reached a staircase.

"*Elbow*," not-Mummy said to not-Daddy. "You remember that Christmas when . . ."

Not-Daddy squeezed Freesia's elbow. "Hold the banister."

Freesia grabbed the railing that ran along the stairs. Her pulse quickened.

Stairs meant danger.

She couldn't remember ever being in this place, yet she recognized it far back in her brain, like snippets from a fuzzy dream.

Stairs meant pain.

"Can I go home now?" she croaked. (What was wrong with her voice?)

"You are home, Francine." Not-Daddy held tight to her elbow.

"Every time, we go through this," not-Mummy muttered.

She made it down the stairs without falling. At the bottom, a sitting room had white walls and tan furniture. Heavy shutters covered the windows. Down the hall was yet another white room, this one a kitchen with plain tan countertops.

"Is there no color in your world?" Freesia asked.

Without answering, not-Daddy opened a door at the far end of the kitchen, revealing a big black boxy car just like Freesia had seen in movies. From what Freesia had seen, these vehicles only did two things: speed and explode.

"*Get down!*" Freesia dropped to the ground and buried her head in her arms.

"What the—"

"It's going to blow!"

"The Expedition?" not-Mummy said.

"Can't Dad just stay here and freaksit?" not-Angel begged. "And you can drive me?"

"I need to buy shoe inserts at the mall," not-Daddy said. "For the boots I bought for this summer's Civil War reenactment."

Not-Mummy nudged Freesia's shoulder. "Put your head up. Drink this."

Trembling, Freesia pushed herself off the cold floor and opened her mouth. The liquid was warm, the taste sweet and reassuring.

"Is that happy juice?" Freesia whispered.

"You got it," not-Mummy said.

10

After a few minutes, Freesia was no longer afraid of the big boxy car. The people who looked like her parents said it wouldn't blow up. Why should she doubt them? Freesia felt . . . not happy, exactly, but calm. Calm-ish. Calm enough.

The vehicle backed out of the stuffy garage into a world quite unlike Agalinas. Spiky plants and spindly trees struggled for existence in front of a seemingly endless line of white and beige houses. Instead of lawns, the yards were strewn with gravel. The driveway was white, the road gray. Aside from the vast blue sky, there was, in fact, very little color here.

"What do you call this place?" Freesia asked.

"Phoenix, Arizona," not-Mummy said.

"Will you turn on the TV?" not-Angel said.

A rectangle hanging from the car ceiling lit up and showed pretty, happy people on a beach not so different from the one in Agalinas.

"Are those your friends?" Freesia asked not-Angel.

The girl flared her nostrils. "Can we just not talk?"

Something buzzed. The girl pulled her rectangle from a handbag that wasn't even a little bit vicious.

"Is that your bubble?" Freesia asked.

The girl tapped at the screen and ignored her.

Freesia peered out the window. White house. White house. Tan house. White house. She yawned, her calm-ishness turning to the sleepies.

Big white car. Big silver car. Huge white car. Big white car. Medium tan car.

Spindly plants.

More houses.

At last—color! A column of lights hung from a wire above the road. As they approached, a green circle flickered out as, above it, a yellow one flickered on, only to be replaced by a bright red circle on top.

The car stopped.

A long, low building lay beyond the intersection. Freesia knew that place, and not just from a dream. Heart racing, her sleepies ran away.

"That building. In front of us. I think I've been there before."

"That was your elementary school," not-Daddy said.

"But how . . . ?"

"We'll talk about it when we get to the mall."

*B*ig, ugly cars surrounded the big, ugly mall. But none of that prepared Freesia for the sight of the people who got out of the cars. A very tall, very skinny boy walked past Freesia's car window.

"Oh my Todd. What's wrong with his face?"

"What do you mean?" not-Mummy asked.

"He's . . . disfigured."

"He is not disfigured. He just has acne," not-Mummy said. "All teenagers get it."

"I don't." Angel opened her door. "Give me a thirty-second lead." She slammed the door and ran across the parking lot. Her blond hair shone under the harsh sun.

Two enormous people passed the car. Freesia recoiled. "Those creatures are grotesque!"

Not-Mummy spun around. "You have to stop doing that, Francine! There is nothing wrong with those people. They are just fat. This is America, which means that when we go inside, you will see more fat people. Also people with pimples and people with bad hair and people in wheelchairs—and you can't stare at any of them."

"I would never stare at someone in a wheelchair."

Not-Daddy opened his door. "Thirty seconds are up."

The parking lot was very, very warm.

"Is this summer?" Freesia asked.

Not-Mummy shook her head. "It's only March. Summer's twenty degrees hotter, sometimes more."

Funny how Freesia hadn't even noticed what she was wearing until now, but her black stretch pants and T-shirt, while comfortable in the white-walled house, stuck to her in the heat. Plus: black stretch pants and a black T-shirt? With squeaky white sneakers? Hideosity!

"I need to find a dress shop," Freesia said. "Or a skirt and top shop. Do you have those things on the mainland?"

Not-Daddy pulled open a glass door to the big building. A blast of cold air hit Freesia, and she shivered. But that was okay because just like that, a rack of blouses stood next to a rack of sweaters stood next to a wall of dresses stood next to a display of pants.

"Perfect!" Freesia reached for a fluffy red cardigan. "This sweater will look de-vicious with my houndstooth minidress and my patent-leather pumps."

Not-Mummy snatched the sweater away from her. "I am not buying you cashmere, and besides, you can't wear something from *here* with your minidress from *there* because—"

"Because why?"

"Let's get coffee," not-Daddy said.

Walking through the cold mall with her not-parents, Freesia felt as though she were surrounded by fun-house-mirror people: too fat, too thin, big noses, small chins . . . who knew there were so many ways to be ugly?

"Don't stare," not-Mummy hissed.

Freesia looked at the ground. Good Todd, her sneakers

were ick. How could she have ever chosen them? And why didn't she remember doing so?

"Here we are." Not-Daddy's voice was flat. "Tracey's Famous Coffee. Nothing like a coffee cloud to start your day the Tracey way."

"I hate those commercials," not-Mummy said.

Freesia stared—first at her not-parents and then at the sign over the coffee shop. "We have Tracey's coffee in Agalinas."

"Product placement," not-Mummy said. "Darren, get us lattes, will you?"

Not-Mummy chose a mirrored table in the back and told Freesia to face the wall so she'd stop staring at people. Freesia's chair made a painful squeaking noise when she pulled it out.

"Ow!" She put her hands over her ears.

"Noise sensitivity," not-Mummy said.

"What?"

"Sit down, Francine."

Not-Mummy retrieved something that looked like not-Angel's not-bubble. She tapped and pulled and poked at the little screen. Finally, she dropped it back into her purse.

Not-Daddy placed a paper bag on the table along with three brown cardboard cups with plastic lids. "Three pastries and three coffee clouds."

"I prefer my hot beverages in a mug," Freesia said. No one responded. Fine: she'd drink out of cardboard, but the plastic lid had to go. Carefully, she peeled it off. And then she glanced at the mirrored tabletop.

"*Aaaaaarghhh!*"

"Francine, *Francine*, *FRANCINE!*"

"It's her! It's the girl!" Her chair shrieked against the tile as she pushed away from the table and stood up.

"Stop it, Francine. Everyone is looking at us."

Freesia squeezed her eyes shut and covered her face with her hands. Maybe it was just her imagination. Maybe she just *thought* she had seen the stocky, bumpy-skinned, frizzy-haired girl who'd once looked back from her closet mirror in Agalinas.

She opened her eyes for a peek, but her not-parents had covered the table with paper napkins.

"Sit down, Francine. We have something to tell you."

11

"Francine, I am your father."

"You look like my father, but—"

"It's true, Francine," the woman said.

"Stop calling me that."

"It's your name," the woman said.

"If he's my father, then you're—"

"Obviously."

"But I already have a Mummy. She's in Agalinas—waiting for me, probably wondering where I've gone. I'd bubble her, but—"

"I'm Mummy. Mummy is me. We're the same . . . Mummy. Though I'd actually prefer you call me Mother."

"So when I'm in Agalinas and I talk to Mummy and she answers back, it's really you?"

"Yes. No. Sometimes. I have the option of logging in as . . . Mummy. But my schedule—it's hard to coordinate. Some of the time Mummy is actually computer generated."

"Most of the time," not-Daddy said. "Pretty much always."

"I'm a strong believer in consistency," not-Mummy—Mother—said.

"Should we start at the start?" the man—Father—asked.

Freesia nodded.

● ● ●

It all began sixteen years, six months, and nine days earlier, when Donna Somers gave birth to a furry, wrinkly baby girl, who bawled at her first sight of the world and didn't stop for a good eighteen months, when her parents discovered that educational videos could buy them forty minutes' peace at a stretch. Donna and her husband, Darren, tried to convince themselves that their daughter's crankiness was within the range of normal, but when their second daughter was born, two years after Francine, her placid, pleasant temperament stood in such contrast to her older sister's that her parents considered the baby a gift from the heavens. And so they called her Angel.

"She's not so angelic now," Freesia interrupted.

"She's a teenager," the man said. "All teenagers are selfish and rude."

"And he should know," Mother said. "He teaches high school."

By the time Freesia was three, she'd moved on from videos to interactive electronic games to educational computer programs: early spelling, early addition, early French. By the time she was four, she'd mastered basic reading programs and had begun to tackle subtraction.

Away from the computer, things didn't go so well. Her mother arranged play dates; Francine hid under her bed. Her mother took her to a little kids' gym; Francine buried her head in her mother's lap and refused to participate in the parachute exercises.

And then came school. She cried on the first day. She cried on the second day. She cried on the . . . well, every day. All day long until Donna picked her up, gave her a snack, and parked her in front of the computer.

At first, the teachers assured Donna and Darren that things would get better. But things didn't get better, not really. True, Francine learned to control her crying, at least some of the time, but she refused to interact with the other children, refused to participate in playground games, failed to make eye contact.

"Shy is one thing, but you didn't even try," Mother said.

"The kids were so mean to me!" Freesia blurted.

Why did she say that? How did she *know* that? These people who called themselves her parents were speaking utter nonsense about some other child who did or didn't exist, and yet . . .

The playground. Sharp gray stones glittered in the sun. Children threw them at her legs, at her back. Their laughter was sharp, too. Their voices were high and cruel as they twisted her name. "Freak-cine." "Franken-cine."

Mother said, "It broke my heart, Francine."

"Don't call me that."

"We just wanted to protect you," Father said.

She got older, but things got no better. She complained of headaches. Sore throats. Stomach cramps. Anything that would allow her to stay home with her computer. She begged her mother to homeschool her, but Donna was just launching her career as a vlogger, plus she didn't have the right temperament to educate her child.

"Teaching sucks the life out of you," Father said.

"What is a vlogger?" Freesia asked.

"A vlogger is a person who vlogs," Mother said.

Father explained. "A vlog is a video log. Like a newscast, only the vlogger controls her own site—the content, presentation, everything. And sometimes other websites pick up her videos."

"Often," Mother said. "Other sites *often* pick me up. That's in addition to my links on a wide variety of social networking sites. I am a leading web expert on emerging family-centric technologies."

"She does a lot of stories on smartphone apps."

"And I vlog about Bubble World. Though to maintain our privacy, I don't use my real name. I call myself Donna Flash. The vlog is called *Flash Drive.*"

Donna and Darren investigated online schools and were about to try one when Donna attended a technology convention in Texas. There she met a video game designer and educational software developer named Todd Piloski, who was on the verge of launching a program that would revolutionize education.

Todd Piloski had created a virtual-reality teen utopia,

which he called Bubble World. The program would employ all the senses to make participants feel like they were really there, eating, sleeping, talking, and learning. *Especially* learning.

"Bubble World is a total educational immersion," Mother said. "Where else could there be an English class taught by Shakespeare? Or a biology class that takes you inside a thirty-foot-tall model of the human body?"

"Ew." Freesia shuddered, too repulsed by the thought of slogging through a giant body to ask about that Shakespeare guy.

"We're sorry about your memory issues," Father said. "You weren't supposed to forget *everything* about your life before Bubble World. The memory blockers were just supposed to wipe out a week or two. To make the transition easier."

"How long have I been gone?"

"Three and a half years."

"Have I been back before?"

"Of course!" Mother said. "We bring you home every birthday and every Christmas."

"Except for the last one," Father said.

Mother shrugged. "We got a phenomenal deal on plane tickets to Maui. And the truth is, your transitions out of Bubble World, even the scheduled ones, have always been a bit traumatic."

Happy juice beginning to wear off, Freesia felt the fingers of panic creeping up her spine. "So you're saying that Agalinas doesn't exist?"

"Of course it exists!" Mother said. "It exists in Todd's imagination and in yours and in simulations across the world. Just because you can't touch something doesn't mean it isn't real."

"Agalinas doesn't exist," Father said.

Freesia said, "But I have a house there. And a family and friends and clothes. Lots and lots of clothes."

"Your friends exist," Mother said. "Most of them, anyway. They don't look like their Bubble World avatars, of course, any more than you do. But they are real kids with real bubble stations, just like yours."

"And they don't know that the island is virtual?"

"Well . . . no. The memory blockers were only supposed to erase the previous week or so. Unfortunately, the pharmaceutical company had failed to test the medications on teenagers. We knew more extensive memory loss was a possibility. Still, it was jarring the first time you came home and didn't recognize us. At Todd's request, I haven't dwelled on that angle in my vlog reports."

Suddenly, Freesia was so tired she thought she'd fall asleep on the napkin-covered table.

"Can I go back now?"

"To the house?"

"No, to Agalinas."

"Yes! Of course. Not right this minute—your father needs his shoe inserts, and anyway, the upgrades aren't complete— but soon. We were worried that you might want to stay. Not that we wouldn't enjoy having you around, of course. But you've been so happy in Bubble World, and academically— well, your progress just blows us away."

Father opened the paper bag and pulled out a cupcake, a muffin, and a scone. "Hungry?"

"We'll make it nice for you," Mother said. "Bubble World, I mean."

Freesia reached for the cupcake. "It's already nice."

"We'll make it nicer."

"It's red velvet," Father said.

Tinny music played from Mother's handbag. She pulled out her rectangular thing and held it up to her ear. "Yes, Angel. . . . Not for another half hour or so. . . . Because your father needs to go to that store with the ugly shoes so he can buy inserts. . . . Give us fifteen minutes. . . . Okay, ten . . . five . . . Angel . . . *Angel.*"

Mother tapped the front of the rectangle and dropped it into her handbag. "We have to leave now. Angel will meet us at the car."

"But—"

"She had a fight. With a friend. Or several friends. The usual."

"But—"

"She's crying. Hysterically. Making a scene."

"I guess I can come back later to get my inserts."

"I guess you can."

Freesia bit into the cupcake and squeaked with surprise.

"Something wrong?" Father asked.

"Don't chew with your mouth open, Francine."

"This cupcake! The taste!"

"Don't talk with your mouth open, Francine."

She chewed, swallowed, spoke again. "Food in Agalinas

tastes nothing like this." She took another bite, bigger this time, the sensation of cake and frosting exploding in her mouth. Then she took a sip of her coffee, which had grown a little cold, which needed a little more sugar, but still!

Mother said, "The food in Agalinas—which is to say, the food we give you—isn't food exactly, at least in the traditional sense. We feed you nutrition bars and supplement shakes, all carefully calibrated to meet your dietary needs. Visual triggers make you think you're getting variety."

Music jingled from Mother's handbag again. She checked her rectangle and smiled. "Good news! Updates are complete. Francine can go back to Bubble World."

Freesia shoved the rest of the cupcake in her mouth and took the cardboard cup along with her to the car.

*B*ack in the bubblepod, Father held out a small plastic cup filled with something bright green. "Drink this."

After a tense ride back from the mall, Angel had locked herself in her bedroom, while Mother had retreated to her office. Freesia could hear her on the phone. *"The A-level upgrade. Yes, I've already cleared it with Todd."*

Freesia took the cup of green liquid. "Happy juice?"

"Memory blocker. Some of the things you learned today seemed to upset you. We don't want that. If you're going to live in Bubble World, we want you to believe in it. Also, there's a provision in the contract. You're not allowed to talk to the other students about the outside world. It would take away from the immersion experience."

Freesia took a deep breath. "You said that *most* of my friends in Agalinas are real, more or less. So that means that some of them are . . ."

Father shrugged. "You can't just throw a bunch of kids together and expect everyone to have a great time. So they created buffers, antagonists, and facilitators."

"I have no idea what that means."

"You don't have to. Drink your medicine."

Freesia took the cup, brought it up to her mouth, and hesitated. "Did everyone get updates today?"

"Yes, but I doubt anyone else's system crashed. So things went on as normal."

She brought the cup up to her mouth—and stopped again. She twisted around and nodded toward the very exposed toilet. "If you don't mind, I'd like to use that before I go."

"Of course!" Her father headed for the door. "I'll wait in the hall. Let me know when you're ready."

When Father shut himself in the hallway, she hurried to the toilet and, before she had time to reconsider, dumped the green liquid. She counted to thirty and flushed.

"I'm ready," she called out.

Her father came into the bubblepod and took her empty medicine cup.

She settled into the recliner and gazed at the hard, clear walls. "Tell me how this works."

"This is your monitor," Father said, gesturing toward the

bubble walls. "The images project all around you. Sounds come from speakers in the ceiling and floor. The control ball is your bubble. And this—" he pointed to the black rubber floor—"is a treadmill."

Father twisted open a bottle of clear liquid and poured it into the stainless-steel cup. "Have some juice. It's important for you to stay hydrated."

Freesia peered at the liquid. "Are there memory blockers in here, too?"

"Oh, no—this is what you drink every day. The blockers are just for when you make the transition from the real to the virtual state."

Freesia sipped the liquid. It was sweet with a metallic aftertaste.

"Have some more," Father urged.

Obediently, she took a few gulps and put the cup back on the stainless-steel tray. Feeling suddenly relaxed, she took it all in: the hard white walls, the silver table, the black rubber floor, her father's tired face.

She wouldn't miss this place, not one bit.

"Send me home, please."

12

*S*he expected to find herself on the beach where she'd blacked out, but no: she was back in her pretty room in her pretty house in Agalinas, sitting—slumping, really—in her pink lounger, the peacocks at her feet. Her silver bubble sat in its trumpet-shaped charger. One thing was different. A brand-new holographic poster of Chase Bennett covered an entire wall! That must have been what her parents meant when they said they would make things nice for her.

"Sing," she commanded Ashley.

As the peacock launched into a new Chase Bennett tune, the holograph swayed, gyrated, and moved his lips in close-enough time to the song.

No time for sadness
Here on the island, girl.
We're far from madness
Here on the island, girl.
Forget your worries,

Forget your cares,
Forget who you were,
Forget what you'd wear,
'Cuz when you're on the island, girl,
All that matters is that you're an island girl.

Thank Todd some things stayed the same. Chase Bennett? Was still an artistic genius.

"Mummy?" she called out.

Just like that, Mummy appeared at the door: pretty, happy, shiny Mummy.

"Yes, sweet Freesia? Can I get you something? A coffee cloud? An afternoon snack? Some happy juice?"

"No, thank you. Just . . ."

Mummy kept standing there. Kept smiling. Kept shining.

"What was I like as a child?" Freesia asked.

"You were beautiful," Mummy said. "Also sweet as a cupcake and happy as a hummingbird."

"I love you, Mummy." Freesia's voice cracked, and her nose stung in an odd way. She felt something spill out of her eyes, but when she touched her cheek and checked her fingers, they were dry.

"I love you, too!" Mummy remained in the doorway, smiling.

How could Mummy be make-believe? And this whole room: could she really be back in that awful bubblepod? It all felt so real.

"Should I stay or should I go?" Mummy asked.

Freesia squeezed her eyes shut. "Go."

When she opened her eyes again, Mummy was gone, but Ashley and Jennifer, the peacocks, had wandered over to her feet, along with a tiny cat with extravagant white fur.

"Who are you?" Freesia pushed herself out of the pink lounger and scooped up the warm, silky cat. It rumbled in her arms.

"Yow," the cat said.

"That's your name?"

"Yow," the cat confirmed, closing his eyes and rumbling some more.

Freesia took Yow and her bubble into her enormous closet and checked her reflection in the wall mirror.

Thank Todd: she was back to pretty. No, better than pretty—she was back to herself. She was not, of course, wearing the awful T-shirt and stretch pants from the mainland. Instead she had on a soft blue dress that she didn't remember buying and a long strand of white beads. It was okay, but right now she needed a boost: something extra vicious.

She pointed her bubble at the mirror. "Attire assistance," she commanded.

An image of Freesia holding the cat appeared in the mirror, but this Freesia was wearing an ankle-length floral dress that she didn't recognize.

"Another."

Next up, the Freesia in the mirror wore a strappy black blouse with tight white jeans. She was certain she'd never seen them before.

"This is flippy," she told Yow, placing him on the pink chenille sofa and turning her attention to the racks.

There was a white peasant blouse with pale blue trim. A tiny black dress with cutouts. A red miniskirt. A strapless pink denim dress.

"*I have all new clothes!*"

She had to tell Jelissa. She was bubbling her friend before she thought of all the other things she had to talk about.

Jelissa was transmitting from her balcony, on a street two levels below and a little to the right of Freesia's. She wore enormous red heart-shaped sunglasses and a straw sunhat.

"If you're calling to tell me, I already know," she said.

"*You do?*"

"It's on both their bubble updates, plus I ran into her at the beach club, and she told me they were going to the dance together."

"Wait—what?"

"Dare and Chai. They're linked. But you're better off without him. I hope you know that."

Dare Fiesta. Handsome. Perfect. Dull. Predictable. Just like that, she knew: Dare was an artificial construct. Chai could have him.

"I know that," Freesia said. "Plus . . . I know some other things. Can you meet me at Tracey's in half an hour?"

"Of course!" Jelissa said. "Love you oodles!"

"Love you more!" Freesia said, realizing for the first time just how much she meant it.

Freesia yanked the strapless pink denim dress off its hanger and traded her beads for a skinny white cotton scarf. She gave her thick copper locks a quick brush, dusted peach glitter over her cheeks, put her bubble, some lip gloss, and Yow in an oversized tote, and scampered out of her house.

"Oh! My! Todd!"

Just outside the back door, she froze. Instead of a stepping-stone walkway running through a butterfly garden to the narrow street, a stone bridge arched over a glistening, gurgling swimming pool that disappeared around either side of her house. She crossed the stone bridge and followed the pool around one side, where she encountered a steamy spa with an ocean view.

She went back around the house and followed the pool along the other side. Two steps led up to a ledge, which served as a launching point for the longest waterslide Freesia had ever seen. It traveled through her front yard, over a bridge, through the down-below neighbor's yard, over another bridge, through another yard, and so on until it emptied into a newly roped-off section of the harbor.

"But how can this be?" Freesia wondered aloud. "I wasn't gone long enough for anyone to build this."

Of course. The Chase Bennett poster was only one piece of the A-level upgrade.

Freesia began to giggle. "Thank you, Mother!"

Just like that, Mummy appeared at the kitchen window.

"You're welcome, sweet Freesia."

Freesia forced a smile. Mummy wasn't real. Neither were the pool or the waterslide or even the cat, who'd fallen asleep at the bottom of her tote.

Legs wobbly, she walked to her itty car, which was parked on the street just a few feet from the pool.

Tracey's Famous Coffee was at the end of Front Street closest to Freesia's house. Jelissa was already there, sitting at an outside table, her straw hat shading her creamy face from the sun.

"You're sure you're not upset?" Jelissa said as Freesia pulled out her chair.

"Upset? Oh—you mean about Dare and Chai. No, not at all." Freesia sat down and peered at the oversized white coffee mug.

"It's a coffee cloud," Jelissa said. "Would you rather have a wackaccino?"

"Oh—no. It looks scrummy. Thanks."

"Have you figured out what you're wearing tonight?" Jelissa asked.

"For . . . ?"

"The dance, silly! Meet there at nine, like we said?"

Freesia stared at her friend. "What day is it?"

"Is this a joke?"

"Please. Just tell me. What day is it?"

"I adore a clever joke."

"What day?"

"Saturday, of course. So what's the joke?"

It couldn't be—but it was. After repeating Tuesday, they had skipped all the way to Saturday. Freesia felt dizzy.

"What did you do yesterday?" she asked, trying to keep her voice steady.

"Yesterday was Friday," Jelissa said. "Which means I had French immersion followed by a mani-pedi." She held out her hands, showing off glossy nails, each painted with a different seashell. "Next was lunch, Art Appreciation, a sea salt spa treatment, a beach picnic for dinner, and a night swim with the dolphins."

"Yes, that's what happens every Friday. But do you actually recall doing those things yesterday?"

Jelissa pulled her heart-shaped glasses down her nose and gazed over them for a long, long time. "This is about Dare, isn't it?"

"No! This isn't about Dare! This is about . . ." Freesia looked around to make sure no one was listening and then she lowered her voice. "Yesterday . . . Tuesday . . . I went back to the real world."

Jelissa pushed her glasses back up her nose. She tilted her head to one side. "Is this a trick? So it's a trick and not a joke?"

"Look at the hillside." Freesia pointed to her new waterslide.

"I'm looking," Jelissa said.

"Don't you notice something new? Something long? And blue? And sparkling?"

"Is that a waterslide?"

"It's my waterslide. I have a swimming pool now, too."

"Vicious!"

"No! Not vicious. Well, maybe a little bit vicious. But flippy. How could anyone build something so fast?"

"We have very efficient serfs in Avalon."

"No one is that efficient."

"I'm afraid I don't like this trick very much."

"Jelissa, the trick is this place. The coffee shop, Front Street, my house, your house, all the stores, our school . . . none of it is real."

Jelissa tilted her head to the other side.

"We're not really together at the coffee shop," Freesia continued. "It just looks like we are. And this cat—" She reached into her bag and pulled out a sleepy Yow.

"Pretty!" Jelissa reached out to stroke Yow's silky fur.

"Yes. He's pretty. But he's not real." Freesia slipped the cat back into her tote, where he immediately resumed his nap. "Jelissa, we are living in a multiplayer virtual reality program called Bubble World. Our parents signed us up. Hooked us up. And then they gave us drugs that messed with our memories. We're not really living together on a magical island. Instead, we're all alone in these things called bubblepods and wearing"—Freesia paused to gather her strength—"stretch pants."

Jelissa took a sip of her coffee and then put the mug on the table. "I love you oodles, Free, but this is utterly unfunny."

"It's worse than unfunny. It's odious. Jelly, if you could see me, the way I really look—"

"What are you talking about? You look luminous! And I adore that dress. Is it new?"

"I only *look* like I look luminous. Because everything about me—my hair, my eyes, my long, long legs—it's all fake. In the real world, I have bumpy skin, bushy eyebrows, and seriously bad hair. Also I'm short and, and . . . I'm fat! Only not as fat as a lot of other people. In the real world, people are a hundred kinds of ugly."

Jelissa pushed her chair back and stood up. She pulled off her sunglasses and dropped them in her purse. Her face was pink, and not from the sun. "*Stop.*"

"I know it sounds crazy, and I know it's hard to hear, but in the real world—"

Jelissa covered her ears. "I don't need to hear any more about the so-called real world! I have lots of friendlies, but only one bestie. And now you're telling me that we don't even know each other? That we've never even met?"

"Of course not."

"What?"

"No."

"*What?*"

"You need to take your hands off your ears." Freesia gestured.

Jelissa dropped her hands, but she still looked wary.

"I know you better than I know anyone," Freesia said. "And our friendship is as real as they come. But this table, this mug . . . the harbor and boats . . . your body and mine. They don't exist. I don't even know what you look like."

Jelissa's pale eyes shone with unspilled tears. Her rosebud mouth quivered. "I don't . . . I wish . . . I can't . . ." She shook her head. "I'll see you tonight. And, Freesia?"

"Yes?"

"I really do like your dress." She turned away and hurried down the street.

Hands shaking, Freesia poked around in her tote until she found her bubble under Yow.

"Enemy check."

The silver bubble began to glow: first green, then blue.

CHAI COTILLION . . . TRANSMITTING

TASER LUCAS . . . NOT TRANSMITTING

DARE FIESTA . . . TRANSMITTING

Dash it. She had no desire to watch Chai and Dare getting all fizzy together (though she'd love to see the look on Chai's face if she learned that Dare wasn't real), but she wanted to talk to Taser. No, she *needed* to talk to Taser.

Taser's house lay a few blocks behind Front Street in a flat stretch of land cleverly dubbed The Flats. His house was blue and pointy, with purple shutters and yellow whirly swirls decorating the eaves.

Freesia rang the doorbell.

Just like that, Taser's mother—blond, trim, and pretty, in a tennis dress and bright white sneakers—opened the door.

"Hello, there!"

"Um, hi. Is Taser home?"

Taser's mother turned toward the house. "Taser? Are you here?" After a beat, still smiling, she turned back to Freesia.

"Sorry, but Taser is not home."

"Do you know where he is?"

"Sorry, but Taser is not home."

"I know, but . . . did he go off to play zap wars? Or could he be out in his skiff?"

"Hello, there! Sorry, but Taser is not home." She took a step back into the house. "Taser? Are you here?" Then she turned back to Freesia. "Thanks for stopping by! Sorry, but Taser is not home."

She shut the door.

Freesia began to shake. Now what was she supposed to do? She climbed back into her itty car and pulled out her bubble.

"Friendlies check."

A long list of names popped up. **RICKY LEISURE**, she tapped.

Clad in a plush bathrobe, Ricky lounged in a swivel chair in the vast marble salon room that lay off his even vaster marble bathroom while Nikita, his hair serf, trimmed the edges of his streaky blond hair.

"Don't let her cut too much off!" Freesia called into her bubble, forcing herself to sound jolly.

Ricky's blue eyes widened with pleasure. "I told Nikita one-thirty-second of an inch. That too much?"

"That should be good."

"Come over later," Ricky said. "And let my stylists prepare you for the dance."

"Okay, but I don't want to wait that long to see you. Meet me under the rainbow?"

"Where?"

"On the side near your house—the third bench, just below where the purple bleeds into the blue."

The sun had just fallen low enough in the sky to turn everything golden; that meant Freesia had about a half an hour until the rainbow. She headed for the Dressy Dress Shoppe. So what if the Sweet Seventeen dance was imaginary? She still needed something to wear.

13

icky was waiting on the bench. He'd changed into flowered board shorts and a crisp white T-shirt that showed off his tan. His hair, of course, was perfect. For a flash, Freesia wondered what Ricky looked like beyond Agalinas, but she pushed the thought out of her mind.

"You're early, Ricardo! The rain hasn't even started yet."

Over the harbor, puffy gray clouds cast gentle shadows on the boats below.

"I didn't want to miss any of it." He patted the bench next to him, and Freesia sat down. Together they watched as the shadows below the clouds sprouted blue-gray streaks of rain. Around them, the air grew cooler and the salt smells gave way to something green and just slightly metallic.

As the clouds drifted toward the island, the ocean foamed near the shore, setting loose a flurry of soap bubbles that floated up and around them. And then the rain began: soft, gentle droplets tickling their faces and dusting their hair. Next, the sun shot rays through the clouds and the colors began to appear: red, orange, yellow, green, blue, indigo, violet—faintly at first but quickly gaining saturation and length until a full rainbow stretched above their heads along the entire length of the town of Avalon. Everyone stopped what they were doing to marvel.

And then, just like that, the rainbow faded and disappeared, and the last of the gray clouds drifted over the mountain.

Ricky stood up and stretched. "Nikita is waiting for you. She's even got fresh flowers for your hair."

"Oh, Ricky, you're so . . ."

"What?"

"Just—I'm so glad we're friendlies."

In Ricky's salon room, Nikita waited with two bouquets of every imaginable kind of flower. Freesia chose a dusty pink rosebud to match the dress she had just bought for the second time. Nikita brushed and curled and sprayed her locks until they tumbled and swam over her shoulders, then she pulled and twisted two front pieces away from her face and knotted the flower between them.

"I can summon a cosmetics serf, if you'd like," Ricky said when Nikita had finished her work.

The offer tempted Freesia—she would have loved a set of butterfly eyelashes, as well as some glitter for her cheeks—but she needed to talk to someone about what had happened, and since Jelissa did not want to be that someone, Ricky was next on her list.

"Later, perhaps," she said. "For now let's go up to your rooftop and watch the sky turn pink."

They reached the roof deck just in time to watch the coral sun cast a path on the water. Soon the deep blue sky faded to periwinkle, then lavender, and then a pink so bright it made her shiver.

"I never get tired of this view." As she spoke, Freesia realized that it wasn't true. In fact, she barely ever paused long enough to watch the sky turn pink. Why bother? There would always be another opportunity tomorrow and the tomorrow after that.

Ricky wore a beautiful smile of contentment. She didn't want to ruin the moment for him and yet . . .

"Do you ever wonder if Agalinas is too good to be true?" she blurted.

He kept his eyes on the glowing sun. "Does it matter?"

"Of course it matters!"

"Why?" Ricky turned his face toward her. The sun made him glow like an angel.

"Because . . . because . . ."

Ricky was playing with her. Teasing her. Because he didn't know what she knew.

"Ricky, what I'm about to tell you is—" She stopped. Considered her words. "This may sound hard to believe—" She paused. "I don't want to upset you. . . ."

Ricky pointed at the horizon. "I love it when the sun just touches the water. It's like it's face-linking with the universe."

The orange sun was halfway into the ocean now.

Everything around them—the sea, the sand, the roads and houses—glowed apricot. They stood in silence until the sun slipped into the ocean.

Ricky took her hand. "I need to show you something."

They went into the house and down a hallway to Ricky's room (skylights, mirrors, tropical fish tank), through his walk-in closet (two walls of board shorts, a hundred T-shirts, countless flip-flops, one tie), beyond an herb-scented hot tub, past a salty-snack pantry, and down another long hallway. At a closed door, they stopped.

He turned the knob, followed her into the room, and shut the door behind him.

"I've never taken anyone else here."

The room was small and plain, with nothing but a puffy black couch, a simple wood desk, and a giant dark screen on one wall.

"Movie room?" Freesia guessed.

"It can be. But it's more than that. A lot more. Sit."

Freesia settled onto the couch.

Ricky said, "Up on the roof—were you trying to tell me that Agalinas is a virtual world?"

She gasped. "So you already know?"

"I've known since the beginning. The memory blockers don't work on me for some reason. That's why I've got all this—the giant house, the waterslides. The parties. Because my father thinks I will make a fuss if he doesn't give me everything I ask for. He's afraid I will want to leave."

"But how can you stand it, knowing none of this is real?"

He shrugged. "Who's to say what's real and what isn't? We're really talking to each other. Up on the roof, we really experienced the beauty of the sunset."

Ricky took something hard and flat off the desk and sat down beside her.

"Is that a bubble?" Freesia asked.

"A keyboard." He rested the rectangle on his lap and passed his hand over the surface until lettered buttons appeared. He nodded toward the screen on the wall. "That's a virtual computer monitor—a bubble to beat all bubbles. My link to the outside world." Ricky tapped the keyboard, and the screen on the wall lit up: gray, then blue, then . . .

"Oh my Todd—is that my mother?" Mother's picture smiled from the top left corner of the screen, next to the words *Flash Drive*.

"This is your mother's vlog site," Ricky said. "She has a new entry up. Let's watch."

A white arrow crossed the screen until it reached a triangle in the middle of a black box. With a click, the black box sprang to life. Mother's voice sounded hollow. Freesia recognized the clunky brown desk, the plain white walls.

"Today I had the pleasure of visiting with my sixteen-year-old daughter F. while some updates were performed to improve the Bubble World experience. For those of you who haven't watched my previous posts, F. is an honors student in Bubble World, the Web's first fully interactive virtual education program.

"Normally we spend my daughter's visits home enjoying

family dinners, playing board games, and just talking. But today we took her to our local shopping mall. F. was astonished by how unrefined, unsophisticated, and monolingual the teenagers were."

"I didn't say the teenagers were unrefined!" Freesia burst out. "I just said they were ugly. And what does she mean by mono . . . mono . . ."

"*Some of my viewers have questioned my husband's and my decision to enroll our daughter in an untested program. However, as I've long maintained, somebody has to be the pioneer. Today, at the end of our visit, my husband and I asked F., as we have many times before, if she would like to discontinue as a Bubble World pioneer and reenter the public school system. And her answer, as always, was a resounding no.*"

"That's true," Freesia said.

"*Our daughter is happy in Bubble World.*"

"True," Freesia whispered.

"*She has friends there.*"

"Also true."

"*But most of all, she is proud to be a pioneer paving the way for others in this innovative educational community.*"

The box within the screen went dark.

Freesia didn't say anything for a while. Ricky took her hand.

"What was that?" she asked at last.

"The Internet. It's got everything you want to know, anytime you want to know it. Celebrity gossip, world news, weather, fashion . . . funny cat videos."

At that, Yow woke up and climbed to the top of Freesia's purse, which sat on the couch next to her.

"Yow!"

"I love virtual cats." Ricky reached over and picked up Yow. He cradled the cat in his arm and stroked its soft belly. "I'm allergic to real ones."

Freesia buried her face in her hands. "I don't like this. I don't like it at all."

"Don't be sad!" Ricky balanced the cat on one arm. With the other hand, he tapped at the keyboard.

On the giant screen, another video appeared. An orange kitten snuck up on a giant sleeping dog, slapped its nose, and ran away.

"That one wasn't very good," Ricky said. He tapped the keyboard some more and came up with another mini cat movie, called "Cat Tarzan." It involved kittens and window-shade blinds, and it made Freesia smile. A little.

"That's how people in the so-called real world entertain themselves," Ricky said. "By tapping keyboards and watching stuff on screens. Here in Bubble World, we don't just watch entertainment, we live it. It's much fizzier."

"So that's why our parents put us here? So we could have a fizzy time?"

"Of course not. They put us here so they wouldn't have to deal with us. But they also think we're getting this wicked education. Check out the Bubble World website."

A few more keyboard taps, and the screen gave way to an aerial shot of Agalinas, with words drifting down the screen:

There is a place
Where your child can grow and learn and be happy.
Where she or he can become fluent in multiple languages,
Build friendships and develop social skills to last a lifetime,
Master high math concepts and sophisticated writing conventions,
Devour world history, the sciences, literature, and more,
Explore art, music, dance, theater, and athletics . . .
All in the comfort and safety of your own home.
That place is called . . .
Bubble World.
Click <u>here</u> for testimonials.

Ricky moved the arrow on the screen to the <u>here</u>, and just like that, the screen gave way to a shot of . . .

"Is that me?" Freesia asked.

"Sort of."

A girl appeared on the screen. She looked just like Freesia—except that she wore a formless yellow polo shirt that Freesia wouldn't be caught dead in.

"I can't thank my parents enough for allowing me to engage in an interactive Bubble World experience. Before I came here, I struggled with academics and had trouble forming and maintaining interpersonal ties. Now I excel in my schoolwork, I have countless study partners, and I am fluent in five languages and proficient in two musical instruments."

"What did I just say?" Freesia asked Ricky.

"That you spend all your time studying."

For the first time all day, Freesia laughed. "But how do they make it look like I'm spouting such silliness?"

"Everything in Agalinas, including your voice and appearance, is computer generated," Ricky reminded her. "A Bubble World Enterprises programmer can make your avatar say or do utterly anything."

Freesia shuddered.

"Here's my testimonial." Ricky tapped the keyboard, and there he was, running up the steep hill that led to the interior, a sheen of sweat on his brow. He slowed his pace and faced the camera. "My favorite thing about Bubble World is all the opportunities it provides for physical fitness. Before coming here, I struggled with my weight. Now I enjoy running, biking, kayaking, and ocean swimming. Whatever my mood, there's an activity to meet it!" He held up his hand to wave and sprinted up the hill.

"I thought that would make you twinkle," Ricky said.

Freesia said, "My father told me that some of the people on Agalinas . . . aren't people. I think Dare might be make-believe."

"Oh, no—Dare is real. His real name is David, and he's from Pennsylvania. He's got this rare disease that makes his skin so sensitive that it can't be exposed to sunlight. Bubble World is his only chance to have a normal life."

He put Yow on the couch and reached down to a pull-out fridge under the couch. "Cheesecake?"

"No, thank you. Um . . . you know that's really a nutrition bar."

Ricky shrugged. "It looks like cheesecake. It smells like cheesecake. I say it's cheesecake."

He took a big bite and closed his eyes. Once he

swallowed, he opened his eyes and said, "That's what you need to understand. It doesn't matter what's computer generated and what isn't. Agalinas is real because it *feels* real. Oh! This will make you twinkle. Chai's virtual."

"She *is*?"

"Nobody could be that noxious. But according to the psychologists who advised Todd Piloski, all teenage girls need someone to abhor. But he couldn't have students shunning a paying customer—it would be bad for business. Chai's an easy target. Plus, she was Bitsy's Insta-friend."

"Her what?"

Ricky ate some more cheesecake before answering. "Bitsy had trouble making friends. So her parents paid Todd Piloski to make one for her."

Freesia felt dizzy. "Who else is make-believe?"

"None of our better friendlies," Ricky said.

"Where is Pennsylvania?"

Ricky tapped at his keyboard some more and brought up a map of the United States. He moved the arrow over to the right side. "That's Pennsylvania." He moved the arrow to the lower left. "Your bubblepod is here—in Phoenix, Arizona."

"Where's your bubblepod?" she asked.

He moved the arrow way over to the left, where the land met water. "Newport Beach, California. Number five Sunset Drive. My real name is Richard Levine."

"My real name is Francine Somers."

"I know."

"How do you know all of this?" Freesia asked.

He smiled. "In addition to the house, the boats, the cars—everything—I convinced my father to give me a next-generation bubble. When you were in class, I was writing code, hacking into the Bubble World's mainframe, reading Todd Piloski's e-mails, building this keyboard, this screen, this room. . . ."

Freesia bit her lip. "I don't understand much of what you just said, but it sounds bad."

"Oh, no. It is just something to pass the time when the rest of you are in class. But our true world—Agalinas—is far more interesting than anything we can find online." He clicked a few more times, and the giant screen went dark.

"Does anyone else know the truth?" Freesia asked.

"I don't think so."

"Taser knows something is off. He took me to this cave—"

Ricky gasped. "Down the coast? Past the wild waters?"

"You've been there?"

"I've . . . heard of it. Don't go there again, Freesia. It's not safe. And if you see Taser again, remember: you can't talk about the so-called real world. Not a peep. You never know when they're watching you."

Freesia's skin prickled. "Can they see us now?"

"Not in this room. I was careful to hide the code."

"But . . ." Freesia's head hurt from thinking so much. "Don't they notice when you disappear?"

He shrugged. "They can't follow all of us at once. The program is overloaded as it is. That's part of the reason it keeps crashing. They watch Front Street, the learning center sometimes.

Otherwise, they just follow people if something seems wiggy."

"So I can't let them think anything is wiggy."

"Exactly."

"But what could they do to me?"

"They could close down your account. Make you disappear."

"Poof." Freesia's voice cracked.

"You just need to put all of this out of your mind. Let's not talk about it again. Remember: Agalinas is real because it *feels* real."

Freesia scooped Yow back into her handbag, and they left the secret screen room behind. Stepping out onto the roof deck was a relief. The glimpse of reality, such as it was, had been stressful.

Above them, a blue moon had begun to rise in the sky. Below them, on Front Street, a crowd had gathered—surprising, since everyone should have been home getting ready for the dance right around then.

Ricky had his very own zipline, with stops at the learning center and the Front Street Beach. Within minutes, he and Freesia were on the sand, surrounded by tizzy friendlies.

"It's Chase Bennett!" Cabo explained.

Just beyond the bay, which was lit only with twinkling boat lights and a few final streaks of pink in the sky, a ship far larger than any they'd ever seen glowed as if it were illuminated from within. A helicopter sat on its roof, and a small boat trailed from a rope behind.

In the excitement, Freesia forgot, at least for the moment,

that Agalinas was not what she'd always thought it was. "Mr. Coda said Chase Bennett would be vacationing in Agalinas. But I never dreamed it would be so soon."

"He's holding a bubblecast essay contest," Ferdinand said. "Submissions are due by ten o'clock tomorrow morning. I'm going to compose mine after I get home from the dance."

"What's the prize?" Ricky asked.

"The winner gets to meet Chase Bennett and tour his yacht."

"Oh my Todd!" Freesia jumped up and down on the sand. "I am Chase Bennett's biggest fan. I have to meet him. What's the essay topic?"

"*Why I Want to Meet Chase Bennett,*" Ferdinand told her.

"Clever," Cabo said.

And everyone agreed.

14

$\mathcal{I}$f Freesia owned a calendar, she could have said how many Saturday night dances she had attended at the Rotunda, but keeping track of time was even more bor- rifying than Cantonese immersion class on a day when the in- structor neglected to supply fortune cookies. Costume dances were her favorite because she could dress up as a fairy tale princess (and, on occasion, a wood nymph). But she also en- joyed the Sweet Fifteens and Seventeens (the Sixteens, in her opinion, were too predictable) because they featured tall, sparkly cakes, lush floral bouquets, and unexpected amuse- ments like Ferris wheels and magic shows.

As if the sight of Chase Bennett's yacht moored just outside the harbor weren't enough to take her mind off her recent discovery, a fleet of hot-air balloons covered the hillside across from the Rotunda. A handful had already been set free to drift into the night sky.

On the pathway adjacent to the hillside, Jelissa clapped her hands with delight. "Oh, Freesia, isn't this magical? I've al- ways wanted to go up in a hot-air balloon!"

After their coffee shop conversation, Freesia feared that Jelissa would still be angry with her—or, maybe worse, that she would ask Freesia to explain herself further. Instead, her friend acted as if nothing had happened.

"You should ask Dare to take a ride with you," Jelissa suggested. "I'd love to see Chai go all wiggy."

"I think I'll ask Ricky instead."

Jelissa giggled and gave her a little pinch.

"It's not like that! Ricky's my second bestie. I need to chat with him about . . . things."

Jelissa frowned. "I hope you will not upset him the way you upset me this morning."

"Of course not."

Freesia envied Jelissa's ignorance. If only she could go back in time and take the memory blocker instead of dumping it down the toilet.

Coffee-colored Cabo, dressed all in black, and fair Ferdinand, in white, strolled toward them.

"Four people can fit in a basket," Cabo said.

"And there are two of you and two of us," Ferdinand added. (See? They'd picked up some math skills along the way.)

On the hillside, girls in fluffy dresses and boys wearing all black or all white stepped into the big wicker baskets. Party serfs untied the heavy red ropes that tethered the balloons to the ground and freed them into the starry sky.

"Freesia's saving her ride for Ricky," Jelissa said.

Freesia felt her face grow warm. "We're just friendlies, almost besties, and—"

"No need to explain." Jelissa slipped a hand into each boy's elbow. "Let's go, boys. See you in the sky, Free."

Freesia watched her friends drift away in the twinkling night. Then, out of nowhere, it hit her: were Cabo and Ferdinand real?

Did it matter?

She didn't want it to, but it did.

Freesia pulled her bubble out of her white satin party purse. "Friendlies check."

She tapped **RICKY LEISURE** and saw . . . herself. He'd snuck up next to her when she wasn't looking.

"Were you bubbling me?" He held a silver bucket filled with a bottle of happy fizz and two glasses.

"I was. Let's share a balloon."

Together, they climbed up the wildflower-covered hillside. They craned their necks to examine the giant balloons until they agreed on a turquoise one with a giant purple dragonfly on either side. A serf untied the rope that tethered the basket to the ground, and up they went.

Ricky popped open the happy fizz, poured two glasses, and gave one to Freesia. She clutched the side of the basket and watched the world below grow smaller and smaller. The wind on her face was colder than she expected. She should have brought a wrap.

"Chilly?" Ricky asked.

She nodded.

He stepped behind her and encircled her waist with his arms. Immediately, she felt warm and safe.

The balloon drifted along the coastline. She could see the

Avalon Beach Club and the Agalinas Learning World. The yellow class huts looked like toy houses. Beyond, the rocky coast dropped right into the ocean, gentle waves lapping the land.

A burst of wind hit the balloon, jolting the basket just a bit and steering them farther inland. Ricky gave Freesia a reassuring squeeze.

"It's flippy how real this all feels," she said.

He stiffened. "If something feels real, then it is real."

They were drifting over the hills now. Inland, where the land was flatter, she could make out some tanks and barracks from the zap wars. The other hot-air balloons, a veritable swarm of them, bobbed and swayed farther out, closer to the water. Freesia felt like an ant who had hitchhiked on a bunch of birthday balloons.

"Life here is magical," Freesia whispered.

● ● ●

The Rotunda was the biggest and most beautiful building on the island. Stark white with a red domed roof, curved walls, and columns, it jutted into the bay. In the plaza outside the main entrance, a blue glass dolphin leapt from a saltwater fountain alive with skinny silver fish. Inside, murals covered the walls: sea life in the entryway, Greek and Roman gods in the theater, and scenes from Agalinas in the ballroom. Freesia never tired of gazing up at the mosaic on the ballroom ceiling: rubies, sapphires, emeralds, amethysts, topaz, and pearls.

The ballroom was pleasantly crowded when they arrived.

Freesia delighted in the sight of all the pretty dresses, all the pretty shoes, all the pretty girls, all the pretty boys. Especially the pretty boys. On a small stage, students from the Island Ballet Academy leapt and twirled and spun in perfect time to the Chase Bennett cover band that strummed and drummed on the floor below them.

Freesia scanned the room, searching for Taser Lucas, but he wasn't there.

"Shall we visit the cake?" Ricky asked.

Together, they crossed the ballroom, saying hello to a friendly every few steps, until they reached a towering mass of vanilla and buttercream in the shape of an ostrich. Below the confectionary bird lay a giant chocolate egg.

"Why an ostrich?" Freesia asked the Advanced Pastry student stationed by the plates.

"Why not?"

Freesia could not deny his logic. The pastry class always made duplicate cakes for slicing. The student handed Freesia and Ricky each a serving of ostrich cake sprinkled with chocolate shavings.

"Did you know that some people only eat dessert after a meal?" Ricky asked.

Before replying, Freesia took a forkful of cake: sweet-ish, creamy-ish, not as good as the red velvet cupcake at the Arizona mall, but okay. Ish.

"That makes no sense," she said once she'd swallowed. "After a meal, your tummy is too full to properly appreciate a tasty pastry."

Ricky finished his cake and accepted a second plate, but Freesia held off: she was too anxious to move on to the pasta bar, which offered eleven pasta shapes and fourteen sauces.

Sometime during the evening—long after Freesia had eaten and laughed with countless friendlies and had danced so much that her warm face felt pleasantly damp—it struck her: Ricky was right. Agalinas was real because it *felt* real. Nothing else mattered.

At midnight, party serfs passed trays of happy fizz. They all held up their glasses and said, in unison, "Here's to today. Here's to tomorrow. Happy dreams to all."

Soon afterward, Freesia was back in her bedroom. Yow snoozed on her fuzzy pink pillows. Suddenly sleepy, she longed to join him, but first she had a bubblecast essay to compose.

She sat in her lounger and held her silver bubble in both hands. "Composition."

The bubble glowed green, then blue, then a bright, shiny white.

Freesia said, "Why I Should Meet Chase Bennett, by Freesia Summers." Immediately, the words appeared on the bubble. Freesia gazed at her new holographic poster for a moment before continuing.

"I don't remember the first time I heard Chase Bennett sing. It's like Chase and his songs have always been a part of my life. They are the first thing I listen to in the morning. The last thing I hear at night. If I were ever sad, they would make me happy, but I am never sad. And I think that is because I listen to Chase Bennett's music so much. To me, he is more than a person. More than a musician. He is everything good in the universe rolled into one. So that's why I should meet him. So I can tell him just how vicious I think he is. And also, I don't know if this matters, but I'd really like to see his yacht."

Freesia read back the composition. Satisfied, she said, "Transmit to Chase Bennett bubblecast essay contest."

The bubble glowed blue, then green. Then blue, then green, and finally silver. The composition had been sent.

Freesia placed the bubble in its charger. She crawled into bed and scooted Yow to the other side of the pillow. "If I win, I'll take you with me."

Yow purred.

Freesia fell into a deep, sweet sleep.

15

The next morning, everything went according to schedule: peacocks, Chase Bennett, Mummy with the coffee. . . .

"Nothing like a shot of premium espresso to *snap* your day into shape!" With her free hand, Mummy snapped her fingers.

"What are you talking about? Where's my coffee cloud?"

"American coffees can't compare to Snappi brand imported Italian espresso." Mummy snapped her fingers again. "That's Snappi with an *i*," she added.

"But what happened to Tracey's?"

"We shall not speak of this." Mummy handed her a bitty white cup that said SNAPPI. "Would you like—"

"Pancakes," Freesia said. "In here. And, yes, you can go."

Freesia took an itty sip of espresso, only to discover that Snappi tasted exactly like Tracey's. She tossed it back and hopped out of bed.

● ● ●

F ront Street was overflowing with tizzy teens by the time Freesia arrived, looking especially de-vicious in an apple red sundress and shiny white heels. She scanned the crowd and quickly found Jelissa, Cabo, and Ferdinand. Ricky, naturally, chose to sleep late rather than attend the announcement; he hadn't written an essay, anyway.

Taser was nowhere to be seen, but she wasn't sure what she'd say to him, anyway. *Agalinas is real because it feels real.* If anything, Taser should understand that better than anyone. After all, his zap wars were more real to him than, well . . . than that other thing that up until recently she had assumed was the actual world. But Taser had a fondness for conspiracy theories; if she told him about her visit to "the mainland," he'd never let it go, never let her resume her happy life.

Chase Bennett's bright white ship was right where it had been the night before. At precisely ten o'clock, someone (Chase Bennett? No, this person had darker hair) boarded the skiff at the back and headed for shore. As it neared the long green pier, the engine's buzz grew to a roar.

The man steering the boat was trim, clean-shaven, and ageless. He wore a navy blue polo shirt, khaki pants, and brown boat shoes. Once he tied the skiff up to a slip, he climbed out and trotted down the pier to address the crowd, a large white envelope in hand.

"Chase Bennett sincerely thanks you all for participating in his essay contest. He sincerely wishes he could invite you all to tour his watercraft. Unfortunately, his vessel just isn't big enough."

Everyone paused to gauge the size of the yacht, which was quite obviously more than big enough.

"However, we are happy to announce the lucky Avalon resident who will get to meet Chase and tour his ship. And the winner is . . ."

As he tore open the envelope, Jelissa grabbed Freesia's hand and squeezed so hard it should have hurt.

". . . Freesia Summers!"

She'd won. She'd really, really won. Freesia was so happy she could hardly breathe. But she did breathe, which was good because this would have been an inconvenient time to pass out.

Her friends, who were nearly as excited as she, hustled her through the crowd to the envelope man.

"I'm Freesia," she told him.

"Excellent. Follow me, please." He spun around and headed for the skiff.

"But wait. Don't I have time to freshen up and change my clothes? I have this sailor dress—it would be scrummy with red flats. Plus, I told my cat he could come."

He was at the boat now, untying the rope. If she didn't follow, she might miss the biggest chance of her real and virtual lives combined. She hurried along the pier, wobbling in her heels. "Wait! I'm coming!"

● ● ●

Chase Bennett had named his yacht *Island Girl*, just like the song. Up close, it was even more giganto than it had appeared from shore. Freesia was so awestruck that she barely had time to worry if anything was showing when she climbed a rope ladder ahead of the dark-haired man.

She hauled herself (none too gracefully) over the side of the boat onto a shiny teak deck. A star-shaped pool glistened in the center. Two crisp women in white jackets, their hair slicked back in buns, waited with trays.

"Lemon sipper? Vanilla fizz? A hot cup of Snappi brand imported Italian espresso?"

"Chocolate-covered strawberry? Cucumber sandwich? Peppermint meringue?"

Freesia selected a vanilla fizz and a meringue.

The dark-haired man appeared over the side of the ship. Wordlessly, he and the servers retreated beyond a wooden doorway.

Freesia sipped her vanilla fizz, which, when she thought about it, didn't taste much like vanilla and wasn't fizzy at all. (In Freesia's experience, it was generally best not to think about things too much.)

A door opened, and yet another woman in a white jacket with a slicked-back bun appeared. "Mr. Chase will greet you now."

Freesia scampered over the teak deck and into the giant ship, where she found herself in a kind of entryway with a circular white couch, a gurgling fountain, and surprisingly high ceilings.

At last, a set of double doors opened, and there he was, Chase Bennett—or, at least, some reasonable facsimile, which was the best she could hope for under the circumstances. He wore his signature white baseball cap, a sleeveless white T-shirt, blue board shorts, and leather flip-flops. A thin silver hoop glinted in his left earlobe. Lit from behind, he looked like an angel.

Freesia began to babble. "I'm so . . . this is such . . . you have no idea how many times—"

He said, "My fans mean everything to me. Without you guys, I'm just a guy who likes to sing."

"I utterly adore your music!" Freesia's voice quavered.

"I'm so glad. And I really liked what you said in your, you know, essay. Would you like a tour of the ship?"

Freesia could only nod.

"I've got a recording session with Felicity Flufferhaus in an hour—I sent my helicopter to pick up Felicity and my producer from the mainland. Until then, I'm all yours."

He grinned. His teeth were super white and just a little bit pointy, though not in a creepy vampire way. He had a dimple in his left cheek but not in his right (which she already knew from hours spent staring at his picture).

"I have a holograph of you in my bedroom. But you're even more de-vicious in person." She paused. "I hope that's not a squiggy thing to say."

He laughed. "No. I'm flattered."

Chase held the door open for her. (Not only was he wicked talented, he was wicked polite.) Now they were in a giant atrium, three stories high with a glass elevator, wicker furniture, and a shiny white baby grand piano. Purple koi swam in a fountain. Birds sang in gilded cages. Sunshine from the transparent ceiling nurtured a veritable jungle of flowering plants, their perfume making her an itty bit dizzy.

Chase slid onto the piano bench. "Would you like me to play something? You can sit next to me if you like."

She would like.

The bench was smooth and cold. His fingers were long and square and almost seemed a part of the piano, so effortlessly did they scamper across the keys.

"I've been working on a new song. It's called "Then You Smiled." He tilted his chin, half closed his eyes, and began to sing.

I woke up one day, not feeling wild,
No wind in my sails, no wag in my tail,
Didn't think I could win, just thought I could fail.
Then you rang my phone and came to my door.
And then you smiled.
Yeah, girl, that's when you smiled.
And when you smile, girl,
You make me wild, girl.
Oh, yeah, girl, I love your smile.

He turned and smiled. "It's not done yet. But you get the basic idea."

"I think it's done! I think it's vicious!"

He shook his head. "I have to be careful. Not to settle, you know? Because this teen idol thing, it's not going to last forever. If I want to make the transition to being a serious artist, I have to push myself."

He stood up and, miraculously, held out his hand. "Let me show you the rest of the ship."

Rooms fanned off from the atrium like petals on a flower. There was a bowling alley, a dining room, an exercise studio, and a movie theater with a special snack alcove.

Still holding her hand, Chase led Freesia to the glass elevator. A sound system played a piano track of "Island Girl." Freesia's stomach lurched as the elevator began its ascent. The second- and third-floor hallways ran like railed racetracks around the vast open space.

"My recording studio is on the second floor," he said as they passed it. "Also some guest rooms. And on the top deck, next to the helipad, I've got a lazy river that surrounds a dance floor. I'll show it to you after this."

The elevator stopped on three, and they got out.

"This is basically where I live," Chase said. "My bedroom's here, and my game room and sauna."

He led her down the hall. Finally, he stopped. "Here's the room I most want you to see."

He dropped her hand (Todd dammit!), turned the knob, and pushed open the door. "After you."

Freesia entered the room, not knowing what to expect, but definitely anticipating something better than the borrifying office that lay ahead. It had gray walls, gray carpet, a big white desk, a black guest chair, a black leather couch, and framed photographs of woodsy wildlife: raccoons, bears, deer.

She was trying to think of something nice to say when she realized that there was something far stranger than the furniture in this room. Behind the big desk was a big window. But the window didn't offer an ocean view; instead, it looked out on a vast parking lot similar to the one outside that odious mall in Arizona.

"I don't understand how—" Freesia turned to face Chase Bennett. And screamed.

Chase Bennett was gone. In his place stood a skinny middle-aged man with thin, sandy hair, wire-rimmed glasses, and a sharp nose.

"*Chill out*," he said.

"Who are you?"

"Todd Piloski, founder and CEO of Bubble World Enterprises. Otherwise known as the man who made everything good and happy in your life possible."

"But . . . where are we?"

"You're where you've always been. In your bubblepod in Arizona. I'm in my office in Silicon Valley. Thanks to huge advances in virtual reality achieved by *my* educational program, it looks and feels like we are in the same room. Awesome, yes?"

He settled himself at the big desk, his back to the window, and motioned to the black guest chair. "Sit."

Freesia lowered herself slowly, nervously, as if someone

might pull the chair out from under her. "But . . . where is Chase?"

"I dunno. Vegas, maybe? I licensed his appearance as well as the rights to a good chunk of his back catalog, but his involvement pretty much ends there. Guys in product development have been working on this ship and Chase's avatar for the past year. That was me taking the avatar for a spin. I even wrote the song myself. Not bad, I thought."

"But . . . but . . ." Not only hadn't Freesia spent the past hour talking to the real Chase Bennett, she'd been holding hands with this creature. Even at a virtual level, that was odious.

"I didn't bring you here to talk about Chase Bennett," he said. "I brought you here to talk about Francine Somers."

Freesia stiffened. "I don't like being called by that name."

Todd opened a drawer and pulled something out. "Have a look." He reached over the desk and handed her a mirror.

"No!" She squeezed her eyes shut, but not before she'd gotten a good look at her bumpy skin, frizzy hair, and bushy eyebrows.

She turned the mirror facedown on her lap, opened her eyes, and glanced down at her black tee and stretch pants.

"Was it your mother's idea?" he asked. "Send you back without the memory blocker so you could report from the inside, give her new material for her vlog?"

"No!"

"Your father's, then?"

"Of course not. He gave me the medicine and told me to

take it. But I flushed it down the toilet. I couldn't stand the idea of erasing everything I knew, everything I'd learned. Though now . . . maybe I should have. But it doesn't matter. Agalinas is my home. I don't want to be anyplace else. So please—just let me go back."

Todd laced his fingers in front of him on the desk and held her eyes. "You told."

Freesia stiffened. "What do you mean?"

"Jelissa. At the coffee shop. You couldn't wait to spill everything. Spread the news about the so-called real world. Don't you know that we can see you? Hear you? That everything you do is recorded and stored on our hard drive?"

Freesia shivered. "But my parents said you only meant for the memory blocker to knock out a few days."

"That's what I told them. They believed it because they wanted to. And yet they signed the medical release forms. All the parents did. They all agreed to let their children be treated by the Bubble World staff doctor, who just happens to be on the payroll of a very large pharmaceutical firm that wanted to research memory blockers."

"Why does it matter whether we know about the outside world? Everyone would want to stay in Agalinas anyway."

He shook his head so energetically that his wire-rimmed glasses slid down his pointy nose. He didn't bother pushing them back up. "Bubble World can only be the utopia I envisioned if students believe it is the *only* world. I had to cleanse you of all earlier associations and beliefs. The two worlds must be kept separate. Always."

"But why?"

He cleared his throat. "Your parents—in fact, everybody's parents—believe that you have been receiving more of a, shall we say, traditional education."

"What do you mean?"

"They think you are learning stuff."

"Like?"

"American government. Calculus. Eighteenth-century British literature. All those languages." He rolled his eyes.

"But that's so borrifying!"

"Exactly! The program started out with all that drivel. It was the only way to sell it to parents. A team of PhDs created lesson plans. There were lectures and tests and blah, blah, blah. And everyone was miserable, as I knew they would be. You know why? Because kids don't need curriculums. They need time and space and freedom. That's the only way they can truly create and innovate." His face was turning red. "You know why I dropped out of Harvard after one year?"

"Because it was borrifying?"

"Yes!" He paused. "No. Because the traditional educational system did not allow me to follow my bliss. If I'd spent three more years in the education mill, do you think I would have had the vision to create Cranky Hamsters? Or the Phonics are Phun educational software programs, preschool through third grade? Or Bubble World?"

Freesia shook her head.

"*Exactly.* In Bubble World, you are free to experiment and create. To follow your bliss. You learn by *doing* and *being*, not by reading boring textbooks. Example: what do you like to do in your free time?"

"I really like to shop," Freesia said.

"Anything else?"

She considered. "I enjoy experimenting with eyeliner."

"That's what I'm talking about," Todd said.

Freesia nodded, even though she had no idea what he was talking about.

"I was never in this for the money," Todd said. "But as it turns out, Bubble World has made me a small fortune, with the potential of a large fortune in sight. If my customers—by which I mean the parents—discover that their children are receiving a less traditional education than the promotional materials perhaps led them to believe, the party will be over—for you, for me . . . and for everyone in Bubble World."

"I won't tell anyone," Freesia promised.

"No. You won't." Todd leaned back in his chair. "You've already been penalized for your misbehavior. And if you say one more peep about any of this to anyone, your account will be terminated."

"Does this mean I won't get to see the lazy river and the dance floor on the upper deck? Because if you'd just give me five more minutes to take the ittiest peek—"

Todd Piloski scowled at a spot on the wall behind her. "Reset," he said.

And everything went black.

16

The ick news: She didn't get to float in Chase Bennett's lazy river.

The wick news: She didn't get sent back to her bubblepod in Arizona.

Okay, technically she was in the pod. Now and always. But it didn't *look* like the bubblepod. It looked like Agalinas. Like . . . home! Freesia was back in the backyard of her pretty hillside house in Avalon. There was her stone walkway! There was her butterfly garden! There were her flowers and her grass and—

Oh, smack! The pool was gone. The spa and waterslide, too. Ruining her yacht tour wasn't enough of a penalty; Todd Piloski had messed with her upgrades.

Did that mean the Chase Bennett poster had been removed? Freesia yanked open the back door. She scampered up the stairs to her bedroom and . . . *no!* How could he do that to her? Not only was the poster gone, so were her pink lounger and puffy pillows and fluffy rug . . . and her balcony!

What was once a set of French doors was now a not-that-big window, sealed shut. (The view was still killer.)

But wait. If her balcony was gone . . .

"Ashley? Jennifer?"

There were no peacocks in the bedroom. There were no peacocks in the bathroom. There were no peacocks in the giganto walk-in closet. And even *that* wasn't the worst of it.

"Oh my Todd! What happened to all my clothes?"

The gold mini fridge and pink chenille sofa were still there, but Freesia's dresses and skirts and pants and blouses and shoes and purses were all gone. This was too much. Too cruel. So utterly un-utter.

"I'm sorry!" Freesia called out, hoping Todd would hear. "I'll never do it again!"

She peered back into the yawning emptiness of her closet, relieved to see her slim, pretty image gazing back from the mirror at the far end.

"Freesia? Is something wrong?"

Angel stood in her doorway, holding . . .

"Is that Yow?"

Freesia reached for the fluffy white kitten. Angel held him tighter. He snuggled under her chin and began to purr. "This is Mischief. Mummy said he's mine."

"But I had a cat that looked just like that."

"Maybe they're brothers." Angel nuzzled the kitten. "I like your dress."

Freesia was still wearing the red sundress and white heels. Angel had on a silver T-shirt and a fluffy pink skirt just this side of a tutu. Angel was several inches shorter than Free-sia, with no curves at all. None of her clothes would fit—which was probably just as well. Not even Freesia, with her flawless figure, could pull off sparkly tween wear, but she needed a new wardrobe, and she needed it fast.

"Want to go shopping with me, Angel?"

"Oh, yes, please!"

Freesia grabbed her bubble from its charger on her night-stand and headed for her closet to find a handbag. And then remembered that she didn't have any.

"Um, Angel—do you have a bag I can borrow? Some-thing not pink? Or not purple? Preferably without any balle-rina designs?"

"Of course!" She turned to go.

"I can hold Mischief until you come back." Freesia reached for the cat.

Angel bit her lip. "He gets nervous around anyone but me."

"I have a feeling he'll like me." Freesia took a step closer.

Angel peeled the cat off her chest and handed him over to her sister, but as soon as the swap was made, the cat yowled and scratched and tumbled to the ground. He crouched low and growled at Freesia.

"Ow!" Her arm was bleeding.

"You can't blame him. Mischief is just a baby." Angel picked up the cat, tucked him under her chin, and trotted off to her room.

Freesia rinsed her stinging, bloodied arm in the sink. Her eyes stung as well, but she blinked away her tears, and then she was fine. When she came out of the bathroom, Angel was waiting with a silver purse encrusted with puffy pink bunny stickers.

"That's . . . that's . . ."

"It's vicious, I know!" Angel opened the purse so Freesia could place the bubble inside.

Freesia swallowed hard and nodded. What choice did she have?

• ● •

Freesia's itty car wouldn't start, so they walked down the hill to Front Street. Chase Bennett's yacht was gone. Had it sailed away, or had the illusion somehow been erased from the collective memory? She didn't dare ask. If Todd wasn't watching her, one of his minions would be.

"What day is this?" Freesia asked Angel suddenly.

"Sunday."

Freesia exhaled. For once, something was as it should be. Besides, Sunday was the day when her account would be refreshed. Mummy and Daddy would have added more shells to reward her for going to cultural immersion and music class.

The Dressy Dress Shoppe was empty except for the two salesgirls, with their bobbed hair, striped tops, and aloof manner. Freesia ignored them and went straight to the racks. Two black dresses, a white miniskirt, a yellow sundress, a blue blouse, a gray tank top, denim shorts . . . Freesia piled her arms with clothes until one of the salesgirls took them off to a dressing room. Then she grabbed some more things.

Angel lingered at the chiffon rack, fingering the filmy dresses, occasionally pulling one off the rack and holding it up to the light. One in particular, pale green with silver threads, especially entranced her. She held it against her slim body, a tiny smile on her face.

"Try it on," Freesia urged, even though she knew Angel had no shells of her own. Even though she knew Angel wasn't real.

"Truly?" Angel said, eyes bright.

"Truly."

In the dressing room, Freesia and Angel sipped watermelon mocktinis as their mirror images modeled the clothes.

Freesia sighed. "It's so hard to choose. Everything looks vicious on me. And I need it all."

"Why not buy it all, then?" Angel asked. In the mirror her likeness, wearing the filmy green dress, did a graceful pirouette.

"Not enough shells."

"In that case, you mustn't buy me the green dress, Freesia."

"Oh, no, I want you to have it." She did, too.

Freesia studied the rack of clothes she had tried on, choosing her favorites: the shorter and tighter of the two black dresses, the shorts and tank top. She was pretty sure she had enough shells to cover them as well as the green dress for Angel—which, at seventy percent off, cost less than the tank top. (Freesia was all for generosity, but one mustn't get carried away).

Freesia pulled her bubble out of the silver bunny purse. Maybe she should forgo the black dress and visit the handbag shop instead. Plus, she had shoes to think about. In her hand, the silver bubble glowed green. How many shells did she have, anyway?

"Personal bubble account balance," Freesia said. The bubble turned blue and then began to flash red.

YOUR BUBBLE ACCOUNT HAS BEEN CLOSED DUE TO INSUFFICIENT FUNDS.

"What? No!" She shook the bubble as if that might make a difference, but of course it didn't.

"What's wrong?" Angel asked.

"My shells are all gone!"

Angel smiled. "I love you anyway. Would you like me to pour you another watermelon mocktini?"

"No! Thank you. I have to . . . I need to . . . I don't know what I'll . . ." Freesia sank to the couch.

"You don't have to buy me the green dress," Angel said.

The dressing room curtains slid open. Wordlessly, the salesgirls swept in, gathered the clothes from the rack, and took them back to the shop floor.

"Let's go home," Freesia said. She gathered up the silver purse and headed out of the dressing room. "We'll ask Mummy for coffee, then I'll look through your closet to see if there are any clothes that aren't too small or too hideous for me to wear."

"I have a white tutu that might fit!"

Freesia shuddered.

● ● ●

*B*ack on the street, she pulled out her bubble and did a friendlies check. Jelissa was offline, but Ricky Leisure was transmitting (panoramic view). He was floating on an inner tube in his pool, sipping something creamy.

"Ricky!"

At the sound of her voice, he paddled to the side of the pool and retrieved his bubble, alarm in his eyes. "Freesia? What's wrong?"

Everything, she wanted to say. But couldn't. They were watching. Now and always.

"Sunday nights are borrifying," she said. "Can I come over?"

"Of course."

"Can you pick me up? My itty car won't start."

Ricky's blue eyes widened. He knew something was wrong. And he knew enough not to say anything about it.

"I'll come by when the moon rises over the treetops."

Freesia nodded. "I'll be ready."

17

Mummy was in the kitchen, stirring something in a pot.

Daddy was at the table, reading a newspaper.

Angel, armed with a ball of purple yarn, played with a leaping Mischief. When the kitten saw Freesia, he arched his back and hissed. She walked as far around him as possible, guarding her delicate ankles.

"Are you making spaghetti, Mummy?"

Mummy didn't answer. Didn't look up.

Dinner was late; the sun was almost down. Freesia's tummy rumbled. Freesia sniffed the air: nothing. She approached the stove and peered inside the pot. Mummy was stirring boiling water.

"Mummy? What's for dinner?"

Mummy kept stirring.

"Mummy? Are you going to cook anything in that pot?"

Mummy didn't look up.

"Isn't anyone else hungry?" As she spoke, she realized just how absurd her question was. But surely even Todd Piloski would consider starvation too extreme a punishment.

The pantry, normally overflowing with scrummy nibbles, held plain crackers. The icebox offered a single pitcher of water. Freesia took a box of crackers and poured herself a glass of water. She went out to the deck where her family normally ate dinner, but the wind blew hard and cold and dusty, so she came back inside, put her crackers and water on the coffee table, and perched on the couch.

Across the room, Daddy continued reading his paper in silence. He turned a page. Turned another page. Reached the end of the newspaper, flipped back to the beginning, and started all over again.

Freesia ate her crackers. She drank her water. She tasted nothing. When her tummy stopped rumbling, she returned the cracker box to the pantry and placed her glass in the sink.

Mummy was still at the stove, still stirring.

●　●　●

When Ricky's bright red convertible itty coupe pulled up later that evening, Freesia was waiting out back in the butterfly garden (which normally turned into a firefly garden at sundown, but Todd Piloski had ruined that along with everything else). She was still wearing her red dress, but from Angel she'd borrowed a hooded sweatshirt (pink with green rhinestones). The hated silver bunny purse still held her bubble. At least it was dark outside.

Ricky drove them down the steep hill. His car exhaust smelled like red licorice. Too afraid to say anything, Freesia tilted her head back and gazed at the stars. They rode in silence through town and up the hill that led to Ricky's mansion, lit tonight with orange lights.

"Why orange?" Freesia asked, breaking the silence.

"Why not?"

At Ricky's front door, a serf waited with two glasses of happy fizz. For the first time in . . . ever, Freesia gulped her fizz faster than Ricky and gladly accepted a refill. Thus fortified, they made their way up the stairs and through the various rooms and hallways until they reached Ricky's secret screen room.

Freesia collapsed on the puffy black sofa. "Oh my Todd, Ricky! I've had the most odious day."

"Did you meet Chase Bennett?" he asked.

"Yes! No. Sort of. I wasn't sure it even happened, or that anyone knew it had happened. I saw Jelissa, and she didn't even mention it."

"Todd prescribed memory blockers all around and rebooted the entire program."

"That explains it," Freesia said. "I met Todd. Only he made himself look and sound like Chase Bennett. It was wiggy. No, worse than wiggy. It was cruel."

She told him about her empty closet, her empty bubble account, her distracted parents, her traitorous cat.

Ricky sighed. "We shouldn't even be here, then."

"What do you mean?"

"You can't disappear off their monitors too regularly, Free. You can't give them any more reasons to watch you. You need to go back to your life. Parties. Shopping. Coffee. Lounging around my pool—"

"I can't go shopping, because they took away all my shells, remember?"

"It's not forever," he said. "Just till they're sure you'll behave. In the meantime, I'll buy you anything you want. Clothes, meals, dolphin rides. You want a sandwich?" He reached into the pull-out fridge under the couch.

She chose tuna salad, thrilled to bite into something that had more taste than the crackers she'd eaten for dinner. Even if that taste was really just the suggestion of a taste.

Freesia thought about Ricky's many perks. "They must know you know," she said.

"I know they know I know." Ricky had downed his cheese and tomato sandwich in three bites.

"Then why don't they punish you like they've punished me?"

"One, because my father is a major investor in Todd Piloski's company. And, two, because I've never let anyone in on the secret."

"Is Jelissa computer-generated?" she blurted.

Ricky's eyes bugged with surprise. "Of course not. She's living through an avatar like the rest of us, but she's a real person. Her given name is Jessica Melissa or Melissa Jessica. I can never remember which. She lives in Canada, one of those far-north provinces that are always cold and really hard to get to. The nearest school was over a hundred miles away. That's why she's here."

"I hate thinking this way!" Freesia rubbed her face. "Who's real and who's not, and where we really live and—"

"Come." Ricky stood up and held out a hand.

She shook her head. "I'm feeling too squiggy to go back out just yet. I can't stand the thought of them watching me."

"No one will see us." Ricky crossed the room and tapped what she'd taken for a plain wall but that, with a tap, turned into a doorway.

"Take my hand."

She did.

"Close your eyes."

She did.

"Now, follow me . . ."

18

*S*he smelled brine and flowers. Felt a breeze that plunged from warm to cool. Thunder clapped. She opened her eyes just as the rain began to fall, and Ricky pulled her into a familiar space.

"Taser's cave!"

It was as she remembered: the stone room with the domed ceiling; the alcove with the green, glowing, teardrop-shaped pool; the surprisingly warm air; the dark doorway that led to unexplored depths.

Hand in hand, they made their way over to the little pool, sat on the edge, and plunged their feet in the water, which immediately sparkled.

"Taser may have found this cave, but I wrote the code," Ricky said.

"When?"

"A couple of years ago, right after I got my screen room up and running. I was into pirates that year, and I was going to hide a treasure chest farther back, but I never got around to it. I haven't been here in ages."

"If you can get here through your screen room, why connect it to the ocean?"

"I was curious to see if anyone would brave the rough water—figured they deserved a reward if they did. I never thought that 'anyone' would be Taser." He wrinkled his nose.

"You're jealous." She tried not to sound as pleased as she felt. "Is that why you told me the cave wasn't safe?"

"Maybe." Ricky's mouth twitched. "Come. Let me show you the rest."

"It's awfully dark back there," she said as he led her to the yawning door trimmed with glittery stalagmites. Beyond, they found deeper darkness. Something dripped and echoed. Around a corner, lights flickered.

Splash! The stone floor gave way and Freesia was over her head in warm water. Her hand slipped out of Ricky's. When she surfaced, she groped for him and opened her eyes. A hundred diamond-shaped lights on the bottom had turned the water purple.

Freesia and Ricky swam toward each other. Freesia began to laugh. "Don't tell me you forgot about your own swimming pool!"

Ricky grinned, the pool's purple light casting an eerie glow on his face. "Nothing like an unexpected swim to cheer you up."

After a little more paddling, Ricky swam to a far side of the pool and hauled himself out. "We should get back soon. I don't want them to wonder where you've gone. But first let me show you the firefly garden."

As soon as Freesia got out of the pool, the purple lights began to dim. Dripping wet as they were, Freesia would have expected to feel cold, but she not only felt warm she felt . . . dry. Probably because in the real world she *was* dry.

Stop thinking this way, she commanded herself. *Agalinas is real because it feels real.*

Ricky took her hand, and they walked very, very carefully toward the flickering lights. They turned a corner and—

"Aargh!" Freesia threw up her hands to shield her face. They were everywhere: skimming her hair, bumping up against her arms, swiping her legs.

Ricky grabbed her elbow and dragged her back into the now fully darkened pool room.

"Those were the biggest fireflies I've ever seen!" Freesia's voice shook.

"Those weren't fireflies." He was breathing hard. "They were illuminated bats."

"Did you write the code for them?"

"No."

Now Freesia really was cold—not from the water but from fear. She didn't dare brave the bat room to hunt for towels, however. Ricky was right: it was time to go. Holding hands, they made their way through the pool room, sticking close to the walls.

At last they made it to the big domed stone room, where they were startled to see a boy unrolling a sleeping bag.

"Taser!" Freesia dropped Ricky's hand and hurried over to her ex-boylink, who continued his task without looking up.

Taser had never been much on personal grooming, but Freesia had never seen him looking so uncombed, unwashed, and underfed. Dirt and dried blood darkened his hollowed-out cheeks. His hair, buzzed into a military cut, stuck straight out as if it were trying to get as far away from his scalp as possible.

Just like that, he broke from his stupor and screamed.

"*Enemy forces! Incoming!*" He gazed in terror at the stone ceiling before sinking to the ground and weeping.

"It's like he can't tell the difference between reality and unreality." Ricky paused. "Or between one unreality and another."

"I don't understand," Freesia said. "He's always played zap wars, but they never had this kind of effect on him before."

Ricky sighed. "The real money these days is in war games—the more realistic, the better. Piloski's looking to open a military academy in the interior—kind of like Bubble World only with uniforms and guns."

"That sounds like a lot for one island."

Ricky shrugged. "It's a lot for one server, that's for sure. Also, Piloski's got the programmers so busy developing war games that they've been neglecting site maintenance. That's why the site has been so wiggy."

"How do you know all this?" Freesia asked.

"Piloski's e-mail. It's not even password-protected. Unbelievable."

Taser was still weeping. Freesia crossed the room and put her arms around him.

"Taser, it's okay. The war is make-believe. And this cave is make-believe, too, and so is Avalon and all of Agalinas. You're safe, Taser. You're home in . . ."

"New Jersey," Ricky said.

"You're in New Jersey. And no one's going to hurt you."

Taser stopped weeping. Freesia tried to get him to look at her, but his gray eyes seemed to be seeing something very far away.

Ricky put a hand on her shoulder. "We'd better get back."

"We can't just leave him here."

Ricky sighed. "I know."

Ricky grabbed Taser under the arms, and Freesia held up his legs. He wasn't that heavy. Together, they hauled him out of the cave. Above, the moon shone almost as brightly as the sun.

They placed Taser gently on the stone dock. He curled into a fetal position.

"How do we get back to your secret room?" Freesia asked.

Before Ricky could answer, two illuminated bats appeared out of nowhere and swooped down. Freesia and Ricky hit the rock floor and covered their heads. When the air cleared, Freesia peeked up. "Bats scare me."

"Bats don't scare me as much as . . ."

"What?"

"Nothing. Let's get out of here."

Ricky walked to the very edge of the rock dock and put out his hand. Just when it looked like he would plunge into the glassy sea, a tall pale rectangle appeared, as if it were floating in the air. He pushed at it, and the rectangle became an open door into Ricky's secret room.

"Vicious," Freesia whispered.

They scooped up Taser and hauled him through the door. They didn't linger in the screen room, hurrying instead through the hallways and doors up to Ricky's roof deck, where they deposited Taser on a puffy lounger. Freesia's arms ached.

Ricky pulled a bottle of happy fizz from a cooler and popped it open. "Drink this."

He held the bottle up to Taser's lips. Taser drank. And drank. And drank. Something like a smile played around his mouth.

Ricky pulled his tangerine-sized bubble out of his pocket. "I need a driver. And maybe a helper."

Just like that, two of Ricky's many serfs appeared on the deck.

"Please take Taser back to his house," Ricky instructed.

Without a word, the serfs helped Taser to his feet. Taser giggled. He wobbled. The serfs each took an arm and helped him off the deck.

"Happy fizz makes everything better," Ricky said. Above them, the stars shone like mini searchlights.

"Do you think he'll be okay?"

"Of course. He's in Agalinas. He'll be better than okay."

Freesia said, "Being with you, it makes me feel happy."

Ricky said, "Being with you, it makes me want to . . ."

"What?"

He thought for a good long time. "Leave my house more often."

Freesia bit her lip. "That would be wicked."

They leaned toward each other, and Freesia's face grew

warm and tingly. This was the best face-link ever, even if it felt like every other face-link she had ever had. For the moment, Freesia forgot who she was and where she was. She forgot about everything in the world except Ricky.

And then, of course, everything went black.

19

"Not now!" Freesia yelled into the darkness. Her voice echoed against the hard walls of her bubble. She felt as if she were being awakened from the nicest dream she had ever had. Yet it was more than just a dream because she had shared it with Ricky. Who was once her second bestie and now . . . something more.

Ricky was right: Agalinas was real because it felt real. And now *this* had to happen. The timing was as bad as it could be.

"Mother!"

Nothing.

"Father!"

Nothing.

"Angel!"

Angel thumped the wall from the other side and yelled something that sounded an awful lot like "shut your stupid face."

Freesia stood in total darkness, presumably on the rubber floor in the front half of her bubble. She took a tiny step backward and then another, until she felt the big leather recliner. She sat down. She waited. And waited.

Status updates, she told herself. Minor malfunctions. *Don't panic.*

Odious Todd Piloski. If he weren't so focused on those doltoid war games, stuff like this wouldn't happen. She could mention the system problems to her mother, but then she'd risk her parents finding out that she wasn't getting quite the education they'd been promised.

All she had to do was . . . sleep! Of course. When she woke up, the system problems would be fixed and she'd be in her ocean-view room, which, with any luck at all, would have her peacocks and balcony and clothes back where they belonged.

She leaned back. The recliner wasn't reclining. She fished around for buttons or levers. Nothing. The chair must be programmed to recline whenever she headed for her bed in Avalon. Or maybe every night she left the bubble to sleep in the narrow bed against the wall?

She groped in the darkness, feeling her way along the smooth walls to the hinged doorway. She fiddled with the lever, pushed it open, and stepped down onto the hard floor. The bed was here somewhere, pushed against a window. On the side of the room? Or the back?

She felt along the wall, along the wall, along the wall—

"Oh, smack!" She banged a knee against the metal bed frame.

She worked her way around the side of the bed, leaned

forward, touched the bedspread, and climbed on top. Just like that, she was asleep.

● ● ●

"What. In the name. Of holy heck. Are you *doing here*?"

Morning.

No singing peacocks. No coffee cloud. Just a dim room with a cranky Mother in a ratty brown bathrobe.

Freesia sat up and rubbed her eyes. "This is where I live. You said I was always here, even when it felt like I was in Agalinas."

"*Here* as in your bubble. Not *here* as in the bed."

"The program crashed. Everything went black and then I found myself here. I tried to go back to sleep, but the recliner wouldn't recline. So I thought maybe this was where I slept."

Mother shook her head. "As soon as you leave the bubble, you leave Bubble World. *Bubble—Bubble World*. Get it?"

"Why is there even a bed in this room, then?" It wasn't a very comfortable bed; Freesia's back was stiff.

"We need it for guests," Mother said. "Oh, don't look at me like that. It was just your grandmother. Once. Okay, three times. What was I supposed to do? Put her in my office?"

Mother crossed to the bubble, which was transparent except for a silver box near the door. She opened the box and poked some keys. "Maybe you need to be in there first before I can reboot."

Freesia pushed herself out of bed and shuffled over to the bubble and into the recliner. She felt funny. Shaky.

"Oh! I almost forgot." Mother hurried out of the room and returned with a plastic cup. "Drink this."

"Memory blocker?" Freesia took the cup.

Mother stiffened. "Is that what your father told you?"

"It was just a guess." How wonderful if the memory blocker actually worked this time and she could go back to believing in everything and everyone in Agalinas.

Suspicion crossed her mother's face. "When I came in, you knew who I was and where you were. In the past, you've been much more confused. Did something happen the last time you were here?"

Freesia didn't say anything, just downed the thick, sweet liquid in four gulps. Within moments, she felt calm enough to face her mother's questions.

Mother, however, had already lost interest in everything except getting Freesia back into a bubble state. "Okay. Here we go." She resumed poking at the silver box.

Freesia took a deep breath, and . . .

Nothing.

"*Come! On!*" Mother poked harder at the keys, which of course accomplished nothing.

"Stay here," she commanded, as if Freesia had somewhere else to go. "I'm going to call tech support. We'll have you out of here in . . . soon. It better be soon."

Alone in the room within a room, Freesia could hear her mother's sharp voice from across the hall. "Somers. With an O. . . . Well, there must be some mistake. . . . No, I'm certain that nothing like that occurred. My daughter would never— Excuse me? I'll have you know that I am a close personal friend of Todd Piloski's and— That! Is not! Acceptable! Hello?"

When Mother returned, she looked dazed. "They said your account has been closed due to breach of contract. They said you caused undue harm to others by making derogatory comments about Bubble World and thus detracting from the total educational immersion experience."

"I'm so sorry, Mother, but . . ."

"Yes?"

"I didn't understand a single thing you just said."

"They say you told people that Bubble World wasn't real."

"But . . ." And then it hit her. The cave: it wasn't safe. They could see her there after all.

"Mom? Is there anything for breakfast?" Angel stood in the doorway. She wore tiny white shorts with fuzzy brown boots and a bright blue sweater that rode up and showed her navel.

"There's cereal and Pop-Tarts in the pantry," Mother said.

Angel glared at Freesia. "What's it doing awake?"

"It's having technical difficulties. I mean, *we're* having technical difficulties. Or maybe legal difficulties. How did you know?" Mother asked Freesia. "Didn't your father make you take your meds before you went back?"

"I dumped the memory blocker down the toilet when he wasn't looking."

"Do we have anything for breakfast that isn't *processed*?" Angel asked.

Mother thought about it. "No."

Angel left in a huff.

"But everything is okay now," Freesia told her mother. "It was flippy at first, knowing that nothing was as it seemed. But then I realized that it doesn't matter. Agalinas is my home. I won't say anything to anyone ever again. I promise."

"It's not me you have to convince." Mother shook her head. "Look. Tech support says you've been expelled from Bubble World. You know, deleted. And they said no one will even look at your application for readmittance until the end of the week. But I'll call Todd today, get everything sorted out."

"They *deleted* me?"

Just like that, she was gone. Poof.

Mother said, "I need to shower and dress, after which I'll make every effort to sort this mess out. There are Pop-Tarts in the pantry—you always loved Pop-Tarts—and television in the den. You can use Angel's computer after she goes to school. Just don't tell her."

As Mother turned to leave, Father showed up carrying a plastic bottle and several foil-wrapped packages. He was dressed up in tan pants that were too tight at his belted waist, a rust-colored shirt, and a black tie with awkward square edges. Being dressed up did not mean he looked good. But at least he looked tidy.

"I've got her nutrients," he told Mother. And then he saw Freesia, awake and aware, looking at him. "Another malfunction?"

"Worse." Mother explained the situation.

"But you told me you had to go to the restroom," he said to Freesia when they got to the bit about the memory blocker.

"I wanted to know what it was like," Freesia said. "To be in Agalinas knowing what I knew."

"How was it?"

Her shoulders slumped. "Odious."

"I'm sure things will be cleared up in a jiffy. Todd Piloski is a close personal friend of your mother's." Father entered the bubble. He poured the contents of the bottle into Freesia's metal cup and began unwrapping the packages.

"I told her she could have Pop-Tarts," Mother said. "So she doesn't need the nutrition bars. But . . . you might as well leave them, just in case. If I can get Todd into the loop, maybe we can reboot by lunchtime."

Mother went off to shower, while Father and Angel left for the high school. And then Freesia was alone as she'd never been alone before, at least within the narrow limits of her mucky memory. There was no one to bring her coffee. No one to meet for shopping or dancing. No parties to go to. No besties to bubble.

The unwrapped nutrient bars sat on the metal tray where her father had left them. She sat in the recliner and took a bite, expecting the taste of a cookie or waffle. But no. The nutrient bar tasted like stale nuts and dust. On the bright side, there were Pop-Tarts in the kitchen. And she knew what they were, even if she didn't know how she knew. Strawberry was her favorite, followed by fudge. But she wasn't ready to leave this room. Not yet.

Maybe the clear liquid in the tall metal cup would help wash down the bar?

Nope. It tasted bad, too, though in a different way: a sweetness that gave way to a bitter bite and ultimately left a metallic aftertaste. But she was hungry and thirsty, so she forced herself through most of a bar and more than half the contents of the cup.

She felt better. Almost . . . too much better. She was so relaxed she felt sleepy, though not enough to go to bed. She wasn't happy, but she wasn't sad, either. And she wasn't angry or frightened or anxious or excited . . . or anything. She was just kind of flat. What was in that cup, anyway?

She sat in the recliner for a while, but that got boring, so she got up and explored a closet she hadn't noticed before. On the floor were a taped-up cardboard box, a pair of slippers, and some ugly slip-on shoes. A few oversized sweatshirts (gray, another gray, black) dangled from wire hangers. Plastic bins held socks and underwear, a pile of stretch pants, and a stack of oversized T-shirts.

That was it. Forget about a sofa and a fridge filled with sips and nibbles. Freesia's closet held no jeans, no dresses, no skirts, no scarves, no handbags, no blouses, no jackets—nothing she would ever in a gajillion years want to wear. How could her parents do this to her? Anger seeped through her medicated numbness. She was so mad, she wanted to . . . she was ready to . . . she was driven to . . .

"I need a Pop-Tart!"

Her mother came into the room. She wore sweatpants, a pilled and ill-fitting sweater, and velour slippers. She'd combed her hair, but it was dull and frizzy. Just like Francine's.

"I've put a call in to Todd."

Freesia pointed to her metal cup. "What did I just drink?"

"If he doesn't call back within the hour, I'll try him again."

"The stuff Father poured from the bottle. What is it?"

"It's normal for you to feel disoriented. This experience has been a shock."

"Mother. What have you been giving me?"

Mother opened the bubble door and stepped inside. "Your medications, of course. They reduce your anxiety, increase your focus, and help induce the proper hypnotic, semi-hallucinatory state. It's all perfectly safe."

She picked up the metal cup and peered inside. "You drank half of it already? Normally you pace yourself—a few sips every hour, all day long. Oh, well. It's not dangerous. But it might make you sleepy. Don't drink any more for now. If you're thirsty, get something else to drink. I think there's lemonade in the fridge." She looked at her watch. "You know what? I'm going to try Todd again. The squeaky wheel gets the grease."

And then she was gone.

Lemonade. Pop-Tarts. Now Freesia had two reasons to leave the room.

The hallway was just as she remembered (how strange to remember things): plain white walls, with closed doors and framed pictures of ugly people. Oh—wait. Those pictures were of her. Plus some other people who were probably relatives. Ugly must run in the family.

And then she saw Angel. *Her* Angel, not the nasty girl who slept in the next room. She was maybe eleven years old, on a stage and wearing a pale leotard and en pointe shoes, her hair slicked back in a bun, her arms forming a graceful U over her head. Her eyes were wide, and she was smiling.

No wonder she loved virtual Angel so much. She wasn't entirely make-believe—more like her actual little sister, frozen in time. She blinked back tears and headed for the stairs.

Ugh! *Stairs!* Thanks to whatever was in that cup, she didn't panic, but still. She had to be careful. She clutched the banister, took one little step, another little step, put a foot into the abyss, and—

This wasn't going to work. Having spent the last few years in two dimensions, she wasn't sure how to negotiate the level changes. She had to get down a different way.

Freesia sat on the carpeted floor and slid her feet and legs over the first step. She scooted forwarded, and . . . *bump.* One step down, a whole bunch more to go. She leaned back, pushed her bottom forward and . . . *bump.* Two down.

Finally she made it to the landing, stood up, and walked on wobbly legs to the kitchen, which was just as plain as she remembered it. But who cared? In the pantry, Freesia found the promised Pop-Tarts, along with cheese curls, chocolate chip cookies, Thin Mints, granola bars, fruity cereal, and box after box of macaroni and cheese. The refrigerator held chocolate milk, orange-guava-strawberry juice, diet soda, leftover pizza, bottled smoothies, and bacon. Also lots of Styrofoam containers.

She started with a frosted strawberry Pop-Tart and a glass of the complicated juice, both of which tickled her taste buds. As much as she longed to be back in Agalinas, she would miss the basic sensation of fully experiencing food.

So really, she had no choice but to eat more.

Chocolate chip cookies: check.

Chocolate milk: check.

Another Pop-Tart.

At that point, her taste buds protested. Freesia took that as a call for salt. She chased a bag of cheese curls with a handful of pretzels and a small slice of pepperoni pizza.

She didn't get sick, but she felt so awful, she almost wished she had. To distract herself while she digested, she went into the den, in search of the television her mother had mentioned. Like *banister*, the word *television* stuck in her mind. It was a happy word.

She recognized the gray box immediately, but she couldn't remember how to turn it on. Figuring the contraption might work like a bubble, she placed her hands on the cold, hard screen.

"Program check."

Nothing.

"I want to watch you."

Forget it.

A nubby tan couch faced the set. Freesia sat down, rubbed her belly, and stared at the blank screen. What did it matter whether she got something to appear on the screen? She had no interest in watching people she didn't know have grand adventures while she was stuck in this house doing nothing.

When her stomach felt a bit more settled, she returned to

the stairs. Going up was easier; she simply crawled on hands and knees. Unfortunately, her mother came out of her office just as Freesia reached the top step. Mother cringed.

Freesia stood up and brushed off her knees. "You're out of Pop-Tarts," she said as casually as she could manage. "Also, you said I could use Angel's computer?" Perhaps she could find the Bubble World website.

"As long as you don't tell her."

"How could I tell her? Won't I be back in Agalinas by the time she gets home?"

Mother's mouth twitched. "I'll try Todd again."

Angel's room had candy pink walls with a ballerina border, purple polka-dot curtains, and a canopy bed so tall it came with a step stool. Clothes overflowed from a cramped closet and a low white dresser. A white desk lay buried under papers and makeup.

A bulletin board hung over the dresser. Freesia moved closer to inspect the high school football game ticket stubs, a couple of hand-drawn birthday cards, assorted fashion model and teen idol pictures, and a certificate of eighth grade completion. There were photos, too: Angel, slightly younger, with a friend, posing in someone's bedroom; Angel, younger still, sitting on the edge of a concrete swimming pool with a group of curveless preteens in bikinis.

A third photo, mostly hidden behind the eighth grade certificate, startled Freesia. Two smiling little girls, maybe three and five years old, beamed at the camera from a green turtle sandbox. The older one, with dark hair, had her arm around the younger one, a blonde who held up a red shovel like a torch.

Could it be—? There was a family resemblance, certainly, but the little girls could easily be younger cousins. And yet . . .

No. Angel despised her sister. There was no way she'd keep Freesia's picture in her room.

When something moved in the corner of her vision, Freesia jumped—but then she realized it was just a full-length mirror hung on the wall. Freesia took a deep breath and looked. Prepared as she was for an utter troll, her reflection didn't seem as horrifying as before. Her curls were out of control, but if styled properly, could be fun and flirty. A good foundation could do wonders for her skin. Her eyebrows could be plucked, and her thighs . . . well, her thighs were a problem.

Freesia searched the room for a computer—a difficult task, since she wasn't exactly sure what a computer looked like. Nothing in this room resembled either Ricky's giant screen or Mother's glowing box.

With nothing else to do, Freesia retreated to her bedroom. To her bubble. She closed the hinged door behind her, sat down in the recliner, and downed the rest of the liquid in the metal cup. Before long, she was asleep.

20

When she woke up, the light was gray, her neck hurt, and her mouth tasted like synthetic cheese. Worst of all, she was still in Arizona. She brushed her teeth in her bubble bathroom and ventured into the hallway. Voices drifted up from downstairs, but she couldn't hear what they were saying.

She bumped down the stairs on her bottom, relieved that no one saw her, and followed the voices.

Mother was in the kitchen, stirring something in a pot.

Father was in the den, reading some papers.

Angel darted between them, alternately poking that hand-sized glowing rectangle she loved so much and saying things like "worst day ever," "care about me at all," and "ruin my life."

"Hello," Freesia said, entering the kitchen.

Mother grunted. Angel said nothing.

"Is that spaghetti?" Freesia asked Mother.

"Macaroni and cheese."

"Macaroni and chemicals and artificial coloring is more like it," Angel said. "I'll have carrots and dip."

"I like macaroni and cheese," Freesia said. "Almost as much as spaghetti."

"We're out of carrots," Mother told Angel. "Also skim milk, cashews, and frosted strawberry Pop-Tarts. I'm using a new grocery shopping app, which means I know exactly what we don't have."

Freesia knew better than to bug Mother about her Bubble World status, so she went into the den and bugged Father instead.

He looked up from his papers. "From what I've heard, the situation is status quo."

"English, please."

"We haven't heard back."

At last dinner was ready. Freesia knew better than to expect a harbor-view meal at sunset; still, she was surprised that dinner meant a stack of plates next to the stove. Mother scooped some bright orange macaroni onto her own plate, filled a glass with faucet water, and headed for her office. Angel grabbed a granola bar and a glass of chocolate milk and stalked off to her room. Father took his portion and returned to the den. Freesia stood in the kitchen, baffled.

At last she filled a plate with a generous helping, poured herself a glass of chocolate milk, and perched on a counter stool. Chemicals or no, the macaroni and cheese was silky, creamy, salty, and delicious. She cleaned her plate and helped herself to some more. When that was gone, she finished what was left in the pot.

When she heard noises from the den, she went to investigate. Father, still surrounded by papers, had somehow turned on the television. The picture was a lot like a bubblecast, only flatter and with duller colors.

"You like soccer?" he asked.

Onscreen, men with nice legs ran around in shorts.

Freesia said, "It might be my favorite sport."

Mother came in, looking tense. But then, she always looked like that, so it didn't necessarily mean anything.

"I received an e-mail from the account services department at Bubble World Enterprises," she told Father.

"And?"

"It said *Request Denied*. That's it. No 'thank you for writing.' No 'we're reviewing the situation.' No 'thanks for all the Web coverage.' *Request denied*."

"But Todd—"

"Is going to get an earful from me. I'm shocked he hasn't responded personally yet. He's probably off in some woodsy lodge in a brainstorming session or something. You know how those Internet types are."

"So tomorrow—"

"Tomorrow Francine is going to school with you."

"*What?*" Father and Freesia spoke at once.

"It could be days before we clear this up. Weeks, even. I cannot have her moping around the house, interrupting my work. Plus, we have her education to think about," she added as an afterthought.

"Weeks?" Freesia said.

"It's possible. Not probable, but possible. Don't stay up too late. The first bell rings at seven thirty A.M., and you'll have to get there early so Father can speak to the counselor."

"How do you expect me to explain the situation?" Father asked.

"You say what we've told people all along—that Francine has been enrolled in an online high school. It's the truth, after all."

Angel appeared in the doorway. "Is there any macaroni left?"

"There should be," Mother said. "The box makes enough for five people."

"Why is the pot empty, then?"

Freesia said, "I can't possibly go to school tomorrow—or any other day. It would be so *un-utter.*" She shuddered.

Mother turned to Angel. "Presumably, the pot is empty because someone finished the macaroni." To Francine she said, "You made your bed, and now you have to lie in it."

"They have beds at school?"

"No. They do not have beds at school. What I meant was that you got yourself kicked out of Bubble World, and now you have to live with the consequences."

"I finished the macaroni," Freesia said.

Angel said, "Wait. Francine is going to school? *My* school? What will everyone say?"

Father said, "They'll say your sister is lucky to have been educated in a place that values interactive learning over test scores. They'll wonder why her skills and knowledge are so advanced. And they'll be shocked that she finds the classics and history more mesmerizing than MySpace and reality TV. You know what? I'm glad that I can take Francine to school tomorrow. She can really open people's eyes to the possibilities of a nontraditional educational environment."

Angel rolled her eyes. "MySpace is over, Dad. Duh."

"Even I knew that," Mother said.

● ● ●

*A*ngel's door was closed, but Freesia could hear music, so she knew she was awake. She knocked and then knocked some more. Finally, the door swung open.

"What?"

Angel had washed her hair, taken off her makeup, and changed into pajamas, baggy bottoms patterned with rosettes and a lavender tank top. Her skin was smooth, her eyes wide and clear. She looked so much like her younger self that Freesia half expected her to fall to the floor and start playing with dolls.

"I need to borrow clothes," Freesia said. "Also makeup and a hair dryer. Tweezers, if you have them. I can't show up at school looking like this." She had showered in the bubblepod and put on yet another pair of stretch pants and a boxy T-shirt. Her hair was still damp.

Angel didn't speak. Didn't move.

Freesia took a deep breath. "From what I've seen, you have absolutely no fashion sense. But with all those clothes in your closet, there's got to be something on the larger side that's not too odious."

"When did you see my closet?"

"Today. Mother said I could use your computer as long as you didn't find out."

"You used my computer?"

"No, I couldn't find it. But I like your room. It made me think of my little sister in Agalinas."

At last the door opened all the way. An odd expression on her face, Angel retreated to her canopy bed. She picked up a silver tablet and began tapping at some keys. The people in this family spent a lot of time tapping and poking.

"Do you still dance?" Freesia asked, remembering the photo in the hallway.

Without looking up, Angel shook her head.

"Why not?"

"I tried out for the freshman dance team and didn't make it." Her fingers tapped.

Freesia was confused. "You mean you want to dance, but they won't let you?"

"Yes."

"That's nonsensical."

Freesia turned on the closet light and started pushing through the clothes, pausing to pull out a scratchy fuchsia lace minidress with an uneven hemline.

"That won't fit you," Angel said.

"Did you actually wear this? Out of the house?" Freesia fully extended her arm so the dress was as far away from her as possible.

"I wore it to my friend's fifteenth birthday party. Except we're not friends anymore."

"No wonder! That is the most odious dress I have ever seen. I'd tell you to burn it, but I think it's made of plastic." She chucked the dress on the floor and returned to the closet.

She caught sight of her dumpy reflection in Angel's full-length mirror and shuddered. How unfair that Angel, with the same parents, had turned out so much prettier. And what a waste! Angel always had a sour look on her face, and her clothes were inexcusable.

Freesia returned to the closet. "Ick. Ick. Ick . . . holy mother of Todd!" Freesia pulled out another dress, this one made of some slippery material patterned with lime, turquoise, and black splotches. "Did I say that last one was the most odious dress I've ever seen? Because this one is worse." She chucked it on top of the first one.

"I look hot in that dress!" Angel rescued the garment from the floor and shoved it back in her closet. Then she rummaged in the back and pulled out an armful of clothes. "Stop going through my stuff. You're too fat to fit into any of it, anyway. Here. These are hand-me-downs from our cousins. They're too big for me." She pushed the clothes into Freesia's arms and pointed to the doorway.

"Did I hurt your feelings?" Freesia asked, leaving the room. "When I said your clothes were ugly? Because I was only trying to—"

Angel slammed the door.

"That was short of triumphant," Freesia said to no one.

But something did work: a long, thigh-hiding gray cardigan

with a plain white blouse and—there was no way around it—black stretch pants. Freesia returned to her sister's room and knocked . . . and knocked . . . and knocked until she answered.

"What?"

"Do we wear the same size shoes? I need boots. Also a long string of chunky beads and a scarf. Plus maybe you have some foundation I could borrow? You don't need it, but I clearly do."

Silently, Angel handed the items over.

"I'll see you in the morning, then," Freesia said from the hall.

Angel shut the door. But at least she didn't slam it.

Father was coming out of Freesia's room. "I put sleepy juice in your cup. And I reclined the recliner, just in case. Maybe you'll wake up in Agalinas and this will all seem like a bad dream. Though not too bad, I hope."

He forced a laugh. Freesia forced a smile, and they said good night.

21

Freesia's Bubble World account was not reinstated during the night. She didn't wake up to ocean sounds, coffee smells, and peacock songs. Instead, she was jolted into consciousness by her mother, who flung open her bubble door and snapped, "Aren't you up yet? You leave in thirty minutes!"

Freesia was painfully fuzzy from the sleepy juice she'd taken the night before, but she knew better than to ask her mother for a coffee cloud.

Less than an hour later, Father's car pulled into the staff lot next to a long, low, nearly windowless building surrounded by concrete walkways, spiky plants, and gravel. The stars and stripes fluttered high on a pole above the Arizona state flag.

When Father turned off the ignition, Angel said, "Give me twenty seconds." Almost, but not quite, running, she fled from the car and crossed the lot to a side door.

Beyond the school's tennis courts and dusty fields, a sea of red rooftops and white stucco walls stretched for miles. In the distance, jagged gray-brown mountains loomed against a baby blue sky.

The parking lot was hot for such an early hour.

"Supposed to hit ninety today," Father said, as if that were a good thing.

They rounded the front of the school, weaving among groups of chattering students, and went right into the guidance office.

"It's a shame she doesn't have a transcript," said Mrs. Appel, the guidance counselor responsible for students with last names *N* through *S*. "It would make the transfer process easier."

Tall and angular, Mrs. Appel wore a brown blouse with pleated tan pants and brown boots. A plastic cylinder crammed with red licorice sticks sat on the front of her giant desk. The room smelled lemony, but not in a good way.

Nervous perspiration soaked Freesia's palms and armpits. Even in the air-conditioning, the gray cardigan was much too warm. She wanted to go home—if not to Agalinas, then at least to that bland stucco house with the cranky mother and the baffling television set.

"How long has Freesia been out of the public education system?" Mrs. Appel asked.

"Since eighth grade. Though her program was affiliated with a public high school in Alabama."

While Freesia remained silent, Father and Mrs. Appel put together her class schedule: AP Calculus BC; AP American History; AP English; Honors Physics; AP French. Mrs. Appel stood up. Her tan slacks were wrinkled already, and it was just past seven A.M.

"It's a demanding load. But from what you've said, Mr. Somers, I'm sure Francine will have no problem. In fact, her classes may be too easy. We can talk later about getting her registered for the upcoming SAT test. And again—sorry about the locker situation." Due to overcrowding, Francine would have to wait till next year to get her own locker. As if she'd still be here next year. Ha!

The counselor glanced at her computer. "One last thing for our records, Francine. May I have your cell phone number?"

"My what?" At last, she spoke.

"She doesn't have a cell," Father said. "The academy frowned on any technology that could detract from the learning process."

The counselor sighed. "The academy sounds like a wonderful place. I only wish . . ."

"I know," Father said.

Mrs. Appel held out some papers. "Here's your schedule and a map of the school, Francine. Welcome to Tumbleweed High."

The only thing Tumbleweed High School and Agalinas Learning World had in common was—well, nothing. Outside the relative calm of the guidance office, Freesia plunged into a heaving, chattering mass of teenagers, easily twice as many as a building this size, massive though it was, should hold. The long hallways turned this way and that in no discernible pattern. On the plus side, at least there were no stairs.

Her first class of the day was Advanced Placement American History—which sounded utterly borrifying, but Freesia was too nervous to ask if Tumbleweed had a course in lip gloss techniques or the origins of freak dancing that she could take instead. Since Father was a history teacher, his room was on the same wing, so he walked her to class. To calm herself, she stayed half a step behind him, focusing on the stripes of his shirt. Blue, white, purple. Inhale. Blue, white, purple. Exhale.

She hadn't taken any happy juice that morning. Her father was too concerned it would make her sleepy or dopey. But her breathing was shallow, and her head buzzed from fear. Sleepy and dopey were sounding pretty good.

Her father smiled. "When you were little, you used to ask me to take you to work with me. And now I am."

Freesia tried to smile back, but she was too nervous.

Blue stripe, white stripe, purple stripe. Exhale.

At last, after several turns that left Freesia with no sense of where she was, they arrived at the history wing and Freesia's first classroom, where Father introduced Freesia to a storklike woman named Ms. O'Leary before hurrying off to his class.

"So, Francine," Ms. O'Leary said, standing in front of a white board covered with homework assignments, "what's your favorite period in American history?"

Freesia's throat was so tight that when she spoke it came out like a croak. "Um . . . now?"

"Ah! You're a current events gal!"

And then an earsplitting alarm went off and Freesia hit the ground and covered her head.

"Oh my goodness! Francine! Francine?"

Rubber footsteps surrounded her. She peeked beyond her arms and saw a sea of sneakers, a forest of blue-jean-clad legs.

"Didn't you have bells at your old school?" Ms. O'Leary said, leaning down.

Freesia wanted to crawl into a hole. Unfortunately, there was no hole in the floor (and if anyone could see one, it was her). She got on her hands and knees, retrieved the binder she had dropped, and then pushed herself to standing.

"No," she said with dignity. "We didn't."

Once she took a seat in the windowless classroom, in a chair-desk about three-quarters of the way back, things got better—which is not to say good, just less awful. There were so many students in this class (including herself, Freesia counted thirty-seven) that no one paid much attention to the new girl. They just listened as Ms. O'Leary talked about something called the Industrial Revolution and wrote things in their note-books.

Well, the kids in the front listened and wrote, anyway. Back where she was, two girls played with their cell phones (she knew what they were called now) while one boy doo-dled battle scenes: tanks, guns, soldiers.

She thought of Taser. She hoped he was okay.

When the bell rang again, she jumped a little, but at

least she didn't dive to the ground. She was making progress.

"You know how to get to your next class, Francine?" Ms. O'Leary asked. How Freesia hated that name.

"I have a map, but . . . isn't there a break before the next class?"

Ms. O'Leary glanced at the clock. "If you consider four minutes a break. You'd better hurry."

Freesia followed the swarm of students out the door and into the hall and along the lockers until the hall split and she stopped dead. A boy bumped her from behind, mumbled "sorry," and continued around her. She found refuge against a cold metal locker.

She pulled out her school map. It had lines, numbers, boxes—all of them, apparently, corresponding to rooms and hallways within the school. But which ones?

After a few more wrong turns, the bell rang. Freesia was the only one left in the hallway. She stared at the map. It remained incomprehensible.

"Lost?" She opened her eyes to a gangly boy a whole head taller than her. Sandy bangs fell in his gray eyes. His nose was long and slightly crooked. When he smiled, two comma-shaped dimples framed his wide mouth.

She was still clutching the map. "Extremely."

"Where do you need to be?"

"Room . . ." Dash it—she'd forgotten the number. She pulled out her schedule. "Five thirteen. AP French."

He looked at her schedule. "That's a pretty intense class load."

"It is? I mean—yes. Utterly."

"Foreign languages are on the other side of the school. I'm headed that way. I'll show you."

"Don't you have a class now?" she asked him.

"Film studies, yeah. But I spend so much time in the editing studio on nights and weekends, the teacher lets me come and go whenever. So—where did you move here from?"

"What do you mean?"

"Since you don't know your way around the school, I just assumed . . ."

"Oh. Right. My move. It was . . . local."

"I've been here since August," he said. "Moved from Portland."

She gave him a blank look.

"Oregon," he said.

"I knew that!" (She didn't.)

"Well, there's a Portland in Maine, too."

"I knew that too." (She actually did.) "Do you like Arizona?"

He looked at the ceiling, considering. "I miss the rain. I know that sounds weird, but it's true."

She nodded. "Yeah, the sunshine here is awfully . . . sunny." She wasn't just saying that. After spending the last few years indoors, the bright sky made her eyes ache. And for someone who'd lived all her life in the Valley of the Sun, her skin was a shocking shade of pale.

He shrugged. "I guess I miss my old friends, too."

"I know what that is like." Freesia's eyes stung. If only she were going to Spanglish class with Jelissa instead of French class with a bunch of people she didn't know. She could use a good giggle right about now. She wouldn't mind a big plate of nachos, either.

They turned another corner, and the boy stopped. "But people here have been pretty cool. People are people, right? Anyway. Room five thirteen—here you are."

The door was shut. She wished she could walk on by and keep talking to this gangly boy.

He held up a hand. "I'm Adam, by the way."

"Freesia," she said, forgetting for the moment that she was supposed to be Francine. "Thanks for getting me here."

"No problem." He shot her a final grin before turning around and heading back the way he had come.

Freesia straightened her long gray cardigan, took a deep breath, and turned the doorknob. Inside the classroom, the young woman standing in front of the whiteboard—according to Freesia's schedule, her name was Mademoiselle Chu—stopped whatever she was saying and glared. The students all looked at Freesia, too, though with curiosity rather than irritation.

Fighting an urge to flee, Freesia croaked, "*Bonjour.*"

"*Qu'est-ce que c'est?*" Mademoiselle Chu was small and tidy, with thin lips and piercing black eyes.

"English, please."

The teacher's thin lips got thinner. "What is it? I am in the middle of teaching."

"I'm a new student." Hands shaking, Freesia held out her schedule.

The woman gave it a quick look before handing it back. "*D'accord. Assieds-toi.*"

Not understanding the teacher's instructions to sit down, Freesia remained where she was. She scanned the room, hoping to see some food laid out or perhaps a door to an outside patio. Advanced Placement French sounded like a cultural immersion class, and yet—

"*Quel est le problème?*"

Freesia's tummy grumbled. "Where are the snacks?" she whispered.

"*Pardon?*"

Maybe the teacher hadn't heard her. She raised her voice. "*Les* snacks. They must be here somewhere. I haven't eaten anything but a bowl of fruity cereal today, and I could really use a crepe or maybe a warm baguette with a hunk of cheese."

Giggles rippled through the classroom.

With a poisonous glare, Mademoiselle Chu pointed to the field of desks. "*Assieds-toi.*"

Head down, Freesia scurried down a row of students. The only free seat had a wobbly desk arm. Freesia folded her body into the chair, put her binder on her lap, and didn't look up again until the bell rang.

Map reading skills improving, Freesia made it to the rest of her classes without any more student assistance, but she cringed every time she had to stand in front of a class and introduce herself to a new teacher. Also, she was hungry, and she had to go to the bathroom.

At last fifth period ended: only one more class to endure before her father would take her back to the beige house.

Clutching her binder and map, she wound her way through the school, ending in a classroom across the hall from noxious Mademoiselle Chu. Relieved to have made it through the door before that frightful bell, she scurried over to the English teacher's desk.

"I'm new."

Mr. Janz was eating a sandwich. He blinked at Freesia a couple of times, held up a finger, chewed, and swallowed. "Um—hi."

Younger than her father but older than Mademoiselle Chu, Mr. Janz had close-cropped blond hair and pale, wide-set eyes. He wore a beautiful silver watch and a platinum wedding ring, a starched shirt in a lovely shade of royal blue, and perfectly pressed gray trousers. He was the best-dressed person Freesia had seen in school. No, he was the best-dressed person she had seen in Arizona. On the spot, she decided that he was her favorite teacher.

She thrust her schedule at him. He scanned the paper and nodded. "You're in my AP class."

"Yes."

He handed the schedule back. "Excellent. See you sixth period."

For the first time, it struck her that the classroom was empty. "Isn't this sixth period?"

He shook his head. "It's lunch. For another"—he checked the clock above the door—"twenty-six and a half minutes. And then it will be sixth period."

"Lunch? Now? But school is almost over."

He took a swig of Mountain Dew. "Yeah, I know—it's stupid. Though, officially? I didn't say that." He motioned to the empty desks. "You're welcome to hang here till class starts, if you'd like."

She shook her head. "Thanks, but I'm famished, so I think I'll go get some nibbles. Where would I find the spread?"

"The . . ."

"Is there some kind of buffet?"

He considered. "There's a portable food service station in the student commons."

"That sounds scrummy enough." She handed him the school map. "Can you show me where the commons is?"

With only a couple of wrong turns (and a quick stop in the girls' bathroom, which had toilet paper on the floor and mirrors so scratched they didn't count as mirrors), Freesia found her way to the vast, noisy, crowded space where lunch was being served. The food at the portable food station was not only not scrummy, it was possibly not food. As it turned out, it didn't matter because the line was so long that Freesia was unable to score so much as a square piece of pizza.

Minutes before the bell rang, when it was clear she wouldn't be eating, Freesia spotted Angel standing on the edge of a large group. Angel was smiling. And laughing. But they weren't like a real smile and laugh—more like forced contortions.

Freesia edged closer, careful to stay out of Angel's line of sight.

A blond girl in short shorts sat on a plastic chair in the center of the group. She was very pretty, very blond, with just a touch more black mascara than Freesia would have advised. She had broken a bone, apparently—a highlighter-pink cast covered her right calf and foot, leaving her perfectly manicured toes peeking out. A boy sat on the ground by her feet, signing the cast. Another boy held her crutches.

She was telling a story—something about a basketball game and a cheer section and a ball bouncing off someone's head. Around her, everyone listened and laughed in all the right places.

She's like Chai, Freesia thought—only not so over the top that the other girls realize they should just ignore her.

As if she sensed that she was being watched, Angel looked around and met Freesia's gaze. Recognition flickered for just an instant before she turned and took a step closer to the sea of backs.

● ● ●

At least she made it to sixth period on time. Mr. Janz assigned her a seat and said, "Hey, class—this is Francine. Make her feel welcome."

Dutifully, the class ignored her.

She slid into her seat and put her binder on the desk.

"We meet again."

Surprised, she looked up to see Adam sitting next to her.

He said, "Is your name Francine? I thought you said it was Freesia."

"It's both. Freesia is . . ." She had no idea how to explain this.

"A nickname?"

"Yes."

He nodded. "That's cool. How was your first day?"

"Odious."

"It gets better."

"Truly?"

He considered. "Maybe. Maybe not. But it's the kind of thing you're supposed to say." He smiled.

She liked his smile. If only Adam had a straighter nose, a less-wide mouth, a better haircut, and more muscle, he'd be kind of good-looking. Freesia wasn't shallow. Yes, okay, she was shallow. But she'd spent the past three and a half years surrounded by flawless beauty. Physical imperfections jarred her.

By the end of the class, Mr. Janz was still her favorite teacher. He made jokes. He asked questions. He got students talking. But Freesia was just as lost in English as she'd been in French, which was really disappointing, since she actually spoke the language.

At last, the bell rang. For once, it struck Freesia as a happy sound.

Adam said "see ya" and was out the door before she'd closed her binder. She'd almost made it to the door when a girl said, "Francine! I can't believe it's you!"

Freesia turned around and immediately felt unbalanced. Somehow, she knew this girl. She'd seen her wavy orange hair before, her apple cheeks, her rosebud mouth. An oversized blue sweatshirt was insufficient to hide her ample curves.

Jelissa. That's who she looked like—not exactly, but

enough to be her sister or maybe a first cousin. But this girl wasn't Jelissa, of course. Jelissa lived in Canada, and probably looked nothing like this in real life.

Freesia said, "Hi, um . . ."

"Erin." She clutched her bulging book bag in front of her like a shield. "Do you really not recognize me?"

Erin. Freesia knew that name. She knew this girl. It was more than the resemblance to Jelissa. She recognized the freckles above her lip and the way her ears stuck out a little bit. *Erin.* Who was she?

"Of course!" Freesia said. "It's just—been a while."

Erin nodded. "Your dad said you liked your new school."

"I did. I do."

"It was online, right?"

"Uh-huh."

"I asked your dad—last year, or maybe the year before— I asked him for your number, but he said you were so busy with your classes and activities that you didn't really have time to . . . you know."

"Right."

"But you're going to finish up at Tumbleweed?"

"I don't think so."

"Oh. Well, it's really good to see you. And I'm glad you're in my English class. Call me if—you know."

"I will."

Erin put her bag on the floor and rummaged around until she pulled out a cell phone. "Can I have your number?"

"I don't have a cell phone."

"*Really?*"

"I know. I'm kind of a freak."

"I didn't mean—"

"No, it's okay." Freesia couldn't believe she had found someone who was even more uncomfortable in her own skin than she was.

"I'd better go find my dad," Freesia said. "He's driving me home."

Erin nodded. "Yeah. Well, see you tomorrow, I guess. And . . . it really is good to see you, Francine."

"It's actually . . . I go by Freesia now. It's my nickname. So if you could call me that—"

"Of course! *Freesia.* It's nice. I like it."

Freesia nodded. "Me too."

22

"Who is Erin?" Freesia asked.

It was dinnertime in the Somers house, but tonight there was no pot on the stove, just a freezer full of premade entrees that probably wouldn't taste as pretty as their pictures. Mother had already confirmed Freesia's greatest fear: despite countless calls, e-mails, and texts, she had made no progress getting the Bubble World account reinstated.

Mother ripped open a cardboard box. "Erin Reilly?"

"I don't know. Erin in my English class. She has red hair?"

"Erin Reilly." Mother nodded. "Your best friend." She pulled a plastic-covered tray out of the cardboard box and stuck it in the microwave.

"I had a best friend?" Freesia was stunned.

"Of course." Mother pushed some buttons on the microwave.

"But you said I didn't have any friends."

Mother said, "You had friends when you were little. Not a lot, but some. But by the end of seventh grade, when you enrolled in Bubble World, you didn't have any friends at all. I'm sorry, Freesia. I don't mean to stir up any painful memories."

"You can't stir up painful memories, because I don't remember anything."

"So that's a good thing, right?"

The microwave beeped. Mother took her dinner and disappeared upstairs.

● ● ●

Freesia devoured a (surprisingly tasty) piece of lasagna in front of the television set while watching a history show with her father. The show was about World War II in England, which, from the look of it, was even worse than Phoenix of today. There were air raids and food shortages. Also, hemlines were a good five inches below flattering.

During a commercial break (for a computer program that could teach you to speak Italian in six months or your money back), Father told Freesia that he loved history so much that every summer he traveled to Pennsylvania, where he dressed as a Union soldier and reenacted the Battle of Gettysburg. Freesia smiled and nodded as if this were a normal way to spend one's holidays.

When the show was over, Freesia went upstairs and knocked on Angel's door. And knocked. And—

"*What?*" She opened the door a crack.

"May I borrow your computer?"

"No." She shut the door.

From the hallway, Freesia heard muffled voices coming from her sister's room. Angel's and . . . someone else. A boy.

Freesia put her ear to the door and tried to hear what was being said. She knocked. And she knocked. And she—

"*Leave me alone!*" Angel yanked open the door.

"Leaving you alone is my greatest wish." Freesia tried to see beyond her sister into the room. "But I can't do that unless I get back to Agalinas. And I can't get back to Agalinas unless I use your computer."

The door opened just a crack. Angel went back inside, murmured something to whoever was in there, and returned holding the silver tablet Freesia had seen her tapping at the day before.

"What is this?"

"It's my computer. Duh." She handed the thing to Freesia. "Be careful. And give it back to me as soon as you're done."

"I don't know how to use this thing."

Angel looked at the ceiling. "Fine. I'll show you." She pulled her door open wider and took her computer over to her desk. Unfolded, it had a screen on the top half, a keyboard on the bottom.

To Freesia's surprise, there was no one else in the room. "Were you talking to someone just now? I thought I heard another voice."

"Yeah. So?"

"Was it just your phone?"

"I was video chatting. My boy—my friend has a laptop,

too, so we can see each other when we talk. I still have home-work. Can we get this over with?"

"I need to send one of those letter things."

"An e-mail?"

"I guess."

"Do you have an e-mail address?"

"No."

"Do you have an e-mail for the person you want to write to?"

"No." Freesia rubbed her face. Her whole body ached with fatigue. "Is that a problem?"

"Depends. Who do you want to write to?" Angel asked.

"Todd Piloski. The—"

"I know who he is." Angel tapped a few keys. "What do you want your e-mail name to be?"

"My what?"

"I'm creating an e-mail account for you. I'll try Francine, see if that's available."

"I hate that name. Try Freesia."

Angel tapped the keys. Onscreen, a message read,

That name has been claimed by another user. Still available:

Freesia249
Freesia177
Freesia621

"You want any of those?" Angel asked.

"Try Sweet Freesia."

"You're calling yourself sweet?"

Freesia kept her eyes on the screen. "It's what my mother calls me. My mother in Agalinas, I mean."

Angel poked at the keys until a message popped up:

Congratulations! Your new e-mail address will be: sweetfreesia@botmail.com.

Angel tapped a few more keys, and the Bubble World website popped up. Looking at the home page's aerial shot of Agalinas, Freesia felt a big lump in her throat. She swallowed hard.

"Almost like being there, huh?" Angel said.

"No. Not at all."

Angel clicked and tapped some more until she found Todd Piloski's e-mail address. "Okay, it's ready. You can write your e-mail."

Angel retreated to her canopy bed, stuck a couple of buds in her ears, and opened a textbook.

Freesia leaned close to the screen. "Hi, Todd. It's me, Freesia. Francine. But I'd rather be called Freesia. I'm in Arizona. I went to school today, and it was odious."

"*What.* In the *world.* Are you *doing*?" Angel pulled the buds out of her ears and gaped at Freesia as if she were an utter freak. Since Freesia was used to having her sister look at her this way, she wasn't fazed.

"I'm—what do you call it. E-mailing Todd."

"Unbelievable." Angel shut her textbook and scooted off the tall bed. "Just tell me what you want to say. Stick to the important stuff."

"Okay, here goes." Freesia bit her lip, closed her eyes, and began to dictate.

Hello Todd,
I want to come back to Agalinas. It is my home and where my friends are. I understand why you punished me. I am sorry. I will never do it again.

You might be wondering if I told people here what was going on there. You know what I mean. I haven't said a word. And I won't say a word if you let me come back. But if you make me stay in Arizona, I will be forced to tell the truth.

That is not a threat.

Okay, maybe it is.

Sincerely,
Freesia (don't call me Francine) Summers/Somers

"I sent it." Angel looked up from the computer.

"How will I know when he answers?"

"I'll check for you."

"Thanks."

Angel held her gaze. "What haven't you said?"

"Huh?"

"What's the truth that you'll be forced to tell?"

"Nothing." Freesia's mouth twitched.

Angel's face shut down. "Fine. Close the door on your way out."

23

After Freesia's first day at Tumbleweed High, things could only get better.

Except they didn't.

First was the problem with sleep—or, to be precise, with lack of sleep. Freesia's sleepy juice prescription had been written by the official Bubble World doctor, and after just two nights, the supply ran out, and they couldn't get more.

No Bubble World, no sleepy juice.

No sleepy juice, no sleep.

Happy juice didn't help. If anything, it made her even more awake at bedtime, but during the day it made her head feel all fuzzy and odd. The medication was calibrated for a virtual world, not a real one.

To combat her fatigue, Freesia's parents pumped her full of coffee that left her edgy and tense. Her hands shook. Her heart raced. But at least she was awake.

At school, the mass of students made her nervous. She perspired into her cousins' hand-me-downs. Her hands trembled. Her back ached from hauling around so many books.

No one noticed.

Erin continued to say hello and sometimes to chat a little bit. So did Adam. A couple of girls in her math and physics classes did not befriend her, exactly, but included her in their between-class homework-is-killing-me complaint sessions.

Truth was, homework was not killing Freesia because she was not doing any. The textbooks were so big, the print inside so itty, the words, the paragraphs, the pictures—all so far beyond her grasp.

Surely someone would say something? Do something? But no one did.

Once upon a time, Freesia had felt ugly. Now she felt invisible. Somehow that was worse.

"You want to be in a group together?" Erin asked in English class.

"What?" Freesia had been doodling clothes: palazzo pants with a wide belt and a body-hugging top.

"The Ralph Waldo Emerson group project," Erin said. "Mr. Janz said we could have up to four people in a group."

Adam looked up. "I'll be in your group."

"Great!" Erin said. "Let's all go to my house after school tomorrow."

"Sounds like a plan," Adam said.

Freesia nodded. Her hands trembled. She perspired.

"Nothing," her mother said when Freesia walked into her office after school. It had been the same every day: no word from Todd Piloski.

"Nothing," Angel told her, checking Sweet Freesia's e-mail.

Today Angel wore tight black jeans, a tight peach T-shirt that accentuated her orangey blush, and about fifteen strands of long, mismatched beads: red, gold, silver, turquoise, orange, purple. Purple!

Freesia couldn't stand it anymore.

"Can I give you a makeover?"

"Excuse me?"

"You're really pretty. Way prettier than me. Obviously. But your choice of clothes . . . your makeup technique . . . the way you do your hair . . ."

"What are you trying to say?"

"You always look so . . . un-utter."

Freesia braced herself for one of Angel's nasty comments. Instead her eyes got all shiny and her nose turned red. And still she looked better than Freesia on her best day.

Without a word, Freesia went to the closet, which was so crammed she couldn't even see what was in there. She pulled out an armload of clothes and dumped them on Angel's bed.

First up, a lime green sleeveless blouse. "Will you ever wear this?" Freesia asked.

"No."

"Good answer." She chucked the blouse onto the floor. A fraying tube top and a faded floral sundress followed.

When she came across a long, see-through filmy black blouse, Freesia said, "How about this?"

Angel shrugged. "I've never been able to figure out what to wear it with."

Freesia lit up. "Black tank top, skinny jeans, granny shoes, and one strand—*one*—of long beads. You'll look de-vicious." She slung the blouse over Angel's desk chair and then went back to the pile on the bed, rescuing only a handful of items before retrieving another armload from the closet and tackling that as well.

When she'd finished purging the closet, the pile of give-away clothes was so high it toppled over. There was plenty of room left in the closet—maybe too much room.

"You're sure all that stuff looks good on me?" Angel asked.

Freesia paused. "Of course. But here's what you need to understand about fashion. It's not about how you look. It's about how the clothes make you feel about yourself." She considered. "Okay, maybe it's a little bit about how you look."

Freesia moved on to the dresser. As she yanked open a drawer, her gaze fell on the photo of the two little girls tacked to Angel's bulletin board.

"These little girls—are they us?" Her index finger grazed the edge of the picture. She didn't dare turn around. As nice—or at least apathetic—as Angel was being, she couldn't count on her to hold back a biting remark.

"Oh—that. Yeah, Mom gave me that picture a long time ago. I don't even know why I put it up there."

"We were cute," Freesia said.

"Whatever. Are you going to go through my dresser, or what?"

Her back still turned, Freesia smiled and pulled out a white T-shirt with a kitten decal. "Odious," she proclaimed, chucking the shirt over to the toppled pile.

Within an hour, Freesia was using the camera on Angel's phone to create an outfit catalogue of potential ensembles, fully accessorized.

"I won't be around forever to help you pick out clothes," Freesia said optimistically, holding the camera phone up to record Angel wearing the filmy black shirt for a second time, now with a lacy tank top, white jeans, and black ballet flats.

"You promise?" Angel said, holding a pose.

Freesia grinned at her sister's presumed joke and snapped the picture. Angel did not grin back, which kind of ruined the sisterly bonding moment.

Angel's phone vibrated in Freesia's hand. Words appeared on the screen:

Tyler <3
Skype?

"Who's Tyler?"

"Give me that." Angel snatched the phone and began tapping.

"Is he your boyfriend? The one you're always talking to at night?"

"None of your business." Angel's eyes flicked over Freesia.

"Yes, he is. Okay, we're done. You can leave. Thanks for . . . you know."

"We haven't even done your makeup yet. Or your hair."

"Later. I want you to go."

"Fine. Sure." Freesia retrieved a couple of larger-size items she'd uncovered in the closet blitz: a plain white top and a long black jacket, along with a plaid scarf that Angel thought was ugly because Angel had no taste.

Out in the hallway, Freesia thought, It's not just about looking good or feeling good. It's also, in some small way—or maybe not so small—about being good on the inside.

What a flippy idea.

24

dam's car was small and orange and looked nothing like the big boxy vehicles that always blew up
in Bubble World movies. No—cars as small as Adam's typically flipped off freeway overpasses or bounced
down rocky canyons. Erin sat up front. Freesia belted herself
into the middle back seat, which would be safest in the event
of a rollover.

Erin's house was maybe ten minutes from the school, down
a route Freesia had never traveled before.

And yet.

There is a McDonald's on the next corner, Freesia thought,
an instant before the arches came into view. She'd barely re-
covered from the shock of premonition when another thing
popped into her mind. *We're coming up to the little park with
the twisty green slides and a tire swing.*

There it was!

She peered out the car window with increased intensity.
She knew that crosswalk. That stoplight. That clump of bushes.

That house . . . and the next. Freesia remembered this place, every last bit of it. Had she spent that much time at Erin's?

At Erin's direction, Adam turned the car onto a narrow tree-lined street with long, low houses set far apart. An adobe-style house covered with pink and peach bougainvillea came into view. Immediately, Freesia recognized the stone walkway, the old mesquite tree with low-hanging branches, the towering saguaro cactus. A towering playhouse and a swimming pool dominated the backyard. She couldn't see them, but she knew they were there.

"That's my house!" Freesia blurted.

"Um, yeah," Erin said. "I mean, it was."

"But . . . do you live there now?" Freesia was even more confused than usual.

"In your house? No, of course not. I live where I've always lived. There."

Across the street from the adobe was a bright white house with heavy wood beams. *Erin's house.* Of course.

Adam parked his little orange car next to the curb. Freesia longed to dash across the street, to burst into her old house and run to the hall where the bedrooms were. The first room on the left was hers. There were books on the shelves, dolls and stuffed animals in baskets, and a computer on the desk. Oh, she had loved her computer.

She couldn't let Erin and Adam see her reaction. As far as they knew, she had spent the last few years enrolled in an online high school, fully aware of her new beige house and all the beige things that were happening in and around it.

She took a deep breath and followed Adam and Erin out of the car and into the hot afternoon.

"FRANCINE!" Mrs. Reilly stood in Erin's eerily familiar kitchen. She looked the same as always, pink-faced and pleasantly chubby, with hands in constant motion as she talked. "It is SO good to see you after all this time. How ARE your parents?"

Mrs. Reilly used to make slice-and-bake cookies that she'd set out on the kitchen counter so they could help themselves. The Reillys' plates were white with a flower design around the rim. Erin had an older brother nicknamed Buddy (real name Sean) and a golden retriever/poodle nicknamed Peanut (real name Chief Inspector Doodle).

Erin gave her a Princess Grace Barbie for her eighth birthday. Erin's favorite ice cream flavor was mint chip. Her mother made really good meat loaf but tended to burn the cookies.

She remembered everything.

"My parents are fine" was all Freesia could manage to reply to Mrs. Reilly.

"When Erin TOLD me you were back in school and in her English class, I said you MUST have her over! I said, I haven't seen Francine Somers since I don't know when."

"It's Freesia now," Erin said. "That's what she likes to be called."

"*Freesia?*" Mrs. Reilly said.

Freesia nodded.

"OKAY, then!"

Sounds came from farther back in the house: Gunfire. Shouting. A great big boom. They turned down a hallway, and the sounds got louder. They stopped outside a dark-ened bedroom. A husky teenage boy with a blond crew cut and shiny eyes sat hunched on the room's only bed, clutching game controls. Soldiers and explosions flickered on a bulky television set.

"Hey, Buddy. It's Francine from across the street. She came over to work on our Ralph Waldo Emerson project."

Buddy grunted.

"You remember Francine?"

"Hey," Buddy said, his eyes never leaving the screen.

In Erin's room, they unloaded books, notebooks, pens, and pencils. Plus phones, of course. Immediately, Erin began texting someone and then Adam did, too. How strange to be together and yet not.

Freesia didn't mind, though, because it gave her a chance to examine Erin's room. A double bed with a cloud-patterned comforter had replaced her old bunk beds. Freesia longed to throw open Erin's closet and hunt for the doll with the ponytail that changed length—at least, until Freesia and Erin played hairdresser and chopped the ponytail off.

More than dolls, Erin had adored mice, of the cartoon va-riety, that is. She wore mouse T-shirts, covered her walls with mouse pictures, and collected mouse Beanie Babies.

One Halloween when they were older, sixth grade, maybe, Francine and Erin had dressed as the three blind mice. But there was another girl—the third blind mouse. Something had happened. Something about that girl . . .

"Have you guys thought about the project?" Adam asked.

"Huh?"

Erin said, "We're supposed to work as a group to create something that demonstrates Emerson's principles of self-reliance and independent thought. Didn't you read the handout?"

"Oh. The handout. Sure."

Adam said, "We could do a film."

"I was thinking a poster," Erin said.

Without knowing why, Freesia sided with Adam, though of course her only real opinion about Ralph Waldo Emerson was that he would have benefited from a choose-your-own-name option.

But there was something about that third blind mouse girl. And Erin. Something had happened. . . .

● ● ●

"How long did you live across the street?" Adam unlocked the orange car and opened the passenger door for her: gentlemanly, yes, but for safety reasons she wished she could sit in the back.

"Oh, you know. From when I was little."

She closed herself in and fiddled with the seat belt. The front seats were low and black. She felt as if she were sitting in a hole.

In front of Freesia's old house, the giant saguaro held up its green arms as if worshipping the sky. In the distance, the jagged mountains, turning purple in the late afternoon light, seemed lit from within.

Adam got in and started the car. "The light in the desert is unreal. I can't wait till the cactuses start blooming. I'm going to film a saguaro opening at night."

"Do you really think it's pretty here?" Freesia wrinkled her nose.

He considered. "When we first moved here, I thought that Arizona looked like the moon. But you have to get beyond this set idea that pretty means green and leafy. Once you start noticing all the shades of brown and gray, and you start seeing how intense the shadows get and the way the mountains change color—yeah, I actually think it's really beautiful."

He pulled out his phone. "What's your address?"

She told him and was relieved when he plugged it into his phone rather than asking for directions. It might have seemed weird that she didn't know how to get from her old house to her new one.

It was weird.

"When did you move?" he asked, pulling away from the cub.

"Um . . . three years ago?" It was as good a guess as any.

Adam turned on the radio. Some rap thing was on. He fiddled with the dial, pausing at a few different stations until—

"Wait! Go back!"

"Huh?"

They'd reached the end of the street. Adam's phone told him to turn right.

Freesia said, "That last song—it was Chase Bennett."

"Who?"

Freesia twisted the radio dial, and sure enough, the sounds of Chase Bennett filled the little car.

It's another day.
On the island we say, Hey,
Hey, oh. Hey, oh. Hey, oh.
Don't wanna see you frown,
Girl, turn it upside down.
Hey, oh. Yeah, turn it upside down.
Girl.
Hey.

"That's my favorite song!" Freesia bounced in her seat.

"Seriously? Isn't it, like, really old?"

"Not old-old. A few months, maybe. I used to listen to it every day back when I lived on—" Freesia stopped herself before she said too much.

"Let's find out." Adam turned right and then pulled over to the curb. He tapped the front of his phone a few times and held it up to the radio speakers. Chase Bennett crooned his final verse.

Adam checked the screen. "Yeah, I thought so. Ben Chase, 1986."

"What are you talking about?"

"The song's called 'Island Girl.' I've got this app, if you hold it up to the radio, it tells you what's playing." He handed Freesia the phone.

Sure enough there it was: "Island Girl," Ben Chase, 1986.

Freesia might have thought it was a technical glitch of some sort, but an album cover showed young, smiling Chase Bennett. He was sitting in a red rowboat in shallow water. His hair glowed like a halo.

"You okay?" Adam asked.

"What? Oh—yes. Utterly." Hands trembling, she gave him back the phone.

Chase Bennett really did exist. Only he wasn't named Chase Bennett. And his songs were old. Not just that—if he recorded that song in 1986, that meant that *he* was old. He might as well have been one of Todd Piloski's inventions.

Adam pulled back into traffic, and the smooth confident female voice on his phone alerted him to his next turn. The voice wasn't a real person, even though it sounded like one. And he didn't think that was weird. No one did.

When they got to her house, Adam said, "So I guess we'll all get together after school on Monday to work on the project."

She hesitated. "That's the plan."

Mr. Janz had said that groups could be between two and four people. Erin and Adam would be fine if she went back to Agalinas before then.

He scribbled something on a strip of paper and handed it to her. It was a number. "Give me a call if you ever want to get together to do homework. Or, you know. Drive out to the desert or go see a movie or whatever."

She shoved the paper into her overloaded book bag and opened the door. "Thanks, but I can't call you. I don't have a phone."

She was halfway to her door before it hit her that Adam had just asked her out. And she had said no, rather rudely.

She wheeled around to apologize, but he was already pulling away.

Adam had asked her out? How could that be possible? He was no Dare Fiesta, no Ricky Leisure, no Taser Lucas, even, but he was appealing in his tall, skinny, slightly gawky way. She, on the other hand, was so unattractive that she wouldn't even have looked in the mirror if she could have gotten dressed and accessorized and made up without one.

The real world was a strange and confusing place—in more ways than she had imagined.

25

Mother was in her office, tapping at her computer keyboard.

"Why did we move?"

"What? Oh—Francine. Your father said you were going over to a classmate's to work on a project."

"I went to Erin's house."

Mother's eyes widened and her lips pursed, but she remained quiet.

"I remembered it—her house. Our house. The street. I remembered it all."

Mother nodded.

Freesia waited for her mother to say something. To explain. When she didn't, Freesia asked, "Did we move to this house before I went to Bubble World? Or after?"

"After."

"But our old house—it was pretty. Why would you leave it? I loved that house." Freesia hadn't even known that was true until she said it.

Mother took a deep breath. "The first time we brought you back, you got upset."

"Brought me back from Bubble World, you mean?"

She nodded. "It was Angel's birthday. Her eleventh. We knew it was too soon—recommendations were to wait at least two months before interrupting the virtual state, and it had only been a few weeks. But she missed you. We thought if you could join us for cake and ice cream, a half hour or so, it wouldn't be too much."

"What happened?" Freesia was almost afraid to find out.

Mother turned back to the computer and hit a few keys. Then she dropped her hands in her lap. "You didn't recognize any of us, which upset Angel quite a bit. We told you who we were and what was going on, but instead of calming down, you started screaming. We tried to put you back in your bubblepod, but you fought us. Said you wanted to stay. But we'd watched you in Bubble World. We knew you were happier there. You had friends, you were doing well in school. You had a *life*."

"Obviously, you did something to get me back there."

"We gave you happy juice. And sleepy juice. A double dose. The doctor said that it would be fine under the circumstances. When you woke up, you were back in Bubble World, as cheery as could be."

"So when did we move?"

Mother cleared her throat. "A few months later. The situation with the neighbors . . . people kept asking where you were. We knew they wouldn't understand or appreciate

Bubble World's educational philosophy. I needed extra space for my office, anyway. It was best to make a fresh start."

"Was I awake during the move?"

"Oh, no. Given the severity of your reaction, the doctors recommended we wait at least six months before interrupting your virtual state. They prescribed a heavy sedative, and the movers dismantled your bubblepod. By the time you woke up, we were here."

"Why pick such a plain house, though?" Freesia pictured her old house: the pink and peach bougainvillea, the stone walkway, the giant cactus.

"The other place was too much work," Mother said. "Father and Angel are at school all day, and I've got my career. Who cares whether our house is pretty, as long as it meets our needs?"

Freesia's house in Agalinas looked like a birthday cake. Every time she saw it, she smiled. She didn't know why pretty mattered; she just knew that it did.

"What did you do with all my things?" Freesia asked.

"The furniture we sold or gave away. Same thing with your toys and clothes. You'd outgrown them, anyway."

Freesia shivered. It was like her parents had deleted her from reality. Like she had disappeared. Poof.

"We saved a few mementos," Mother said. "They're in a box in your closet." She rubbed her head. "Have you changed your mind? About going back?"

"No."

"Because you can stay if you want. You've only got a year

and a half of high school left anyway. When you started the program, Todd said that he'd have a virtual university set up by the time everyone turned eighteen, but progress has been slow, and I'm not convinced it's going to happen."

"I want to go back."

Mother nodded. "I still haven't heard anything from Todd, but I'll keep trying."

Upstairs in her room, Freesia pulled the cardboard box out of her closet and peeled off the tape. Mother had saved her Barbie dolls. She picked one up. It had auburn hair and green eyes. Vaguely, she remembered dressing this doll for make-believe parties. She remembered wishing she looked just like it.

Underneath the Barbies were books, school papers, and photos. She pulled out a report card from first grade. In the comment section, her teacher had written, "Francine lacks self-control and cries easily."

Freesia threw down the paper in disgust. Of course she'd cried easily. She'd been six years old! Tears were a reasonable response to the horrors she remembered of elementary school.

A thin chain snaked among the loose photos. She plucked the necklace out of the box and examined the pendant: half a heart. She had something similar in Agalinas. This one had something engraved on it: *BE.*

"Be?" With a shrug, she added the necklace to the pile of papers and moved on to the photographs.

She dug through various school and birthday party shots

until she found it: the Halloween picture of her, Erin, and that other girl dressed as the three blind mice. *Taryn*—that was the girl's name. She'd moved to their neighborhood at the beginning of sixth grade.

Taryn was pretty. The girls all wanted to be her friend, Erin most of all. The boys, their hormones just starting to kick in, became either mute or obnoxious in her presence.

On that awful Halloween, all three girls had gone to school in costume: leotards with ballet skirts, mouse ear headbands, and giant sunglasses. In the morning, they walked together in the school parade. But then, during lunch, Erin told Francine she couldn't be friends with her anymore. She didn't want it to be this way, but Taryn had made her choose. Taryn thought Francine was too babyish. And she cried too much. And wore ugly clothes. Also, Taryn wouldn't have anything to do with someone who still played with Barbies.

Francine, to her credit, did not cry—at least until she got home. She didn't even want to trick-or-treat, but her mother made her go with Angel and her friends.

One blind mouse. See how she runs.

Her memory of the incident restored, Freesia wished she could erase it. She dumped everything back into the cardboard box and shoved it to the rear of her closet.

Angel's door was closed, as usual. Freesia knocked. And knocked. And knocked. And—

"All *right!*" The door swung open. Angel looked good today, in one of the outfits Freesia had put together, but her blush was still too orange.

"Have you checked my e-mail since you got home from school?"

"My life does not revolve around your e-mail."

"Is that a no?"

Angel rolled her eyes and stomped back into her room. Freesia took the open door as an invitation.

Freesia nodded toward Angel's open computer. "Have you been video chatting with Tyler?"

"I never should have told you about him."

Without sitting down, Angel poked furiously at the keys.

"Mother told me about your eleventh birthday."

Angel froze. "What about it?"

"That you wanted me there. But it didn't turn out so well."

"Nothing ever turns out well." Angel's fingers flew over the keys with renewed vigor. "What do you know? Todd wrote back."

She angled the computer so Freesia could see the screen.

To: sweetfreesia@botmail.com
From: Todd Piloski <t_piloski@bubbleworld
enterprises.us.com>
Re: Bubble World Account #S673395 (inactive)

NO.

Todd Piloski
Founder, CEO, and Chairman of the Board
BUBBLE WORLD EDUCATIONAL ENTERPRISES, INC.
"providing the education of the future . . . today"

Learn more about our innovations at
www.bubbleworldeducation.com

"*No?* That's it?" Freesia said, flabbergasted. "He's not even going to write me a note?"

"Looks that way. Do you want to reply, or can I close this out? I have to write a three-page essay for English, which might be kind of hard, since I haven't actually read the book."

Freesia couldn't take her eyes off the screen. "But he knows that I can ruin everything for him. He knows I can tell."

"Okay, you go away and think about what you want to do. I'm going to go online and look for SparkNotes." Angel reached for the computer and then stopped. "Wait. You can tell *what*?"

• • •

Freesia asked her parents to sit down at what everyone called the dinner table, though no one ever actually ate dinner there.

"There's something you need to know about Bubble World."

Mother's hand grazed a pile of glossy catalogs. The dinner table was mainly used as a dumping ground for mail.

Freesia said, "The whole thing is a sham. We spend most of our class time chatting and snacking. No one learns anything."

That got Mother's attention. "That's not possible. Your evaluations have been excellent. Plus, I've seen your classes in action. The second Monday of every month is classroom observation day."

"Which of my classes have you observed?"

"Oh—everything. Microbiology, Latin, History of Ancient Cultures, computer programming, immunology—"

"Immunology?"

"That was a tough class," Father said. You seemed so overwhelmed by the project work at first, we thought we might have to get you a virtual tutor. But you pulled it off in the end."

"I don't even know what immunology is."

Mother leaned forward. "Of course you do. Don't you remember making a three-dimensional model of the streptococcus bacteria? I vlogged about it."

"I never made a model of . . . whatever you just said."

Father said, "With all the memory blockers she's been taking, it's possible that she's forgotten some things." He pulled out his phone, checked it, and slipped it back into his pocket.

"I haven't forgotten anything about Bubble World," Freesia said. "Don't you get it? The entire thing is Todd Piloski's creation. His minions can make my avatar do or say whatever they think you want to hear. But that wasn't really me you were seeing."

"But you can speak French," Father said. "And Korean, Cantonese, Latin, Spanish . . . I'm forgetting one."

"German," Mother said.

"I can speak French food. *Je voudrais une baguette, s'il vous plaît.* Also, I'm almost conversant in Spanglish. That's about it."

Father shook his head. "I asked Miss Chu how you were getting on in AP French, and she said fine."

"Well, sure. I don't cause any trouble. But I don't understand a thing I hear or read."

Father stood up. "All Tumbleweed student grades are posted online. I know you've only been there a week, but some marks should have been entered." He headed to the den to get his laptop.

"Did you not go to class in Bubble World?" Mother was angry—she just wasn't sure at whom. "Is that what you're saying?"

"Of course I went to class! That's how I earned my shells. I wouldn't have been able to shop and eat out otherwise. But cultural appreciation was all about food, not language, and I only took the classes that I wanted to. Like Pop Music Appreciation. And Advanced Eye Makeup."

Mother shook her head. "Not possible. Todd is a close personal friend. He wouldn't deceive me in this way."

Father returned from the den with his open laptop. "Oh my goodness."

"Are her grades bad?" Mother asked.

He put the laptop on the table and slumped into his chair, still staring at the screen. "Yes . . . no. Francine doesn't *have* any grades. According to the online gradebook, she hasn't handed in any work at all."

They all looked at her. She felt hot. Small. Ashamed.

"It's all so borrifying," she explained.

They kept looking at her.

"And I get so hungry."

Still looking.

"Plus, I don't understand a single thing any of the teachers are saying." Her voice quavered.

Mother's face was practically purple. "I can't believe this. I trusted Todd with my most precious—with my child. And he treated her education like a joke!"

Freesia said, "Todd believes the traditional education system stifles creativity. He dropped out of Harvard after his freshman year to launch a computer company."

Mother scowled. "Oh, yeah. Like *that's* such an original move."

"Don't be mad," Freesia begged. "Agalinas is a good place. I'm happy there. I have friends. I just want to go back. I'll work hard this time, I promise. There are classes in literature and math and history. No one ever takes them, but they're there. So, please—just tell Todd that you know what's going on. Maybe he'll be so afraid of getting in trouble that we can go back to the way things were."

"You're not going back to Bubble World," Mother said.

"But—"

"Todd Piloski betrayed me. He betrayed you. He betrayed all the people who put their faith in his program. As a member of the Internet community, it is my duty to expose him."

"You can't do that! I have friends there."

"You can make friends here."

"No, I mean—I can't do that to my friends! What if their parents pull them out of Bubble World?"

"People need to know the truth, Francine." Mother squeezed her eyes shut.

"We'll move you into easier classes," Father said. "Get you up to speed. You'll catch up, don't worry."

"But—"

Father's and Mother's phones buzzed and jangled at the same instant.

"I have to take this," Father said.

Mother didn't say anything, just picked up her phone and went upstairs.

26

Monday morning, as Freesia was stuffing a few granola bars into her book bag, Mother announced, "I'm going to break the Bubble World story on *Flash Drive*."

Freesia didn't say anything. She just rummaged in the pantry and pulled out a foil-wrapped package of chocolate Pop-Tarts. Even cold, they were better than any of the food at school.

"I'm sorry you're angry at me, Francine. But I have to do what's right."

Freesia still didn't say anything, not even *Don't call me Francine.*

"I've given the matter a great deal of thought," Mother said. "The only way to give this story the kind of exposure it deserves is to relinquish our anonymity."

"Meaning?"

Mother took a deep breath. "I am going to use our real names."

Freesia shrugged. "Okay."

"*Okay?*"

"Yeah. Sure." What was that word Angel was always using? "*Whatever.* I don't really care what anyone here thinks of me."

● ● ●

𝓘n school, Freesia had to go through the routine of introducing herself to new teachers again. Good-bye, Advanced Placement everything. Hello, "Opportunity" Math and English, along with American History, Chemistry, Art, and Spanish I, which was supposedly easier than French but would probably be impossible since the students were months ahead of her.

Her American History teacher was Mr. Somers, also known as Father. Except in the classroom, she was to call him Mr. Somers.

First thing, Mr. Somers told the class that his feet were still hurting him, so he'd have to sit through the class. Second thing, Mr. Somers instructed the students to take out their homework and pass it to the left. He read a bunch of answers from the teacher book and told the students to grade their neighbors' papers. When that was done, a student recorded scores. The class was about a third over by then.

Then things got even duller, which was kind of astonishing. Mr. Somers (Father) put notes about the Great Depression up on the overhead projector, read them out loud, and told the students to copy them word for word. They spent the final fifteen minutes "working independently."

Father was by far the worst teacher Freesia had encountered at Tumbleweed High. If she cared at all about her schooling, that would have upset her.

Mr. Janz was still her English teacher, though of course her classmates were different. Instead of two or three kids texting instead of listening, there were now that many kids listening instead of texting. Or sleeping.

"There's no shame in dropping down a level," Mr. Janz assured her. "Or . . . three."

English was fifth period now, and art, right around the corner, was sixth. She lingered after class so Mr. Janz could give her some worksheets from earlier in the semester. They were supposed to teach her parts of speech. She was determined to complete them, even if she couldn't imagine when she'd ever need to know what an adverb was. Mr. Janz was still her favorite teacher, and that counted for something.

And then she lingered some more because she dreaded the lonely chaos of lunch period.

"You can stay here if you want a quiet place to do homework," Mr. Janz said (nicely).

"Thanks." Her shoulders relaxed (slightly).

They spent the next half hour in companionable silence. Freesia was completing her adverb worksheet when the bell rang. She finished up and put papers into her binder. She'd just started for the door when Adam strode in, his AP English textbook bumping on his hip.

She hesitated. How would she explain the class change?

She had less than two minutes to talk to him and get to her next class, so she hurried over and blurted it out.

"I'm so sorry, Adam, but I can't do the group project with you and Erin."

"Whatever." He pulled out his phone.

"It's not because I don't want to! But AP was too hard for me, so they moved me down. Way down."

"Okay." He didn't even look up. She wondered whom he was texting.

"Well—bye, then." She hurried out to make it to art class and almost collided with Erin.

"Where are you going?" Erin asked.

"I'm not in this class anymore. I'll explain later."

But when she spotted Erin coming out of Mr. Janz's room fifty minutes later, she didn't explain; instead she hurried in the other direction.

What was she supposed to say? *My parents hooked me up to a computer program because I didn't have any friends in the real world.*

Including Erin.

Especially Erin.

When Freesia, Angel, and Father came home, Mother was pacing around the first floor, practically foaming at the mouth.

"How! Could! This! Happen!"

Angel said, "I'll be in my room," and headed for the stairs.

"It was my story. My! Story! I've been having online conversations about Bubble World for years, and this person comes out of *nowhere*."

Father said, "Soooooo . . . did you post the vlog exposing the Bubble World fraud?"

"No. Yes. No. That is, I posted the vlog and then discovered—*because it was a Yahoo top news story*—that someone had beat me to it. This person. With a blog. So then I took my vlog down. Because it sounds like I was just copying this person's information."

Mother said, "The blogger said he was writing from inside Bubble World. Whether or not he's telling the truth, no one knows, but he had all the details I did and then some. Would you believe that Bubble World students actually dated?"

"We called it linking," Freesia said.

"Did you ever date anyone?"

"Link. Yes. Of course. I was quite popular there." Freesia tried to run a hand through her frizzy hair, but it got stuck in a tangle.

Mother closed her eyes and took several short, sharp breaths until she regained her composure. "You might have mentioned that. It's the kind of detail that gets Google hits."

Suddenly, Freesia understood. "This blogger—what was his name?"

"He calls himself Ricardo Leisure, of all things."

• • •

"Would you knock?" Angel snapped as Freesia burst into her bedroom. "I'm talking to Tyler!"

Her open laptop sat on her desk, the screen showing the head and shoulders of a boy with shaggy dark blond bangs falling in wide brown eyes. In the real world, he passed for cute.

Freesia bent down. "This is how video chatting works? The picture quality is way better in a bubblecast. Hi, Tyler."

He held up a hand. "Hey."

"Do you go to our school?"

"No, I live in Ohio."

"Seriously? How did you two meet?"

He scratched his chin. "My friend's cousin's friend lives in Phoenix. She and Angel hang out sometimes."

"Not really," Angel said. "Not anymore."

As anxious as Freesia was to search for Ricky's blog, Tyler had piqued her curiosity.

"So, you met Angel when you were out visiting . . . that person?"

Tyler leaned back and put his hands behind his head. "Nah, I've never been to Arizona. Me and Angel, we've got a long-distance thing. That's probably why we never fight." He grinned.

"Vicious," Freesia said. "Angel, I need to use your computer. It's an utter emergency."

"But—"

"It's okay," Tyler said. "I need to watch something on TV, anyway. Text later, Angel?"

"Of course."

Tyler kissed his index finger and held it to his screen camera, which made it look giganto. Then Angel kissed her finger and did the same thing. It looked like her tiny finger was being engulfed by his huge one, though presumably it looked the opposite on his end.

Then Tyler was gone.

Angel put her hands on her hips. "If you have some freakish mission to ruin my life, you are succeeding."

"You can get wiggy with me later," Freesia said. "But right now I need you to find someone online."

"Oh, yeah? Who's that."

"My boyfriend."

"Oh? Is this a real boyfriend or a virtual one?

Freesia narrowed her eyes. "He's at least as real as yours."

It took maybe twenty seconds to find his blog, *Ricardo Leisure: When Normal Just Won't Do*. There was no photo of him; instead, the header bar showed a beach chair on the sand, looking out at an unnaturally blue ocean.

"I've heard of this guy," Angel said.

"Really?"

"He writes about music and movies and TV shows. Lives on an island somewhere—he's always talking about surf and sand and stuff. I don't read blogs, but his reviews are always popping up on other sites. I don't know how he manages to write so much. He must never leave his house."

Monday, 3 A.M.

BURSTING BUBBLE WORLD

Had a party at my house tonight—whole bunch of
people, but no one I really wanted to see. It was warm,
the moon was bright, and the air smelled like flowers.
Paradise, right?

For a long time I thought so.

In the two years since I started this blog, I've had a
whole bunch of people ask me about my island. Was it
in the United States or maybe off of Australia? Was it big
or small, famous or obscure, public or private? Or was I
making the whole thing up?

So here's the thing. I wasn't making the whole thing
up. But someone else was. . . .

"Wow," Angel said when they finished the entry, which
went on for quite some time.

"I know. Ricky is so much smarter than I ever realized."

"You really didn't have to do any work?" Angel asked.
"That is awesome."

Freesia considered. "Depends what you call work. I put a
lot of effort into my Foundations of Foundation class."

"Huh. Maybe I will let you show me how to do makeup."

"*Francine? Come here, please.*" Mother called from across
the hall.

Freesia went into the office, where she found Mother . . .
not happy, exactly, but less upset than before.

"Sit." Mother stood up and extended a hand toward her ergonomic chair.

Freesia sat down. On the computer screen, her image blinked back at her. She really needed to do something about those eyebrows.

Mother leaned over to move the mouse. Freesia heard a clicking sound just as the image on the screen froze.

"Perfect," Mother said. "You can get up." She sat at the computer and began typing furiously. Finally she said, "There! That's done." She clicked some more. "And that." More clicking. "And that."

"What?"

Mother let out a deep breath. "This Ricardo person's story isn't an entirely bad thing. There's a hunger for more information. What's more, there's a desire to put a face on the story. And that face? Is you."

"Are you saying you put my picture on your vlog?" Freesia asked, alarmed.

Mother smiled. "Don't worry, honey. You look nice today. I love what you've done with your hair."

27

"Hey! Yeah, you. Bubble Girl."

They were clustered together at the back of her chemistry class: two girls, three boys, one sitting, four standing. Two wore black hoodies, two wore black T-shirts, one a gray shirt. Together, they looked like a ferocious storm looming on the horizon.

"Come here for a second," one of the boys called.

Her mother had posted the vlog just last night. Freesia hadn't expected the news to travel so fast.

According to the clock above the door, she had three minutes till the bell rang. Chemistry was her first class. She could have filled those last three minutes in the girls' room or just wandering down the halls. But she was so tired this morning. She was so tired every morning. She just wanted to get to her desk and sit down and tune out. But today she wouldn't get away with that.

A sixth person, another girl, joined the mob at the back. She wore a red dress and black boots. Her jet black hair was long and full, and her black eyeliner had been applied just right.

Someone showed her something on a cell phone.

"Are you serious?" The girl looked closer at the phone and then swiveled her head to look at Freesia. "Is your name Francine?"

Freesia nodded (though of course she hated that name).

The girl took the cell phone and examined it more closely.

One by one, students filed into the classroom. No teacher yet: he tended to stride in with the bell.

Freesia's assigned seat was about two-thirds of the way back. Should she just go there and sit quietly, hoping no one would talk to her? She could try claiming a seat up front instead, but that could cause all kinds of new problems.

"Bubble Girl—talk to us. We won't bite." That from the boy who was sitting down.

The girl in red slapped his arm. "Don't call her that." To Freesia: "Ignore him. He's a jerk to everyone. All this stuff online, is it true? You spent three years partying in an alternate universe, and you didn't even know it was made up?"

Tear sprang to Freesia's eyes. She blinked them back and nodded.

The girl in red looked straight at her. "That? Is awesome."

"Awesome," one of the other kids echoed.

"Where do you sit?" the girl in red asked.

"Over there." Freesia pointed.

The girl slid into her seat and patted the desk next to her. "Kid who used to sit next to me dropped out."

Too surprised to say anything, Freesia sat down next to the girl in red and slipped her textbooks under the chair.

"I'm Iris," the girl said. "And you're Francine."

"I like to be called Freesia."

"Yeah? Awesome. Iris and Freesia. Flower power. I like what you're wearing, by the way."

The bell rang, and their teacher, Mr. Liu, hurried in on cue, dumping an armload of books and papers on the desk. "Good morning, all! I trust you did your homework that I assigned for the weekend."

"He says that every Monday," Iris whispered. "Even though almost no one does their work."

Freesia stifled a giggle. Maybe Bubble World wasn't entirely different from reality.

● ● ●

It was the same thing all day long.

"Are you . . ."

"Did you . . ."

"Is your name . . ."

Freesia was a star. Like any star, she had her detractors, people who gave her long creepy looks or who glanced at her briefly and then broke out laughing with their friends. But the one time someone came right out and said something mean—"Hey, check it out. It's Bubble Girl! She's even uglier than her picture"—three complete strangers flew to her defense.

"Don't say that, you pig."

"Who are you to talk? Have you checked the mirror lately?"

"She's been through a lot. Give her some respect."

None of her teachers, including her father (especially not her father), said anything about her newfound fame until she got to English class. Mr. Janz called her up to his desk to say that he was always happy to meet her before or after school to give her extra help.

"It does explain a lot," he said.

"What do you mean?"

"Your work. You're obviously intelligent. I couldn't figure out why your skills didn't reflect that. But as long as you stay on top of your assignments, you'll catch up."

"Okay."

"School's not all fun and games. You get that."

"Yes. Of course. But . . ."

"What?"

"Can't school be at least a little fun?"

Mr. Janz straightened. She feared she had offended him. But then he looked out over the classroom crammed with kids who looked like they all wished they could be anywhere but here.

"That's an excellent point . . . Freesia."

She ran into Iris, the stylish girl from her chemistry class, just as she was heading to the student commons for lunch period, which had remained the most excruciating part of her day. As much as she liked Mr. Janz, she was afraid that hanging out in his room would mean more makeup work.

"Hey!" Iris gave her a quick squeeze. "We're going to the inconvenient store. Come with us."

The "inconvenient store" turned out to be a corner market that carried packaged snacks, toxic hot dogs, oily pizza, and frothy ice drinks. "Us" turned out to be Iris and two other fashionable girls, along with a lanky boy with dyed black hair and gold hoops in his ears. The three friends were named Alex, Morgan, and Kendy, though after the initial quick introduction, Freesia was unsure which was which.

"Blue raspberry," the boy (Morgan?) said, sticking an enormous cardboard cup under a spigot and letting it fill with a neon slurry. "Accept no substitutes."

"Are raspberries blue?" Freesia asked. She thought they were red, but since everyone knew she suffered from major memory lapses through no fault of her own, she had almost stopped worrying about sounding like a doltoid.

"Raspberries are *not* blue." He peered at the blue mass. "Ohmigosh, do you think they put something artificial in here?"

Iris came up behind him and smacked him on the arm. (Iris was a big arm smacker.) "Don't tease her, Morgan!" (It was Morgan.)

"I tease everyone I like."

On Morgan's recommendation, Freesia filled her own enormous cardboard cup with the unnatural looking slush. One sip and she almost forgot where she was. Making up for lost time in math and English might be (would be) painful, but exploring foods of every taste, texture, and color—even blue—was a never-ending delight.

Bells on the front door jingled, and a group of kids entered the already crowded store. The blond girl with the pink cast was at the center, hobbling on her crutches while a burly boy carried her handbag. Angel was at the back of the pack.

"That's my sister," Freesia said. Angel hadn't seen her yet.

"What, with Taryn?" Iris said.

Freesia tensed. "Which one is she?"

"The really annoying blond girl with the cast," Iris said. "Bet you anything, her leg isn't even broken. Girls do that to get out of cheer practice. And to get attention. Not that Taryn doesn't get enough."

Taryn. Freesia felt like she had been punched in the chest. She had instinctively disliked the girl when she'd seen her in the commons. Now she knew why.

"I went to sixth grade with her." Her voice was unsteady.

"Ew," Morgan said. "I hope you weren't friends."

Freesia shook her head. "No. We definitely weren't."

Taryn, trailed by the boy with the handbag and also by Angel, hobbled over to the nacho machine, where yet another boy dispensed orange goo onto a cardboard tray of chips. Angel, officially an enemy of articial flavors and colors, pounced on the cheese machine the moment it was free. When she was done, she looked up and caught Freesia's eyes.

Freesia broke eye contact first. "Guess we should pay for this stuff and get out of here. The bell will ring soon."

"Yup," Iris said. "One more class, and we're free till morning."

● ● ●

"So are you like best friends with Iris Franco now?" Angel asked after school.

They were waiting outside their father's classroom. This was the first time Angel had stood next to her rather than hiding around the corner.

Father was staying late to give some kid a makeup test. Father gave tests every Wednesday and had students correct each other's tests every Thursday. That made for a day and a half every week in every class when he didn't actually have to teach. Father was a terrible teacher, but he wasn't stupid.

"I barely know Iris," Freesia said.

"You went to the inconvenient store with her."

"Is that really what it's called?"

"No. Duh."

Freesia took a step away from her sister.

"Iris is really stuck up," Angel said. "And it's kind of weird that you're hanging out with sophomores."

"How would you know if she's stuck up? Have you ever even talked to her?"

"No. Because she's too stuck up. She doesn't even know who I am."

Freesia narrowed her eyes. "So anyone who doesn't know who you are is stuck up? There are a lot of people in this school. Nobody can know everyone."

Angel rolled her eyes. "You don't understand. At all."

"You're right. I don't."

They stood in silence for a while. Finally, Angel spoke up. "People kept asking about you today. They wanted to know if I was your sister."

"Sorry about that." Freesia's voice oozed sarcasm.

"It's okay." Angel was impervious to the ooze. "It's almost like you're a celebrity or something. So that makes me a celebrity's sister."

"Is that why you got to go to the inconvenient store with Taryn?"

"How do you know Taryn?"

"I don't. But it's weird that you're hanging out with juniors. Plus, from what I've heard, she's not a nice person."

"Nice is overrated."

"Hey."

Freesia was so deep in sisterly nastiness, she hadn't noticed Adam approaching.

"Hi!" She looked up, surprised at how glad she was to see him.

He said, "The stuff that everyone's been saying. About, um—"

"It's all true."

"Not the stuff about you getting your own reality TV show," Angel said.

"This is my sister, Angel. And she's right about the TV show, though I hadn't heard that."

Adam nodded. "It makes sense, kind of. I mean, how you didn't want to say much about where you'd gone to school before this. And how you acted kind of strange when we got to Erin's house—no offense."

Freesia shrugged. "I didn't act half as strange as I felt. Anyway, now you know why I had to go down in English. I hope you're not still mad at me for dropping out of the group."

"I was never mad about that. I wasn't mad at all. I was just . . . whatever." His posture changed. He held up a hand. "I hope things work out for you. I wish you the best."

With that, he walked away.

"He *wishes you the best*?" Angel said, once Adam had disappeared around the corner.

"Isn't that a good thing?"

"No. It's what grown-ups say when they never want to see you again. And it's what a kid says when—it's something a kid just *doesn't say.* That guy is a freak."

"He is *not* a freak!" Freesia's anger surprised her. "Just because someone doesn't say or do the exact same things as everyone else doesn't make him odd. It makes him interesting."

Angel's mouth twitched. "And I thought Ricardo was supposed to be your boyfriend."

"I don't even know what a boyfriend is. The rules are different here. Ricky likes me, and I like him, but what does that matter if he's still there and I'm stuck here? I just like Adam as a friend. And I don't want you saying bad things about my friends."

Freesia waited for Angel to point out that her "friend" didn't seem to want to see her. But Angel stayed silent.

28

When they arrived home from school, Mother was waiting in the kitchen looking shiny, happy, stylish—almost pretty. Mother looked like Mummy.

"Three hundred thousand and forty-two," she announced. "That's how many hits my website got today. Last I checked, anyway. I'm sure it's more by now."

"What are hits?"

"That's not even counting the mentions in other blogs and news reports," Mummy continued.

"Nice work." Father patted her arm and headed for the den.

"Some of the reaction has been less than kind," Mother said.

Father, always polite, stopped to listen.

"Some people don't understand that we chose Bubble World because it was the best environment for Francine," Mother continued. "Not because it made our lives easier. But that doesn't bother me. There's nothing like controversy to generate intelligent discussion. Freesia, did you know Ricardo Leisure in Bubble World?"

Freesia willed Angel to remain silent. Miraculously, she did.

"Uh—sure. Everyone knows Ricky."

"Do you know his real name?"

She tensed. "I didn't even know my own name."

Mother sighed. "I've spent the entire day trying to get in touch with him. But there's no contact information on his blog, and he didn't respond to my comments or tweets. I'd do anything to meet him." Mother gnawed on an unpolished fingernail. "According to his latest tweet, he's just been kicked out of Bubble World, too. So he might be available for an interview."

"*What?* Ricky got deleted? Because of me?"

Mother shook her head. "He violated his contract. It's all on his blog."

Freesia met Angel's eyes, and Angel nodded toward the stairs. Together, they hurried up to her room (for once, Freesia didn't trip) and opened the laptop.

Tuesday, 2:22 P.M.

BANISHED

It's not like I didn't expect this. In fact, I'm surprised it took so long.

When it happened, I was floating on a raft in my pool, staring up at the sky. The sun showed the first suggestion of late-afternoon orange. (In Agalinas, you can look directly at the sun. I do not recommend it in the outside world.)

I was thirsty, so I paddled over to the edge of my pool and called out for a tangerine sipper, but before it arrived, everything was gone: the pool, the sky, the sun, the island.

Like they had never even existed.

They never really did exist. But I believed in them anyway.

It took my eyes a few minutes to adjust to the darkness of my bubblepod. I checked my Bubble World account on my laptop. I wasn't surprised to see that it had been closed.

I have been banished from Bubble World for violating my contract. In other words, for telling the truth on this blog. In the ethereal land of Agalinas, beauty is everywhere, entertainment is the order of the day, and no one has to do anything they don't want to do. No homework. No chores. Nothing but laughter and pleasure and fun.

But freedom of speech? Not a priority.

So here we are.

In the real world.

Don't tell anyone, but reality is overrated.

Freesia went back downstairs. Her mother was in the kitchen, brewing an individual cup of coffee.

"When you said you wanted to meet Ricky, did you mean *meet* meet him? Or just video chat?"

Mother pushed a button, and coffee whooshed into her waiting mug. "Meet meet. I can't very well tape footage of myself talking to a screen. Though it wouldn't be the first time."

"But what if he lived far away?"

"This is an important story, Francine. I'd go to Timbuktu if I had to."

Francine almost asked where Timbuktu was, but then she realized she didn't care. Instead, she chose her words carefully.

"I know Ricardo Leisure's real name. I even know where he lives. But I'll only tell if you agree to take me with you."

Mother held Freesia's eyes for a long time. And then she nodded.

29

AN OPEN LETTER TO ALL SUPPORTERS OF
PROGRESSIVE EDUCATION

Ten years ago, I was a respected video game and educational soft-
ware designer. I enjoyed my work. I was doing well. But I wondered:
WHY COULDN'T EDUCATIONAL SOFTWARE BE AS MUCH
FUN AS VIDEO GAMES?

Studies have shown that humans learn faster WHEN THEY
ENJOY THEMSELVES. They retain more information WHEN
THEY ARE ENGAGED IN ACTIVITIES. So why can't school
be fun? Why can't it be interactive?

At that time, I was just starting to explore the possibilities of virtual reality. That's when it hit me. Instead of GOING TO SCHOOL,
children should be able to LIVE IN AN ACTIVE LEARNING
ENVIRONMENT.

In the real world, it is not possible for a child to learn Korean in
Seoul one day and French in Paris the next. It is not practical to dem-
onstrate the laws of physics by having students record their speeds on

a succession of waterslides. It is impossible to teach American History by allowing students to engage in conversation with George Washington. (Yes—*that* George Washington!)

In Bubble World, the virtual education reality community that I developed with extensive input from leading educators and child psychologists, these kinds of experiences are commonplace. VIRTUAL REALITY EDUCATION = ACTIVE LEARNING.

In recent days, you may have read inflammatory posts from discontented bloggers. They say Bubble World is a sham. They say that a school without bells and workbooks and standardized tests is not a school. I say they are wrong.

These bloggers are simply angry because THEIR CONTRACTS WERE TERMINATED. Until this week, THEY HAD NO COMPLAINTS. But in Bubble World, safety is rule number one and respect for others is rule number two. These students were expelled because they posed a threat to other students. Confidentiality prevents me from divulging details.

DO NOT BELIEVE EVERYTHING YOU READ.

Students in Bubble World continue to thrive and grow and learn at a pace unmatched anywhere. To learn more about how your child might benefit from our one-of-a-kind active learning environment, visit our Success Stories page.

Sincerely,

Todd Piloski

Founder, CEO, and Chairman of the Board

BUBBLE WORLD EDUCATIONAL ENTERPRISES, INC.

"providing the education of the future . . . today"

30

*A*long the dusty desert road between Phoenix and the Pacific Ocean, a sprawling outlet mall lay among fields of giant windmills. Freesia could have spent days going through all the stores, but they wanted to make it to Ricky's house before sundown.

Mother hadn't bought into the idea of a makeover right away.

"You need a new look," Freesia announced back in Phoenix as Mother filled her tired beige suitcase with tired beige clothes.

"What do you mean?" Mother's hair looked even more unruly than usual. She wore a men's heather gray sweatshirt and pajama bottoms.

"This is your big moment. Thanks to the Bubble World story, your website is getting thousands of slaps."

"Hits."

"Hits. Right. If you want people to take you seriously, you need to look the part."

Mother appeared skeptical.

Freesia laid it out. "People like to look at pretty people. It's not right, but it's just the way it is. So if you want to build your audience, you need to first build a relationship with a hair straightener and some good-quality foundation. And you need to start dressing like a professional blog, vlog . . . news . . . talker person."

At the outlets, a few hours were enough to steer her mother away from gray pants suits and wrinkle-resistant blouses. Instead, Freesia convinced Mother to adopt a seventies-inspired style: wrap dresses, jaunty scarves, chunky heels, and over-sized sunglasses. Mother had never looked this good. Not just that—even *Mummy* had never looked better.

It was surprisingly easy to convince Mother to buy Freesia the beginnings of a new wardrobe: "If I am poorly dressed, people will think it's because you don't love me."

Perhaps there was enough truth in that statement to frighten or shame her. In any event, Mother flashed her credit card like it was nothing more than a piece of plastic. Freesia even managed to get her to splurge at a beauty supply store.

As for Freesia, picking out clothes was more of a challenge now that she no longer possessed her everything-looks-good Bubble World body. But she had nice arms and pleasantly curved calves, plus she'd discovered that strong colors brightened her sallow complexion. In the end, she opted for flared skirts, ruffled collars, and lots of red, green, and royal blue.

She realized, of course, that real-world Ricky probably looked nothing like Bubble World Ricky. How could he? Her high school had over two thousand students, and none of the boys came close to the perfection of the boy with the streaky blond hair, sculpted cheekbones, washboard abs, and brilliant blue eyes. It was even possible (though unlikely) that the difference between the two Rickies was even more pronounced than the gulf that lay between sweet island Freesia and the girl formerly known as Francine.

But that was okay. (She hoped.) She cared for the inner Ricky: fun, warm, smart, original. He didn't have to be perfect looking. She hoped that he felt the same way.

It was late afternoon when the stylish woman and her equally well-dressed daughter drove their enormous boxy black vehicle up to Ricky's house in Newport Beach.

"You have reached. Your destination," the GPS informed them, just in case they hadn't noticed.

They'd already stopped off to check in at the cut-rate hotel Mother had found on the Internet. You could find anything on Internet, it seemed, with the glaring exception of Ricky's phone number.

Freesia wished she'd been able to call Ricky ahead of time. It seemed so un-utter to show up unannounced like this. Still, a blog comment was far too public, and that Twitter thing was just weird.

The enormous front gate stood open. Behind it loomed a house even grander and larger (though not prettier) than Ricky's Agalinas abode. There were columns. There were fountains. There was a bright green bush trimmed to look like a leaping dolphin. The front windows were two stories tall but coated with something shiny that made it impossible to see inside. Off to one side, a garage had enough room for five cars, yet there were three others parked in the massive, curved driveway. Off to the other side, a break in a hedge offered views of a deep blue, churning sea.

Mother pushed the doorbell.

The intercom above it crackled. "Is this the furniture delivery?"

There were so many disembodied voices in the real world. Freesia wasn't sure she'd ever get used to it. At least this one was attached to a human.

"Uh . . . no," Mother said. "We're here to see Ricky."

After a long, long pause, the voice said, "I don't know what you mean."

"Richard Levine?" Mother said. "He blogs under the name Ricardo Leisure."

Another long, long pause, and then: "You need to go away."

Mother said, "My name is Donna Somers. I'm a vlogger who specializes in technology—perhaps you've heard of me? I've been covering Todd Piloski and Bubble World Enterprises for three and a half years now. I need to talk to Ricardo. Richard. To compare notes and—"

Freesia cut her mother off. "Tell Ricky that Freesia is here."

This time the pause was so long that Freesia was afraid the person on the other end would never answer. But eventually she opened the front door and introduced herself as Valeria, the Levines' house manager. Valeria was short and solid, with chin-length hair that was all the same shade of yellow. She wore a turquoise T-shirt, khaki capris, and white sneakers. Nervous though she was, Freesia looked the woman up and down, giving her a mental makeover.

"Is Richard here?" Mother asked, peering beyond Valeria to the cavernous foyer.

Valeria licked her lips. "Richard is always . . . Richard is here. He was surprised to hear he had visitors. But pleased. His personal assistant is helping him get ready. If you'll follow me into the salon, you can make yourself comfortable while you wait."

Ricky has a personal assistant? AND *his own salon?* That was wicked! If Freesia had known, she wouldn't have bothered fussing with the electric hair straightener and all those defrizzifiers she had bought at the outlet mall.

"Are Richard's parents here?" Mother asked. "I'd like to meet them."

"Richard's father and stepmother are in Asia until next week. Mr. Levine's business requires extensive travel."

"What business is he in? If I may ask."

"Cell phone components. Here's the salon. I'll see how Richard is making out."

The salon was not a beauty salon after all. It was a living room. With a grand piano. And a view of the Pacific Ocean beyond an infinity pool. And a maid who asked if she could get them anything. Mineral water? Passion fruit iced tea? Cappuccino?

"This is almost like Agalinas," Freesia said after the maid left to fetch their beverages.

Why in the world did Ricky need a virtual paradise when he was living in a real one?

Beyond the glass wall, the sky was clear except for what looked like a cloud on the horizon. Freesia crossed the room's black-and-white marble tiles to get a better look.

"Is that . . . an island?"

Mother joined her at the enormous window. "I think that's Santa Catalina. One of the Channel Islands. It's what Todd used as inspiration for Agalinas."

Freesia gasped. She put her hand on the glass as if she could touch the far-off land. "Agalinas is real? You mean we can visit?"

When Mother spoke, her voice was uncharacteristically kind. "Catalina Island is a real place. I've heard it's very pretty. But it's not Agalinas. Nothing is. I'm sorry, Francine."

Freesia dropped her hand from the glass, swallowed hard, and nodded.

The maid brought their drinks (mineral water for Mother, the fruity iced tea for Freesia). They settled down on a white couch and looked out at the water without speaking.

What was taking so long? If Ricky had surprised Freesia in Arizona, she might have taken a few moments to change her clothes and apply lip gloss, but she would have rushed down to see him as soon as possible. Didn't Ricky want to see her? Perhaps he was as nervous as she was.

At last yellow-haired Valeria returned.

"Richard is ready for you."

31

$\mathcal{F}$reesia and Mother followed Valeria back through the vast foyer to a wide marble staircase. About half-way up, Freesia stumbled and smacked her leg against a sharp step.

"Are you okay?" Valeria asked.

Freesia righted herself, holding back a whimper. "I'm fine." Her shin throbbed.

Mother said, "She's had trouble with spatial relations ever since . . ."

She left the sentence hanging, but Valeria nodded.

They walked down a dark, high-ceilinged hall with fluffy white carpet and stark black-and-white landscape photographs on the walls. The doors were all closed until they reached the last one, which was left open just enough to allow an eerie blue light to filter through.

Valeria rapped on the door. "Richard? You ready?"

"Yes." His voice sounded strained.

Valeria pushed open the door. Dread clenched Freesia's

stomach, and not because she was afraid that Ricky wouldn't like her outfit. (Her outfit was vicious.) But something was wrong. Something was very, very wrong.

Valeria entered the vast, murky room first, followed by Mother and then Freesia. The only light came from a laptop monitor inside a bubblepod. Freesia blinked, trying to make out shapes.

"Freesia. You found me." That strained voice again.

She edged closer to the bubble. It was at least three times the size of hers.

"You told me your address, remember?" She tried to keep her voice light and normal, but it was hard. *There is something wrong with Ricky.*

"Of course I remember." He paused to take a breath. "I remember everything."

She'd reached the open bubblepod door. As her eyes adjusted to the darkness, blacks turned to charcoals, charcoals to light gray. Objects began to take shape. A recliner similar to the one she had at home dominated the pod. Only this one was far, far larger than hers and piled with pillows.

Behind the recliner, in the space where her bubblepod had a toilet, sink, and shower, Ricky's had an enormous walk-in Jacuzzi with a showerhead, along with a full vanity and toilet.

But no Ricky. (Not that she wanted to see him while he was . . . you know.)

His voice came from somewhere near the recliner. "I always wondered what you looked like in the outside world. Not that it mattered. But you're pretty, Freesia. You really are."

"Thank you." Sweat dampened her new clothes. She had an awful urge to flee. But she didn't. Instead, she took a small step closer to the recliner. And another small step.

That's when she realized: those weren't pillows on the giant recliner. That was Ricky. He was a pale mass of heaving, wheezing flesh. Forget the food court at the mall. Forget the weight-loss reality shows that her sister occasionally watched. Ricky Leisure was by far the fattest person Freesia had ever seen, and not just because she'd lost so much of her memory. A person that size couldn't make it down the stairs, couldn't fit through a car door, couldn't walk down the street.

Tears stung her eyes. Her sweet Ricky, trapped in so much flesh.

"Secret's out," he said. "I'm a big boy."

Enormous black knit pajamas covered him down to his pale pudgy hands and swollen feet. His face was so distorted, it was hard to tell what he really looked like. His hair, unlike the Agalinas golden boy's, was brown and wispy. But his eyes, lit by the glow from the computer, were bright and sharp and shiny blue. She knew those eyes. Those eyes knew her.

"Oh, Ricky." Without thinking, she rushed over and took his hand. It was warm, soft, dry. Nice. *This is Ricky. My second bestie. Maybe my first.*

She said, "I've missed you terribly."

He said, "Agalinas was borrifying without you. Though not nearly as odious as this."

Freesia lowered herself onto a tiny stool next to the recliner.

Ricky shifted his weight. She pictured the Ricky she'd known in Agalinas lounging on his yellow raft, muscles glistening in the sunshine. All those nibbles, all those sips: they added up. But still. He'd left the raft on occasion, to mingle with his guests at a rooftop party or visit Spanglish class.

Freesia said, "The rubber floor in front of your recliner. Is it a treadmill?"

"It is. But I don't use it if that's what you're asking." With his free hand, he pressed a button, and the recliner buzzed and straightened like the front seats in Mother's monstrous black vehicle. "That's about all the exercising I do. But I like lounging best. Even if it can make breathing difficult."

"My chair doesn't recline anymore," Freesia said.

He said, "Mine had to be custom made. So it has backup controls."

"Richard? I'm Donna Somers. Francine's mother." She entered the bubblepod and got a good look at Ricky. "Oh, my . . ."

Feeling protective, Freesia squeezed Ricky's squishy hand.

"Nice to meet you," Ricky said. "I'd get up, but . . ."

"Please don't!" Mother fiddled with the sleeve of her wrap dress. "I think we should join forces to bring down Todd Piloski. I'd like to interview you on camera. People need to know that Bubble World is not only dangerous to the mind, it's harmful to the body as well."

Ricky plucked an enormous cup from the steel table on the far side of the recliner. He put the straw in his mouth and took a long drink before speaking again.

"I was always like this," he said at last. "You can blame Todd for a lot, but not my size."

Mother chose her words carefully. "Francine's nutritional supplements—the bars and shakes and juices—they were all carefully measured to provide her with the proper amount of calories."

Ricky shifted his massive weight. "When I first got to Bubble World, they tried to limit my food, but I couldn't think. I couldn't sleep. So I stomped and yelled until they gave me what I wanted." He sighed. "I know I could get an operation. They could make my stomach smaller. But I'd rather cut off a leg or pull out an eye." He reached for the cup.

"About that interview," Mother said.

Ricky shook his head. His neck was nowhere to be found. "It's not that I care what people think of me. That bothers my father more than it does me. But I won't be writing any more about Bubble World."

"But—"

"Piloski was going to close it down. It just wasn't attracting enough students to make money. That's why I let the secret out. Because it didn't matter anymore."

"How do you know this?"

"I hacked into his e-mail. But here's the thing. In the past few days, because of all the press, enrollment has gone through the roof. There's actually a waiting list to get in."

Mother was stunned. "Even though the whole thing is a sham?"

"People believed Piloski over us."

"But my vlog," Mother said. "My reputation . . ."

"Piloski is trying to get my father to invest more money in his company. If he does, I'll be allowed to go back."

Freesia gasped.

Mother stared at him. "But how could your father let you go back, knowing you did nothing but play?"

"Not true," Ricky said. "I blogged every day. But that's not all. During my three years in Agalinas, I read the entire works of Shakespeare, Dickens, and Twain."

"Are you serious?" Freesia asked, appalled. "No wonder you never made it to class."

Ricky paused to take a breath. "I miss being free. And I miss the rainbows."

Freesia swallowed hard. "I miss everything."

Mother put her hand on Freesia's shoulder. "You won't be going back, Francine. I'm sorry."

"Don't call me Francine," Freesia muttered.

A woman dressed in blue medical scrubs entered the bubblepod. "It's time for Richard's massage. I'm afraid you'll have to leave."

Freesia sprang up from the stool, shaken by the thought of this Ricky having his body rubbed. The woman in the blue scrubs was right. It was time to go.

"Do you have an e-mail address?" Ricky asked. Freesia told him, and he typed it into his laptop.

"I'd like to talk to some other Bubble World students," Mother said. "Do you have any of their phone numbers? Or addresses?"

Ricky hesitated. "Yes."

"May I have them?"

"No."

Mother said, "I know you think you're doing your friends a favor. But they deserve a decent education. You all do."

"Are you going to keep vlogging about Bubble World?" Ricky asked.

"Yes. But I won't mention you."

"Thank you."

Mother and the masseuse left Freesia and Ricky alone to say their good-byes. He closed his laptop, leaving them in total darkness.

"Did you see Jelissa before you left?" she asked.

"Yeah. She came looking for you the day after you disappeared. She's too sad to shop, even."

Freesia swallowed hard. She couldn't remember ever seeing Jelissa sad, unless you counted that awful afternoon when Freesia tried to tell her that Agalinas was not real.

"What about Taser?" Freesia asked.

"I haven't seen him since we took him out of the cave. But I'll try to find something out."

"Thanks."

Ricky squeezed her hand. "Bubble me later?"

She laughed softly.

"Agalinas was real because it felt real," he whispered.

32

To: Richard2457@wemail.com
From: sweetfreesia@botmail.com
Re: hi

Dear Ricky,

It would be so vicious if we were in Agalinas right now and I could just bubble you. But thinking like that just makes me wiggy so I guess I should stop.

After we left your house we drove down to the harbor but my mother couldn't find a place to park so we just got burgers from a takeout place and went back to the motel and watched movies. The movies here are better than the ones we used to watch at the Rotunda. But the movies here are better than life here, and in Avalon that was never true.

Now I'm back in Arizona. It was kind of flippy to drive up to my house and recognize it. The bad thing is, the more I remember of life here, the more details I forget about Agalinas. Last night I was telling my sister about our group of friends and I couldn't think of Cabo's name for the longest time. When I finally remembered it, Angel said, "That's a stupid name" and made me leave her room so she could video chat with her boyfriend, Tyler, who she's never even met.

I think Tyler is a stupid name.

I've gone back to school. It's so borrifying. I just have to sit there while teachers talktalktalktalk at me, then the bell rings and I go to another class and the teachers talktalktalktalk some more. But yesterday I took a math test and I couldn't believe it but I knew how to do all the problems. That seems nonsensical because I didn't like learning how to do them but apparently my brain was paying attention.

School would be so much better if they offered good snacks. I would also appreciate softer toilet paper in the girls' room.

I'm glad you are still writing your blog. I read your last entry about how you want to learn more about music. Did you know that Chase Bennett's real name is Ben Chase?! Also, he was famous a long time ago, when he was young, but now he's old and no one even remembers him. I think that's really sad because he has so much talent.

Friendlies forever,
Freesia

●　●　●

FLASH DRIVE

Featuring Donna Flash, leading expert on emerging family-centric technologies.

BUBBLE WORLD SCANDAL UPDATE

In case you were not one of the 562,132 people who logged on to my website or YouTube channel to see my testimony about how Silicon Valley con man Todd Piloski cheated my beloved daughter Francine out of an education and fooled us into giving her untested medications, I encourage you to watch the video posted below this one. As of today, Todd Piloski and Bubble World Enterprises are still taking people's money for an education he is not delivering. Check back for updates. Or follow me on Twitter!

Next up—A host of grocery list smartphone apps are available, but which one should you choose? In recent weeks, I tested the four most popular, and here's what I found. . . .

●　●　●

To: sweetfreesia@botmail.com
From: Richard2457@wemail.com
Re: Re: hi

Freesia,

I'm so glad you wrote to me. I didn't know if you would. I never wanted you to see me outside of Agalinas. But then, I never wanted to live outside of Agalinas. I'll never forget our last face-link (or our first face-link). I hope it doesn't ruin the memory for you, knowing how I look in the outside world.

I've decided to go on an anti-hunger strike. I'm going to keep eating until my father convinces Piloski to let me return or until I explode—whichever comes first. I know my father has been talking to Piloski (my health aide told me), but he won't tell me about it. Piloski has put new controls on his e-mail, and I haven't figured out how to hack it yet.

Since I can't go to a regular school, my father got me a private tutor. His name is Franklin, and you can tell that he thinks I'm disgusting but tries really hard to act like I'm just a normal kid.

Friendlies forever,
Ricky

AN OPEN LETTER TO THE HATERS, THE DOUBTERS,
AND THE ENEMIES OF PROGRESSIVE EDUCATION

I've tried to stay quiet. To ignore the absurd claims about Bubble World flooding the Internet. But the haters keep on hating and the liars keep on lying. So I will respond to LIES with TRUTHS.

LIE: I tricked parents into medicating their children.

TRUTH: Like parents could medicate their children without knowing they were doing it?? Many of the children in my program, as in any school, require medications to increase focus or reduce anxiety. So I hired a doctor to monitor these prescriptions with the goal of REDUCING THEIR DOSAGES OR ELIMINATING THEM ENTIRELY.

LIE: The children in Bubble World are not learning anything.

FACT: Does Latin not count as learning? World History? Art Appreciation? Calculus? Economics? Chemistry? Physics? SEVEN languages? I could go on. Instead, I encourage you to visit the Curriculum page. Just because students are HAPPY, that does not mean they are not learning.

LIE: I am just in it for the money.

FACT: If I were just interested in money, I would stick to war games.

LIE: I am giving up control of Bubble World.

FACT: Bubble World is not going anywhere, and neither am I!

Sincerely,

Todd Piloski

Founder, CEO and Chairman of the Board

BUBBLE WORLD EDUCATIONAL ENTERPRISES, INC.

"providing the education of the future . . . today"

Ricardo Leisure: When Normal Just Won't Do

Friday, 9:17 P.M.

DISCOVERING NEW (OLD) MUSIC

If you're under forty, chances are you've never heard of Ben Chase. I hadn't until a friend introduced me to his music. At first, his lyrics and melodies seem simplistic. But the more you listen, the more you hear. . . .

http://www.bubbleworldeducation.com
You are being redirected to our new site. . . .

http://www.brightplaneteducation.com
There is a place
Where your child can grow and learn and be happy.
Where she or he can become fluent in multiple languages,
Build friendships and develop social skills to last a lifetime,
Master high math concepts and sophisticated writing conventions,
Devour world history, the sciences, literature, and more,
Explore art, music, dance, theater, and athletics . . .

264

All in the comfort and safety of your own home.
That place is called . . .
Bright Planet.

Thanks for checking out the brand-new website of Bright Planet (formerly known as Bubble World). Our web designers have been busy redesigning this site to keep parents more involved than ever in their child's virtual reality educational experience.

That's not all. Bubble World has been a tremendous success since its launch four years ago, with a student and parent satisfaction rate of 96 percent. But here at Bright Planet, we believe in continuous improvement. That's why we've hired a new team of award-winning educators to design an immersion curriculum that is better than ever.

To learn how your child can benefit from Bright Planet's total immersion virtual education program, visit our <u>Tell Me More</u> page.

TOP STORIES, WAHOO NEWS
- Roasted kale proven to burn belly fat in mice
- Eighties idol Ben Chase slated to appear on *So You Think You Can Dance with a Star*
- Cat survives ten days in cruise ship supply room
- Levine Technologies purchases Bubble World Enterprises for an undisclosed sum

33

Ricky was going back. One day they were both stranded in the so-called real world; the next he was making plans to stable a herd of unicorns at his newly expanded estate on the hillside above the Rotunda.

According to Ricky, his father would do anything to get rid of him, even purchase a company with an embarrassing track record and an uncertain future. Even pay programmers overtime to get the new site up and running as fast as possible. Even hire a game developer to design the perfect unicorn.

Richard Levine Sr. did not approve of unicorns (he'd tried to talk Ricky into a giant sea horse instead), but he'd give Ricky pretty much anything he wanted as long as Ricky agreed to cut all ties with the outside world. No blogging. No e-mailing. No communication with anyone besides his father.

For now, Freesia and Ricky e-mailed at least once and sometimes five times a day. It wasn't half as good as bubbling him or an eighth as good as seeing his virtual self (Freesia was relearning fractions), but it was all she had. And even that wouldn't last.

For now, Bubble World was still up and running, albeit slowly and with frequent crashes. If everything stayed on schedule, Bright Planet would launch within a week. And then Ricky would be gone for good.

Of course Ricky wanted Freesia to go with him. Of course Freesia wanted to go. But her parents refused. "Just because they're calling the program something else, that doesn't mean it's any better," Mother said.

"Ricky could talk to his father," Freesia suggested. "Maybe work out a reduced rate."

"No," Father said. "We can't risk letting you fall even farther behind."

Freesia was staying at Tumbleweed High. That was that.

● ● ●

"Freesia? Can you hang out for a sec?"

She was gathering her books after English class and looking forward to a brief lunch period drinking frosty blue things with Iris and the gang.

"I won't keep you long," Mr. Janz assured her.

She went to his desk, and he pulled out a paper she had handed in a couple of days before. The assignment: write a persuasive essay on a topic you feel passionate about. Her thesis: for the crime of ugliness, Crocs shoes should be outlawed for all but medical professionals.

He grinned. "I liked your topic. But you still need to work on topic sentences and conclusions. Can you come in early or stay late sometime this week? I'd be happy to give you extra help."

A knot formed in Freesia's stomach. "Thank you, Mr. Janz. But I abhor this school so much that the thought of spending an extra second in here makes me squiggy."

His eyes widened.

"Not because of you," she said. "Or any of my other teachers. Well, except maybe my Spanish teacher. She's a bit of a sea sow."

"Are the other students giving you a hard time?"

She shrugged. "Some of them stare and whisper, but I honestly don't care what they think. But I can't stand being in this place. The halls are so crowded, and the desks are uncomfortable, and there's way too much information to cram into my brain. Plus, the bells make me want to jump out of my skin. And there are no windows! Who would build a school with no windows?"

"It's to keep out the heat," Mr. Janz explained. "Also, it reduced construction costs."

"I know you appreciate beauty, Mr. Janz. I can see it in your fine Italian leather shoes." She hesitated, not wanting to offend him. "You don't have to work here. You could get a job in a pretty office with big windows and framed artwork and floral-scented bathrooms."

Mr. Janz reached under his desk for a brown paper bag and pulled out a can of Mountain Dew. He popped open the soda. "Before I became a teacher, I worked in advertising, and I had an office just like that. Though I can't remember whether the bathrooms were scented."

"What happened? Did they fire you?"

He laughed. "No. I got bored. And I wanted to do something more important than convincing people to buy stuff they didn't need. So I got my teaching credentials and came here."

Freesia was confused. "So you actually like teaching?"

"Nope—I love it. Do I wish the classes were smaller and I didn't have to buy my own supplies? Yes. Do I like wasting so much time preparing for standardized tests? No. In a perfect world, teachers would get more respect, better pay, and a real say in how their schools are run. But the world isn't perfect and never will be. So I just do the best I can for my students."

Freesia chewed her lip. "My father says students are too busy texting and MySpacing to care about education."

"Nobody goes on MySpace anymore. As for texting . . ." He shrugged. "Students used to pass notes, now they text and tweet and Facebook. Their parents are just as bad. Maybe worse. We've all got too many distractions now. The world has changed. But kids are still kids. And most of them are more interesting than most adults I've met. I'm never bored, that's for sure."

"But this place is so ugly!" Freesia looked around the classroom. Mr. Janz had made it as nice as he could by hanging student artwork, but it wasn't enough to offset the acoustic tiles on the ceiling, the hard, scuffed, oatmeal-colored floor, the fluorescent lighting, or the cinder-block walls painted a sickly shade of yellow.

Mr. Janz pulled a sandwich out of his paper bag. "I know it's hard for you to understand, Freesia, but there are things in life more important than beauty."

She squinted at him, not understanding.

"Though I'm with you on the Crocs," he said.

To: Richard2457@wemail.com
From: sweetfreesia@botmail.com
Re: I never know what to write in this line

Dear Ricky,

I don't have anything new to tell you, but I wanted to write because it annoys Angel when I use her computer. And also because it makes me feel closer to you.

Thanks for checking on all our friends. I'm glad Taser is acting more normal (at least for Taser) but sorry that Jelissa is still sad. Last night I found myself wishing that Jelissa would leave Agalinas so I could see her in the real world, but then I realized that was a bad thing to wish on a friend. It's like the way I'm sad you're going back but happy for you too.

Friendlies forever,
Freesia

"It's been six minutes!" Angel, sitting on her bed, smacked her pillow.

Freesia hit the Send button and got up from Angel's desk. "I'm done. Calm yourself."

Angel retrieved the laptop and took it to her bed. "Were you writing to the whale again?"

"Don't call him that."

Sitting cross-legged, Angel pecked at her computer keyboard. "It's just so weird when you think about what a Garibaldi he was in Agalinas." Angel's phone buzzed. She checked the display and tapped the screen a few times.

Freesia stared at her sister. "Did you just call Ricky a Garibaldi?"

Panic flickered in Angel's eyes. "Everyone in Bubble World was good looking. It said so in all the Web reports."

"But why did you use that word? I've never heard anyone outside of Agalinas say it."

Angel's phone buzzed again. She moved her hand but didn't pick it up. "A Garibaldi is an orange fish. Look it up. Now, can you please let me—"

"You were there," Freesia said. "You've been to Agalinas."

Angel took a long time to answer. She picked up her phone. Put it back down without texting.

Finally she said, "I had my own Bubble World avatar. Like Mom and Dad, except I logged on to mine way more than they did. I would see this little girl on the screen, and I could make her move and talk. It was just something to do when I was bored. One time you took me to the beach and Ricky was there, lying on the sand."

Freesia crossed to Angel's dresser and stared at the photo

on her bulletin board: Freesia and Angel as little girls. Sisters. Then and always.

"So when I talked to Angel in Agalinas, it was you all along," Freesia marveled.

"No, it was *not* me all along." Angel sounded angry. "Unless you took me somewhere or invited me up to your room, all I could do was hang out in the living room and dance and play with dolls and stuff. When you first went away, I'd log on every day so I could talk to you. And sometimes we'd do stuff together. Like go to the café or the dress shop or the beach. But it was just because you didn't have any friends yet and didn't want to be alone. Once you turned into Miss Popularity, you forgot all about me. Finally I stopped visiting."

"It's not like I asked to be sent away," Freesia said. "So you have no right to be angry."

"I am *not* angry!" Angel said angrily. Her phone buzzed. She picked it up and tapped furiously at the screen.

"I didn't even know where I was," Freesia said. "Or who I was." When Angel didn't respond, she gave up and retreated to her own room to tackle her remedial homework.

"**K**nock, knock." In the open doorway, her father held a shopping bag.

She looked up from the worksheets scattered across her bed. "Hi."

Father gestured to the bubblepod. "I guess we should get rid of that, huh?"

"No rush." Freesia wasn't ready to say good-bye to her last physical link to Agalinas, even if it did crowd the room.

Father held up the bag. "I got you a present."

"Really?" Freesia loved presents.

It was a phone. Not just any phone, but a *smart*phone. (Which was good, because Freesia didn't want to get stuck with a stupidphone.)

"I added you to our family plan," Father said. "You can talk, text, e-mail, check the Web, take pictures, play games . . . and other stuff I'll never figure out." He shook his head. "Sometimes I think I was born a hundred years too late. Or maybe even two hundred. Guess that's why I like history so much. The world was so much simpler then."

Freesia ran a finger over the shiny phone. "This is vicious. Thank you, Father."

He patted her shoulder. "You're welcome. And I'd actually prefer if you called me Dad."

Freesia cradled the rectangle in her palm and gazed at the blank screen. The phone wasn't as pretty as her bubble, and it didn't change sizes, but from what she'd seen from Angel as well as the kids at Tumbleweed High, it was pretty magical. Plus, unlike her bubble, the smartphone was—this word still made her uncomfortable—real.

"You know, Father—I mean Dad—earlier today I was thinking about teaching."

Father shook his head, "For goodness' sake, Francine,

don't become a teacher! It's like a life sentence. I'd rather see you in prison. The food's probably better."

"I was thinking about you, I mean. Maybe you'd be happier doing something else."

He sighed. "It's too late. Teaching is all I know."

"That's not true! You know so much about history, I'm surprised you can fit it all in your head."

"I do possess a lot of knowledge."

"And passion! You have passion for history. And you know what knowledge plus passion equals?"

Father considered. "What?"

"It equals *something*," Freesia said. "Something wonderful. You just have to figure out what it is."

reesia rapped on Angel's door. No answer.

She tried again, harder this time. Still no answer.

She opened her palm and pounded full force.

"Stop! That! Now!" Mother appeared at her office door.

"What is Angel's phone number?" Freesia asked.

Mother told her.

Freesia sat down on the floor outside her sister's room and leaned against the white wall. She pulled out her phone and pecked at it with her index finger. She might be here for a while, but it wasn't like she had anyplace else to go.

Angel, can we talk? (Send.)

Dad got me a phone. (Send.)

I know you're in there. (Send.)

How do I put in the numbers of people I might want to call? (Send.)

At least I won't be using your computer anymore. At least as much. (Send.)

Come on, Angel. Give me five minutes! (Send.)

Angel flung open the door. "We have limited text messaging! If you don't stop texting me, there will be extra charges on both of our phones and Mom will make us pay!"

Freesia scrambled off the floor and grinned. This hadn't taken long at all, and she was getting faster with the keypad.

"How do I put names in my phone?"

"You mean like contacts?"

"I guess."

Angel's eyes narrowed. "What? You want to text Iris?"

"I don't have her number. The only numbers I have are Adam's and yours."

"Who's Adam? Film guy Adam or waterpolo player Adam? Or the Adam with the pierced tongue and the plugs?"

"Uh . . . film guy."

Angel considered. "He's pretty cute."

"Does that mean you'll show me how to add . . . whatsit—contacts? Because Adam's cute?"

Angel rolled her eyes. "I didn't say he was cute. I said he was *pretty* cute." She took Freesia's phone and showed her what to do.

Back in her room, Freesia settled on the recliner (it was her only chair) and composed a text.

Dear Adam, You gave me your number once but I didn't have a phone then but now I do. So now you have my number. I hope you are having a nice day. I tried to sit outside but it was too hot. And also my dad said he saw a big snake in the yard last week. Your friend, Freesia

Hand starting to cramp, Freesia hit Send, thinking how weird it was to launch words out into the universe.

Less than a minute later, the phone buzzed. Adam had responded.

thx

Knock-knock . . . knock, knock, knock . . . KNOCK!
The door swung open. It was getting easier to wear Angel down.

"What does *T-H-X* mean?" She showed her sister the message.

"Thanks." Angel shut the door, just missing Freesia's nose.

Dear Adam, You're welcome! I forgot to say this in my last text but you were right about the blooming cactuses. They're really pretty. I can't wait to see more. Your friend, Freesia

(Send.)

Adam, I forgot to say this in my last last text but my mother says it should be cacti not cactuses but I think that sounds weird. YF, Freesia

(Send.)

After a longer pause than before, her phone buzzed with Adam's response.

Cool.

Freesia stared at the message for a while, not quite comprehending. And then she sent a text to Angel.

What does it mean when you send someone a long text and he answers with one word?

(Send.)

If you answer with one word I will go back to pounding on your door.

(Send.)

Angel texted back right away.

It means he doesn't like you. Or maybe he's mad
at you. He's not that cute so don't feel bad. I have
a few minutes if you want me to show you how to
use your phone.

34

When Freesia stumbled into the kitchen a few mornings later to toast a strawberry Pop-Tart and brew a strong cup of coffee, she found Mother, in full makeup, wearing one of her new wrap dresses.

"Wow. You look—"

"I tried to do the bronzer like you showed me, but it makes me look orange, so I'm going to take it all off and start over." She checked her cell phone. "Shoot. There isn't time."

"Are you—"

"I have an interview. Some distance from here. I'll be flying. I told your father to get takeout on the way home, because I won't be home till after dinner. Does the bronzer make me look orange?"

Freesia squinted at her mother's unnaturally colored face. "It'll look good on camera," she said at last.

● ● ●

*L*ater that day, Freesia was at the inconvenient store with her new friends when Iris said, "Jack's party Saturday night. Yay or nay?"

Alex said nay, but Kendy and Morgan said yay, so Alex changed her vote.

"Who's Jack?" Freesia asked.

"Basketball player." Iris stuck a piece of greasy pizza in the microwave. "A moron and a jerk. But he's got a big house and a huge backyard and his parents go out of town a lot, so who cares."

"I adore parties!" Freesia was so excited, her voice squeaked. "Is there a theme? Like luau or carnival or ballet?"

Everyone laughed, but not in a mean way.

"Is that a no?" Freesia asked.

"That's a no," Morgan said.

Freesia forced a smile. She was always doing this—saying things that people found weird or amusing. Back in Agalinas, that never happened. Back in Agalinas, her friends understood her. She and Jelissa were so close, they could practically read each other's minds.

The microwave beeped, and Iris took out the pizza.

Kendy pulled out her phone, so Freesia did too. Their phones were the same except Kendy's phone case was bright green and Freesia's was bright pink. After school and between classes they all texted each other. No one had anything to say, but there was something reassuring about feeling your phone buzz. It meant you weren't so alone in the world.

With her entire circle of friends surrounding her, Freesia

had no one to text, so she put the phone in camera mode. She posterized shots of the slurry machine, the hot dog warmer, the magazine display. Then she changed the setting to vintage and aimed at Morgan's sneakers.

In the real world, everything looked better through a distorted lens.

A half hour later, she was drawing a bowl of fruit in art class when her phone vibrated in her back pocket. Phones were supposed to be off in class, but if you put your phone on silent, no teacher would ever say anything, even though at times the layers of low vibration sounded like a swarm of bees.

Freesia snuck a peek at the display: Ricky.

How odd. Since she got her phone, Ricky had sent her occasional texts but had never made an actual phone call. What could be so urgent?

● ● ●

After the final bell, she was heading outside to find a quiet place to call Ricky when she almost tripped over Erin on the concrete steps in front of the school.

"Francine! I mean Freesia." Erin scrambled to her feet. She was wearing a black T-shirt two sizes too big and gray jeans that might have been comfortable if it were thirty degrees cooler outside. "I keep seeing you in the halls, but you never see me, I guess. Can you talk?"

"Um, I need to make a call." Freesia had seen Erin in the halls, but before this she'd been quick to look away.

"Oh, right. I guess, then . . . does that mean you got a phone? Because if you give me your number, I'll call you or text or whatever. Maybe we can get together sometime. You can come over again or—"

Oh, no. Freesia did not want to go to Erin's house. She didn't want to talk to Erin, either, but it was better to get it out of the way.

"I guess I can talk now. Just not for long."

"Oh, right. Awesome. I . . ."

Freesia's eyes flicked over the students milling about. With the temperature climbing, most students had traded jeans and hoodies for jean shorts and T-shirts. It wasn't much of an improvement. This weather was perfect for sundresses and seersucker. Why didn't anyone see that?

". . . and I know it's largely my fault," Erin said.

"What did you say?" Freesia refocused on her former friend's normally pink face, which was now closer to red. Whether that was from the heat or her discomfort, it was hard to say.

Erin cleared her throat. "I said we're not close like we used to be, and it's largely my fault. But I hope we can be friends again."

Freesia blinked. "It's not largely your fault."

Erin put a hand on her heart and smiled with relief.

Freesia shook her head. "It's *all* your fault. We stopped being friends because you told me you no longer wanted to be friends."

Erin made a funny little noise and tried to speak. "I . . . it's . . . when . . ."

"I've got to make a call." Freesia headed down the steps.

"Wait!"

Freesia turned.

"I'm sorry! I was just a stupid kid, and I hate that I hurt you. You're the best friend I've ever had. All these years, I've never found anyone to replace you." Erin reached under the neck of her black T-shirt and pulled out a pendant. It was the right half of a broken heart. "Look. Our best friends necklace, remember?"

There was writing on the necklace: *ST*. Erin's broken heart was the missing half to the one Freesia had found in the cardboard box in her closet. Together they spelled *BEST*.

Erin slipped the necklace back into her T-shirt. "It's stupid that I wear it, I guess. I mean, a lot of things I do are stupid. But I've had it forever. It's my good luck charm."

Sweat slithered down Freesia's back. She had to get out of the sun. She had to get away from Erin.

"I found another best friend. I'm sorry you didn't."

Long ago, Erin had abandoned Freesia. Now it was Freesia's turn to walk away. They were even. So why did she feel so icky inside?

● ● ●

Around the side of the school, Freesia found a semi-shady spot under a straggly excuse for a tree. Since she'd started school, the temperatures had crept up from the high eighties to the midnineties, and it was only April.

She leaned against the tree as she pressed the button to call Ricky. She didn't dare sit; mixed in with dust and gravel there could be spiders or scorpions or prickers.

The phone rang three times, and then Ricky answered. "Your mother is here."

Freesia was confused. "You mean in your room?"

"No, in my house." He paused to wheeze. "Though she stopped by to gawk at me earlier."

Freesia forced herself to focus on the content of what was being said and not on Ricky's labored breathing. "My mother told me she was traveling someplace for an interview, but I had no idea that it would be to you. Did she ask you questions? Did she try to film you?"

"She didn't come to see me. She came to see my dad." He wheezed again. "But she wasn't interviewing him. It was the other way around."

"I don't understand."

"It was a job interview. I think your mother is going to work for Bright Planet."

● ● ●

"I didn't tell you that I was going to see Dick Levine because I thought you'd want to come with me," Mother said later that night.

Freesia shook her head. "I had a quiz in chemistry. I couldn't have gone anyway."

That wasn't the real reason. Freesia couldn't have gone

because she couldn't bear to see Ricky trapped in his prison of flesh.

"And also, I didn't want you to get your hopes up. I didn't want you to think that just because I'm Bright Planet's new social media coordinator—it has a nice ring, don't you think?—that your father and I would entrust you to yet another untested education program."

Freesia swallowed her disappointment. "What does a social media coordinator do?"

"I'll spread the word about Bright Planet's innovation. I'll build social networks and make friends all over the world . . . without ever having to leave my office." Mother cleared her throat. "Dick Levine offered to enroll you in the new program for free. But I told him that we'd fallen for slick talk once before and that you're paying the price."

"I understand."

"I told him that your father and I would need proof that Bright Planet was more than just a gimmick."

"I understand."

Mother paused for effect. "And then he showed me a video that laid everything out. The research, the curriculum—everything was mapped out before the Bubble World launch, but Todd Piloski went and scrapped most of it. Bright Planet will take everyone back to the basics, with a core curriculum that emphasizes literature classics, building-block math concepts, *mwah, mwah . . . mwah mwah mwah. Mwah and mwah and mwah. . . .*"

Freesia tuned out. This was beyond borrifying.

Her phone buzzed. She pulled it out of her pocket.

Kendy

I ate two plates of spaghetti n now I have a food baby

Freesia tapped her reply: **O no!**

"Francine? Did you hear what I just said?"

"Huh?" She slipped her phone back in her pocket.

"I said the video Dick showed me, along with his impressive list of medical and pharmaceutical consultants, was all the proof I needed that Bright Planet will be everything that Bubble World was supposed to be. Dick impressed me. I can see him becoming a close personal friend."

"So . . ."

"The Bright Planet launch is scheduled for Monday. You can go back to Agalinas. If you want to, I mean."

Freesia stared at her mother. In her pocket, her phone buzzed. She ignored it.

"I want to," she whispered.

35

$\mathscr{S}$aturday night found Freesia in the living room with Angel, both of them waiting for rides to Jack's house. She'd almost texted Iris to say she wasn't going to the party. It seemed weird to go on acting like everything was the same, but it would be weirder still to tell them that she was going back to Agalinas. They wouldn't understand. But Freesia had two more days to get through, and she did adore a sparkly celebration.

Besides, Mother would only let Angel go to the party if Freesia went. "So you can keep an eye on her."

"You better come," Angel snarled. And Freesia agreed even though her sister could have at least said "please."

Monday morning, right before she got back in her bubble-pod, Freesia would send Iris and the others a group text to let them know she was gone. That way, she wouldn't have to see their reactions.

Angel looked her up and down. "You're not wearing that."

"I *am* wearing this. Obviously." Freesia tossed her temporarily straight and glossy hair and smoothed down her dress.

I look vicious, Freesia told herself, though of course she didn't. The dress was ivory lace, with a scoop neck and long sleeves. Too late, she realized that the color washed her out and the cut of the dress accentuated her body's pear quality.

She'd spent the afternoon at the mall; Mother wanted some "bonding time" before Freesia left, and Freesia never said no to shopping. The lace dress looked so pretty on the hanger. She pulled it off the rack and admired it for a moment before accepting that it wouldn't suit her real-world shape. But Mother swooped in and said she should have something nice to wear to her first (and final) high school party.

When Freesia had looked in the dressing room mirror, she had seen a lovely girl looking back. Now Angel was trying to ruin everything.

"You are in no position to offer fashion advice." Freesia wrinkled her nose at Angel's tight jeans, gray hoodie, and bulky brown boots. Aside from her overgelled hair and orange blush, she could have been going camping.

Their rides pulled up at the same time.

"Will there be parents at the house?" Mother asked, a little late.

"I don't know." Freesia tried to remember what Iris had said.

Angel said, "Yes."

"So there won't be any drinking," Mother said.

"Of course not," Angel said.

Freesia was confused. "I would hope there will be water and maybe juice."

● ● ●

She was beyond overdressed. Even Iris was wearing jeans (though not a hoodie; Iris had her standards). Jack's party was nothing like the dances or get-togethers on Agalinas, and not just because tonight's recommended attire appeared to be "slovenly." There were no pretty cakes. There were no amusing entertainers. There were no rides or games. And the music hurt her ears.

As soon as they walked into the hot, crowded, ripe-smelling house, all she wanted to do was leave. But since Kendy had driven (and seemed to be enjoying herself), she was stuck.

"Let's dance!" Iris said once they'd tried talking to three different sets of people over the earsplitting music.

Freesia looked around for a dance floor. "Where?"

"Anywhere!" Iris grabbed her wrist and pulled her to an empty patch in the living room. The other three followed. Iris, arms up in the air, closed her eyes and swiveled her hips.

Right away, Alex, Kendy, and Morgan began dancing, clapping hands, and saying "woo!" a lot.

In Agalinas, Freesia had been a good dancer, but here she couldn't seem to find the beat of the music. Or maybe she couldn't stand the sensation of having people stare at her and her friends. In any case, once Freesia began to sweat in her lace dress, she couldn't stand any more. When one non-song ended and began to transition into the next nonsong, she shouted, "I'm going to get something to drink."

Iris grinned. "Naughty girl."

Morgan clapped.

Kendy said, "Woo!"

The kitchen was even more crowded than the rest of the house, and her shoes stuck to the floor. A door had been left open to let in the cool night air, so at least the smell was better. Plastic red cups, filled to the rim with something equally red, stood in rows on the counter. Freesia picked up a cup and sniffed: fruity.

"Chug it!" A boy spoke right into her ear.

She just managed to avoid spilling the drink. "Is this . . . happy juice?"

He threw back his head and laughed. His tongue was red, his teeth were pink.

I hate this place, Freesia thought.

"There's root beer, if you'd rather have that," someone else said.

Freesia turned, and there was Adam. He was wearing jeans, sneakers, and a plaid shirt over a T-shirt. Adam looked relaxed. Like he belonged there.

The boy with the red teeth leaned too close to her ear again. "Hey! You're Bubble Girl, aren't you?"

"Root beer sounds good," she told Adam.

"Here's what I keep wondering about that bubble place," the obnoxious boy said. "What about going to the bathroom? Where did you do that?"

Adam filled a red cup with soda. "Let's get out of here."

Outside, the cold air came as a relief. A kidney-shaped pool dominated the small backyard, which was surrounded on three sides by high stucco walls. Kids clustered in small groups on the concrete.

"You look nice," Adam said. "I like your dress."

"I should have worn jeans like everyone else."

"But you're not like everyone else."

"Thanks for pointing that out."

"It's a good thing," he said.

She sipped the soda. It was warm and a little flat. "I'm not so sure about that."

They claimed a rubber lounge chair and sat down next to each other. The air smelled sweet; something was blooming. Above them, a big moon lit up the sky. She'd be gone before it turned full.

"How's the Emerson project going?" she asked.

"Ugh." He rolled his eyes. "Erin's useless. Every time I suggest something, she's all, 'Yeah, I don't think that will work.' But she's so wishy-washy, she doesn't have any ideas of her own. I'd heard she was the worst person you could possibly work with."

"Why'd you offer to be in her group then?"

He shrugged. "Because you were in it."

"Oh." She felt her cheeks turn warm.

"How are your new classes?" he asked.

"Oh, you know."

"Right."

"I'm not—" She stopped. Drank some more soda.

"What?"

She looked at his face. He was cuter than she remembered.

"I'm not staying," she said. "They've changed Bubble World. Made it better. Well, made it so we'll learn stuff, anyway. I'm going back."

"When?"

"Monday. I haven't told anyone else."

He was still for a long time. Then he nodded and looked across the pool.

She followed his gaze. A few girls were getting loud and giggly while some tall boys loomed over them.

There was a squeal, a shout, and a storm of laughter, male and female. And then she saw her.

"Oh, no."

"What?"

"My sister. She just spilled her drink all over herself."

Across the pool, Angel stumbled next to a large boy in a backward blue baseball cap. He steadied her and then draped his arm around her shoulders. She put the red cup to her mouth and tilted it high.

"You mean the one with Jack? The big guy in the baseball cap?"

"Yeah."

"What year is she?" Adam asked.

"Freshman."

Adam squinted at Angel and shook his head. "She shouldn't even be here. And she definitely shouldn't be with him."

"Why?"

As if in answer, the large boy, Jack, scooped up Angel and carried her to the edge of the pool. She squealed with hysteria and said, "No! No!"

She dropped her red cup, but it was empty.

"Do it, Jack!" a blond girl called out. *Taryn*. Her highlighter-pink cast was gone.

Jack turned away from the pool and bent over as if to release Angel onto the deck. Then he spun back around and launched her into the water, where she landed with a sickening splash.

Jack and his friends bent over with laughter. Freesia and Adam sprang off the lounge and hurried to the edge of the pool. When Angel surfaced, Freesia first thought she was laughing, but no: those were sobs.

The pool wasn't very deep; the water came up to Angel's waist. She staggered to the edge and scooped out as much water as she could, trying to splash Jack.

"Why did you *do* that?" She wailed. "That was so *mean*." She splashed again but only managed to drench the pool deck as Jack and his friends, still laughing, retreated to a drier spot.

Adam and Freesia circled the pool. Freesia squatted at the edge and held out a hand.

"Come on, Angel."

Angel stumbled backward and just stood there, arms floating at her sides, tears streaming down her red face.

"Let's go home, Angel."

Angel shook her head and kept crying.

Freesia reached her hand out as far as she could without falling, but Angel wouldn't take it.

"I have a towel in my car," Adam said. "I'll get it. And then I can drive you both home."

"Thanks," Freesia said.

Around the yard, kids laughed and pointed at the girl in the pool.

"Jack is a doltoid," Freesia told Angel. "Taryn too. You shouldn't waste your time on them."

"Nobody likes me." Angel's voice squeaked.

"I like you." Freesia's eyes filled with tears, and when they spilled over, her face was actually wet.

There was no point squatting at the edge, reaching out her hand. Angel wouldn't take it. Freesia had no choice. She put her pink phone on a plastic table, strode over to the edge of the pool, kicked off her shoes . . . and jumped.

"Oh my Todd!" Jack's pool was nothing like the tropical waters off Agalinas. It was nothing like tropical waters any-where. She had never been so cold.

Angel was so shocked that she stopped crying. And then she laughed. And then she cry-laugh-hiccupped. "There goes—*hic*—your new—*hic*—dress."

"I don't really like it anyway." Freesia pushed her wild hair off her face.

Kids moved closer to see what was going on, to see who had fallen in.

Freesia submerged herself and then popped back up. "Everybody in the pool!"

One girl ran to the edge and then, seeing herself alone, retreated.

"Or not."

Angel sniffled. "You're a freak, Francine."

"I don't mind being a freak. But please don't call me Francine."

● ● ●

et, Angel's gray hoodie weighed about five pounds. Freesia wrung it out as best she could and put it in Adam's trunk. Bundled in the towel, Angel staggered onto the back seat and lay down.

"My phone," Angel moaned. "I think it's broke. The water broked it."

"She's acting weird," Freesia murmured to Adam. "I know she's upset. . . ."

"She's pretty wasted," Adam said.

Freesia shook her head with confusion. She shivered from the cold.

"Plastered," Adam said. "Polluted. Drunk."

"You mean . . . from the happy juice?" Freesia hugged herself and jiggled up and down on the pavement.

"That's a new one," Adam said. "But yeah. From the happy juice. Sorry I don't have another towel for you."

"Sorry I'm going to get your car all wet."

"I don't mind."

They got in the car, and Freesia twisted around to look at her bedraggled sister. Freesia tried to think of a single time when a party on Agalinas had ended badly, but she came up with nothing.

When they pulled up in front of Freesia's house ten minutes later, Angel was asleep.

"I'll help you get her in the house," Adam said. But he didn't move.

"Thanks." Freesia didn't move either.

"So I guess . . ." He left the sentence hanging.

"Yeah."

They looked at each other and smiled at the exact same time.

"Be nice to Erin," Freesia said. "She's pretty okay when you get to know her. If I were staying, I'd—well, just try to be patient."

"I will," Adam said. "Will you be able to call from . . ."

"No."

He nodded, and they sat in silence for a bit. Then they hauled Angel out of the back seat and helped her up the walkway. Freesia unlocked the front door, and Angel made a beeline to the bathroom.

Freesia and Adam stood in the open doorway. Adam put his hands in his pockets. Freesia hugged herself. Wet, wild curls hung around her face. She thought: I must look like a mess. And then she realized, with a shock, that she didn't care.

"Well," he said.

"Well." She had to crane her neck to look up at him.

He had such an interesting face. The light eyes, the long, slightly crooked nose, the wide mouth. She'd never seen anyone who looked anything like him.

So fast she didn't see it coming, he bent over and pressed his lips to hers. Just as fast, it was over. But she could still feel his warmth, still taste a hint of his root beer.

"Bye," he said.

And just like that, he was gone.

36

"You'll visit me, right?" Freesia asked Angel in the bathroom Monday morning. Angel was putting on makeup. Freesia resisted the urge to tell her to go easy on the glitter eyeliner.

"Well, yeah. It's not like I've got anything better to do."

After Jack's party, Mother and Father had grounded Angel till pretty much forever. Freesia tried to protect her sister by telling them that an obnoxious boy was to blame for her drenched state (her own soaking was a little harder to explain), but they could tell that Angel was under the influence of something even stronger than adolescent hormones.

Apparently, this wasn't the first time Angel had gotten, as Adam put it, "polluted." Or even the second. But she had promised it would never happen again, and her parents had believed her.

It didn't matter that Angel's phone was ruined. Her parents would have taken it away, anyway, just as they'd confiscated her MP3 player. She could only use her computer to do homework or visit Freesia in Bright Planet. Technology, they explained, was "a privilege, not a right."

"They can't watch you all the time," Freesia said. "I bet you can sneak some video chats with Tyler."

Angel shook her head. "That's over."

"Sorry."

Angel twisted her eyeliner tube and chucked it into a drawer. "He dumped me for another girl he's never met."

The bubblepod updates took longer than expected. It was almost eleven when Freesia, wearing her old black stretch pants and a giant T-shirt, gave her mother an awkward hug and settled into the reactivated recliner.

She hadn't sent her Tumbleweed friends a group text after all. It felt too impersonal. And she couldn't find the right words.

"I'm sad you're going," Mother said. "But I'm happy that you're going to be happy."

Freesia forced an expression of pleasantness onto her face, but when she met her mother's eyes, she was shocked to see that they were shiny. Was Mother actually crying?

"All the things that I said on my vlog," she continued, "they were true. We did it for you, not because we didn't want you around. You couldn't find a place for yourself in the real world, but in the virtual world, you blossomed. I'm still angry at Todd for his deception, don't get me wrong, but I'm so grateful that Bubble World gave you the opportunity to grow into the young woman you were always meant to be."

Freesia nodded. Her heart pounded, and her hands shook. She was going home. Why did that make her so nervous?

"You're sure you want this?" Mother said.

Freesia nodded.

Mother handed her a glass of pale orange liquid. Freesia peered at it with suspicion. "Memory blocker?"

Mother shook her head. "The rest of the students will still take them, but not you. I worked it out with Dick Levine. Though of course you're not allowed to talk about the outside world once you're there."

"What is this, then?"

"Something to relax you and induce the right hypnotic state."

The orange liquid was sweet with a slight metallic taste. Right away, she found herself feeling loose and happy—ready to meet her friendlies on Front Street and swim in the sea.

Mother said, "And remember what I told you about the emergency exit system. You ever want to leave Bright Planet, just clap your hands three times and say, 'There's no place like home.'"

"Clap hands? Why not click heels?"

"Copyright issues."

Freesia snuggled back against the recliner headrest. "I won't want to leave."

Mother checked the control panel. "All systems are ready. Are you?"

"Hm?" Freesia felt sleepy.

"Shall I launch the program?"

"Yes, please. Thank you, Mummy."

Mother paused. "You're welcome. Now, close your eyes and count to twenty. When you open them, you'll be there."

37

When a salty breeze stroked her cheeks and the clang of buoys tickled her ears, Freesia knew she was back in Agalinas, her magical Pacific Paradise off the coast of . . . somewhere. It didn't matter where Agalinas was. Or wasn't. For Freesia, it was home. A smile on her lips, she opened her eyes slowly—only to discover, with a start, that she was sitting in an unfamiliar (though comfortable) chair in an unfamiliar (though lovely) room.

"Hey, girlfriend—what's happening! Welcome to Bright Planet. I'm Imelda, and I'm gonna be your BPGC—that's island speak for Bright Planet Guidance Counselor."

Freesia sat up straight in her overstuffed easy chair and checked the surroundings. She was in a sunny room with pale wood floors and floor-to-ceiling windows that looked right at Avalon Harbor, without any hillside, street, or buildings to mar the view.

"Are we on Front Street?" she asked Imelda, an angular

girl with skin the color of milky coffee and eyes an unnatural shade of gold. Imelda sat cross-legged on a low table. She wore jeans and a fluorescent yellow T-shirt that said BPGC.

Imelda spread her arms. "Right now we're in the Taco Hut Guidance Center, conveniently located on the water side of Avalonia's main street."

"You mean Avalon," Freesia corrected.

"Avalonia is the main town on the awesome island of Agalinas," Imelda said. "Also the only town. Anyways." She unfolded her legs and pulled herself to her full height—which was rather high. "I'm here to help you put the final touches on your personalized education program. Also known as your PEP. After that, I'll show you around the island and take you to your new abode. You down with that?"

"I'm, uh . . ."

"Awesome! But first I gotta go over some island do's and don'ts. Number one: you know the Golden Rule?"

"Don't mix with silver?"

"Exactly! Do unto others like you wanna have them do to you. Or not do to you. Sound chill?"

"I guess."

"Awesome. Number two: do what you're supposed to do, be where you're supposed to be. That's, like, for demonstrations and lectures and stuff."

"Okay."

"And last—and maybe least, ha ha—curfew!"

Freesia shook her head. "I'm not familiar with that word."

"Yeah, so when the wind chimes jingle the first time, you

gotta go home, and when they jingle again, you gotta have lights out."

Imelda strode across the room and took what looked like an oversized cell phone off a shelf. "This here's your Personal Education Station—PEST for short. Ha ha!"

Freesia took the tablet. Words lit up the screen: **Welcome to your adventure!**

"Your PEST will be your e-everything," Imelda said. "Phone, computer, book, movie player, game station. And check it out! Here's a special cord so you can wear it around your neck."

Imelda slipped the PEST cord around Freesia's neck. As far as accessories went, it was far from vicious.

"I bet you're jazzed to see what the island looks like!" Imelda beamed.

"I know what the island looks like. I lived here for three and a half years. I'm not a new student. I got deleted and then I—ugh." Talking to this person, this thing, was a waste of time. "I'll be off now." Freesia headed for the door.

"Hey, that's chill. Your PEP is all spelled out on your PEST. And if you ever have any questions—"

Click. Freesia was out the door, through a waiting room, and back on Front Street. It looked just as she remembered it, except for the Taco Hut Guidance Center, which used to be a day spa. But there was the Dressy Dress Shoppe, the shoe store, the coffee shop, and—"

"Cabo!"

He was perched on a bench at the edge of Front Street

Beach, chatting with two pretty girls in bikinis. When he saw Freesia, his eyes widened and a smile spread across his deeply tanned face.

She hurried over and gave him a hug. He smelled like coconuts.

"You disappeared one day!" he said. "We thought you were gone for good!"

"You and me both."

She forced herself to smile at the bikini girls, who glared at her with something close to fury. What? Just because she'd interrupted their fizz to say hello to one of her oldest friends? ("Oldest" being a relative term in Agalinas.)

And speaking of oldest friends, until now, she'd only known Cabo to fizz with Jelissa. She didn't like the bikini girls. Not at all.

"Freesia, meet Allegra and Blu. They're new." Cabo scanned the crowded street. "We've had a lot of new people today."

"Well, yeah. That's because—" She stopped herself. She wasn't allowed to mention the outside world. Not now. Not ever.

Cabo grinned. His teeth were super white.

"Is Jelissa around?" Freesia asked.

He shrugged. "Haven't seen her today. She hasn't been herself ever since . . ."

"What?"

"Since you left." He sighed. "She never goes to parties anymore. Says it's no fun without you. Mostly she just sits in her house."

Freesia swallowed hard. Poor Jelissa! If only she could bubble her with the good news of her return.

"Maybe she'll be in her house now."

Freesia waved good-bye and headed down the street. She weaved among strolling teenagers in shorts and swimsuits until she reached the switchback road that led to Jelissa's house. By the time she arrived, her breathing was heavy, and her face felt damp.

She rapped on the door: no answer.

She circled the house and stood under Jelissa's bedroom window. "Jelly Bean!"

Still no answer. The curtains were shut. Perhaps she was asleep? "JELLY BEAN! I'm back!"

Defeated, Freesia returned to the road and walked up the hillside till she reached her own birthday cake house. It was even prettier than she remembered. The waterslide and infinity pool hadn't been restored, but she didn't care. There was her butterfly garden! There was her flagstone walkway!

She pushed open the back door. There was her kitchen! Beyond it was the living room where Daddy liked to read his newspaper, and beyond that was the breezy deck where they ate Mummy's delicious homemade suppers.

She climbed the stairs. The doors to her parents' and sister's bedrooms were closed; they must be napping. Freesia's door was closed, too. She took a deep breath and turned the knob, terrified of what she might find. But there was no reason to worry. Everything was back just the way it should be, with peacocks roaming on her balcony, Chase Bennett playing on the vicious sound system, and her wide, puffy bed piled high with fluffy pink pillows.

"Thank Todd," she sighed. She unwound the PEST from her neck and put it on her dressing table. She'd take a quick moment to bubble Jelissa, then she'd shower and change and meet her bestie for a frothy coffee or maybe a mango mocktini.

But—oh, no. Her room was not, in fact, just as it had been. The trumpet-shaped bubble charger was gone from her nightstand, and her bubble was nowhere to be seen.

"*You. Have. A. Message.*"

At the sound of the strange voice, she wheeled around. On her dressing table, her PEST flashed pink.

"No one told me it talked," she muttered, crossing to the tablet.

"*Would. You. Like. To. Speak. To . . . RICKY?*"

"Yes!" Freesia squealed.

Immediately, Ricky's face appeared on the screen. The picture quality was even worse than in Angel's video chats, but still. It was Ricky! Best of all, Ricky looked like Ricky: the blue eyes, the tousled blond hair, the killer cheekbones.

"You're here!" she said.

"I got in a couple of hours ago. Isn't it wicked to be back?"

"Better than wicked. It's magical."

"I want you to see my house. Come over, please! Take the zipline. I'll arrange for you to get a ride up from the landing."

"I will, I will! But first I must shower and change." For reasons she didn't understand, Freesia had arrived in Agalinas wearing khaki shorts and a blue polo shirt.

She said good-bye to Ricky and strode over to her closet, wondering as she did so how she'd ever manage without her bubble's attire assistance function. And then she stopped dead. Her closet still had the skylight, pink chenille couch, giant mirror, and mini fridge, but her clothes were gone. No more artfully torn jeans. No more sundresses. No more strappy sandals or filmy blouses or buttery leather handbags. Instead, her wardrobe consisted of khaki slacks, khaki shorts, a blue polo shirt identical to the one she had on, and a plain white blouse. There was a pair of bright white sneakers, a plain black book bag, and two ruffled nightgowns. That was it.

Were they testing her? Punishing her? What?

She was on the verge of feeling unsettled when she caught a glimpse of herself in the big mirror and did a double take, so surprised, after all this time, to see the beautiful lithe girl with auburn hair looking back.

Even in her borrifying clothes, she looked de-vicious.

She would take a shower. She would put on the shorts and white blouse. And then she would zip over to Ricky's house and celebrate her return.

All that really mattered was that she was back where she belonged.

38

The zipline platform stood at the end of her street, right where it had always been. She climbed up and strapped herself into a harness, looped her hook onto the line, and jumped. Below her, white boats dotted the brilliant blue harbor. The stores on Front Street shone pink and purple and yellow, while the houses in the flats were all perfectly proportioned, perfectly maintained. She laughed with the joy of it all, thrilled to the feel of the wind on her cheeks.

The zipline landed her between the beach club and the learning center. An unfamiliar serf waited with a hot-air balloon shaped like a cupcake.

"Vicious," Freesia said. "But wouldn't an itty car be easier?"

Wordlessly, the serf pointed way, way up the hill, where twin turrets sliced into the brilliant blue sky.

"Ricky's house . . . is a *castle*?"

In answer, the serf opened the door to the balloon's basket.

Up they went. And up. And up. Freesia was too excited to be nervous. If Ricky's old house had been out of a dream, his new castle was straight out of a fairy tale, the stone of the palest, glittery gray, the peaked turrets a shiny turquoise. A row of red flags fluttered in the breeze.

At last they landed next to a deep stream dripping with weeping willows. No, wait—that was a moat. (Ricky had a moat!) Freesia climbed out of the basket and crossed a stone bridge. Straight ahead, two cheetahs wearing diamond collars stood guard on either side of a vast open doorway.

The serf held out an arm, instructing her to go inside. She took a deep breath and hurried past the big cats.

Ricky was waiting inside the vast stone entryway, two glasses of happy fizz in hand. He wore red swim trunks. Muscles rippled beneath a white T-shirt. A PEST dangled from a cord around his neck.

When he saw her, he hurried over. "You're here! You're really, really here."

"Of course. I belong in Agalinas."

"We both do." He handed her a glass. They clinked and sipped.

"Your castle is magical."

"I built it with my own two hands." He held out his free hand and wiggled his fingers as if over a keyboard.

She smiled, though, really, she didn't want to be reminded of anything beyond this fairy-tale room. She tilted her glass and downed the contents in three big gulps. Immediately she felt better: relaxed, happy. She felt like herself.

"You should dress like a prince," she said. "It goes with your castle."

"If I am a prince, I will have no choice but to bestow a face-link upon my princess."

He leaned toward her. She leaned toward him. At once, she felt that warm, tingly, slightly numb feeling that always came with a face-link.

This is nothing like a kiss. The thought flashed through her mind. Without meaning to, she stepped back. That's when she caught sight of Ricky's utterly still face. If his eyes hadn't been open—too open—she'd have thought he'd fallen asleep on his feet.

"Ricky? Are you okay? *Ricky?*"

Just like that, he was alert again. He gasped. He looked scared for just a smidgy moment before forcing something like a smile. "I don't know what . . . that was. . . . I'm fine. Really."

Unbidden, she pictured pale, mountainous Ricky in his oversized bubblepod in Newport Beach, blacking out for a moment, struggling to catch his breath.

"Maybe you should take a little time to rest and reboot," Freesia said.

"Not yet. There is too much I want to show you."

He showed her a ballroom built entirely of pink marble. He showed her an indoor lazy river with a swim-up mocktini bar and tiny raised alcoves for resting. He showed her a dining room with a table big enough to seat a hundred. Behind the castle, they walked through a sunflower field to the stable, stopping at a soft unicorn with silver wings and a pink heart on its forehead.

"This one is yours," Ricky said.

"You got me my own unicorn?" Freesia held out a tentative hand, and the creature nuzzled it.

"Of course. You are my princess. All of this is for you."

If the view of Agalinas from a hot-air balloon was magical, the sight from atop a winged unicorn was mythical. Ricky, astride his own winged unicorn, pointed out some of his castle's finer features. Then they headed to the interior, where lush greenery and flocks of colorful birds gave way to wild pigs and buffalo roaming through scrubby brushes and dusty fields.

"Not very luminous," Ricky shouted over the wind.

Freesia nodded, but inside she disagreed. The harsh landscape moved her somehow. There was an unexpected, almost frightening beauty to the sharp shadows, the wild grasses, the graceless creatures.

They swooped around a hillside, and suddenly there were people below: boys mostly, though there were a few girls, all dressed in olive green and jogging in place. Someone shouted something, and they all stood at attention.

"What is that?" Freesia shouted.

"Military academy. Let's head back."

Freesia had so many things she wanted to ask Ricky, but even when they'd returned their unicorns to the stable and no longer had to shout, she found herself struggling. She didn't want to get in trouble by saying anything about the world beyond Agalinas.

Ricky saved her. "You haven't seen my suite yet."

His sitting room had wooden furniture with ornately carved feet and arms, along with a slightly creepy jester wearing a lime green tunic and a floppy triple-pointed hat. Beyond, his bed was big enough for Newport Beach Ricky (*stop thinking that way*) and surrounded by red velvet curtains. In his bath-room, a jetted spa carved out of crystal sat under a wide window with an ocean view. His closet was the size of Freesia's bedroom, with T-shirts, flip-flops, and board shorts in every imaginable color and pattern.

"I don't have any vicious clothes," Freesia sighed, fingering one of Ricky's ultra-soft tank tops.

"So buy some."

"How can I shop without my bubble?"

"You still have a bubb—I mean a Bright Planet account. You just access it through your PEST now." Ricky unlooped the tablet from Freesia's neck and tapped at the screen. "There. Let's see. You have eighty shells available. But don't worry. Once we begin our personal education programs, you'll earn more."

Freesia put the PEST back around her neck. "Eighty shells won't buy me much. I need a whole new wardrobe."

Ricky scooped up his own PEST and began tapping. "There. Now you can shop."

"What do you mean?"

"I transferred some shells—a lot of shells—into your account. You can buy anything you want."

"But, Ricky—"

"Come." He strode to the end of the closet, pushed some hanging terry-cloth robes out of the way, and pressed his hand against the wall. Cracks of light appeared, quickly tak-ing the shape of a rectangle the height of a door.

● ● ●

*R*icky's new secret room looked exactly like Ricky's old secret room. But Freesia was less concerned about interior decorating than she was about asking forbidden questions.

"Why is there a military academy in the middle of the island?"

"It was part of my father's deal with Piloski. In exchange for giving up control of the virtual school, he gets to use the platform to test war games. Only a handful of Bubble World students signed up. Taser's there, of course."

"But that's the last place he should be! He was so wiggy the last time we saw him."

"Don't worry about Taser. They changed his medications. He's fine."

"Okay, then. What's the deal with these awful tablets?" Freesia flicked her PEST in disgust. "I want my bubble back."

"PESTs are more like what people use on the mainland," Ricky said. "A Bright Planet education is designed to prepare us for the so-called real world. In case we ever go back."

"I don't ever want to go back."

"Then you never have to. Here. Let me show you how to send messages on this thing. You should tell Jelissa you're here. And tell her that she's invited to my castlewarming party—tonight after the moonrise."

A castlewarming party! Now that was something to look forward to. Freesia was so happy to have things to look forward to once again.

39

"**Y**ou're back! You're back! You're back!" Arms outstretched, Jelissa toddled across the Front Street cobblestones on hot pink platform sandals. She was retro-fabu as usual, in a white sundress with black polka dots and a wide fuchsia sash. An enormous black-and-white-striped hat shielded her pink skin from the sun.

"I am! I am! I am!" Freesia rushed toward her bestie, enveloping her in a giant hug. Her tablet jammed into her ribs. "Don't you have a PEST?"

Jelissa slipped a hand into her white patent leather purse, pulled out the PEST enough for Freesia to see, and dropped it back in. "I was going to put rhinestones on it, make it glammier, but then I realized it was better to keep it out of sight as much as possible. I'm not fond of gidgets."

"Me neither," Freesia said.

Jelissa laughed. "Here we are talking about gidgets and rhinestones like we picked up a conversation right where we left off. You can't imagine how much I missed you, Free."

"Yes I can, because I missed you just as much."

"Why did you—" Jelissa stopped. She put a hand over her mouth and shook her head. Then she took a deep breath and dropped her hand. "I told myself I wouldn't ask you. Just . . . promise you'll never leave again?"

"I promise."

"Because I couldn't bear it." She wiped away a shiny tear and smiled. "All that matters is that you're back. We're getting a new school program, did you hear?"

"I heard."

"It's okay with me as long as no one messes with our snacks. Or our bestie time. Or our parties."

"That reminds me! Ricky told me to invite you to his castle-warming party tonight."

Jelissa's eyes widened. "Ricky's back, too?"

"Of course! Who else would have a castle?" Freesia pointed to Ricky's palace on the hill.

Jelissa tilted her head to one side. "Wasn't that always there?"

"No. He just built it." Freesia felt cold all of a sudden. "It's the only castle in Avalon."

Jelissa smiled. "You mean Avalonia, of course."

Freesia opened her mouth to speak, but nothing came out.

"You'll never believe who's gone," Jelissa said.

"Who?"

"Chai!"

Freesia bit her lip. It didn't matter whether or not Chai

was gone because Chai didn't exist. But of course she couldn't say that. She shouldn't even think it. Instead, she said, "Where does that leave Dare?"

"He is link-less," Jelissa said. "In case you're feeling fizzy."

"I'm not," Freesia said. "At least not for Dare. But shopping for a frothy dress . . . that's something I could get tizzy about."

After shopping, Jelissa gave her a ride home in her itty car. Ricky was sending Freesia's unicorn to pick her up, so the two girls would meet up at the castle.

Freesia stepped inside the back door, and there they were—Mummy at the stove, Daddy reading his newspaper, Angel on the floor, playing with her ballerina dolls. At last, she was home!

"I'm making your favorite," Mummy said. "Poached salmon with steamed broccoli and tricolor quinoa. Did you know that it's important to eat foods with omega-3 acids?"

"Um . . ."

Daddy looked up from his newspaper. "I'm learning about the Republic of Malawi, a landlocked country in southeast Africa. Did you know that it was colonized by migrating tribes of Bantu around the tenth century? And that it used to be called Nyasaland?"

"Uh, no," Freesia said.

"I read it in Wikipedia, so it must be true. Tomorrow we'll talk about Zimbabwe." He went back to his paper.

"I'll be in my room," Freesia said. "Call me when dinner is ready."

Angel sprang up from the floor and did a graceful pirouette. "Don't you want to hear about my day?"

"Maybe later." Freesia headed for the stairs.

"You always do this!"

Freesia spun around. Her sister smiled.

"Do . . . what?"

"Ignore me. Take off for your room. Leave me here with *them*. I told you I can't go anywhere unless you invite me. But all you care about is yourself." She smiled. Apparently, Agalinas Angel had no other facial expression.

"Oh my Todd, Angel! It's really you."

"Duh."

"How was your day?" Freesia asked.

She crossed her arms over her narrow chest. And smiled. "I don't want to talk about it."

"Would you like to come upstairs and help me pick out my clothes?"

"No." She dropped to the floor and spun around so her virtual back was facing her virtual sister.

"Fine. Don't talk to me, Angel. *Whatever.*"

Freesia hauled her shopping bags upstairs. She spread her new clothes, shoes, jewelry, and handbags over her big bed and began putting together one de-vicious outfit after another. Immediately, she felt better.

40

In Ricky's world, there was no tricolor quinoa, no broccoli, no anything that could be classified as "good for you." Instead, a multicolored candy buffet sprawled along one wall of his entryway, while a chocolate fountain—a big one, not some flimsy tabletop thing—gurgled in the center. Serfs offered trays piled with pound cake and sugared strawberries for dipping.

At the candy buffet, Freesia helped herself to a spoonful of sour scrummies only to discover that they tasted just like Mummy's quinoa. She moved on to spicy Cinna–yums and dark chock-licks. Same thing.

All around, pretty, slender girls in bikinis fizzed with pretty, muscular boys in swim trunks. All newbies began their island adventures with only eighty shells. Real clothes would have to wait. A PEST dangled around each perfectly shaped neck like a clunky pendant. The tablets flashed and buzzed and yapped. The pretty girls and boys patted and stroked the screens like precious puppies.

"The newbies all look alike," Freesia muttered to herself. It was true. The new students came in all colors and a small range of heights, but their curves and muscles were remarkably similar, their facial features distributed just so.

"Happy fizz?"

She turned, and there was Ricky wearing, of all things, a black tuxedo with a white silk scarf.

"You look like a prince!"

"That's the idea. And you look like a princess. The shoes are wicked."

Freesia had not worn a bikini—this was a castlewarming, not a pool party—but instead had donned a just-purchased one-shouldered silver sheath with a surprisingly comfortable pair of glass slippers (which she had no intention of losing).

They toasted and drank. She felt better. Happy fizz made everything luminous. And yet . . .

"What other princely clothes do you own?"

Ricky shrugged. "Just this, I'm afraid."

A boy in flowered swim trunks slapped Ricky's back. "Chill party, bro."

"Um . . ."

"That's a good thing," Freesia said. "But—about your princely wardrobe. Will you show me what else you have? You know how I adore fashion."

Understanding crossed Ricky's face. "Ah, yes. Let me show you my closet."

● ● ●

"Why is the island so crowded now?" Freesia asked once they'd shut themselves in the secret room.

"The media coverage was good for business." Ricky sat on the comfy black couch and retrieved a hunk of cheesecake on a plate from the pull-out freezer below.

"All those people downstairs, and I didn't recognize a single friendly!"

Ricky plucked the cheesecake off the plate and took a big bite. When he'd swallowed, he said, "Our friendlies don't start the night this early. They'll be here soon."

"What happened to our bubbles? Did those guidance counselor people take them all away?"

"Oh, no. The bubbles just disappeared in the night. Poof!" Ricky smiled.

Freesia did not smile back. "And people don't mind?"

"With the right medications, no one minds or questions anything. Would you like a bite of my cheesecake?"

"No thank you."

"Happy fizz?"

"No." Freesia collapsed on the sofa next to Ricky. "Why is everyone calling our town Avalonia?"

"Someone in marketing thought it was prettier than Avalon. You'll notice the new students are prettier too. They changed the avatar templates."

"I don't think they're prettier. They all look the same."

"No one is prettier than you." Ricky stood up. "Come. Let us enjoy the night. Perhaps Jelissa has arrived."

Freesia shook her head. "She told me she'd be late. And that's another thing. Jelissa hadn't even noticed your castle, and when I pointed it out, she didn't seem surprised."

"It's the meds. They keep people from paying attention to anything that doesn't make sense."

Freesia nodded but stayed where she was on the sofa. "You go join the party. Let me just stay here a little while. Please?"

"Why?"

"Because I need a quiet place to think. And out there . . . where people in the real world could be watching—"

"*Stop.*"

Freesia blinked with surprise. She'd never heard Ricky sounding so forceful. Or at all forceful.

"We are here. We are home. Those strangers downstairs— they are just friendlies we haven't met yet."

Freesia bit her lip and nodded. "I know. You're right. Of course you are. But let me sit here for just a few minutes. Please?"

His expression softened. "You know I can't say no to you. But promise me you won't be long?"

"I promise."

● ● ●

She had no real intention of crossing beyond the secret room; she just wanted to see if she could find the door that led to the cave. It took a few tries to find the right spot on the wall, but at last cracks of light appeared in the plaster. She pushed—and almost fell backward when a wild ocean wind hit her in the chest.

Taser's cave lay ahead of her—except of course it was really Ricky's cave. Ricky wouldn't want her visiting the cave without him. But what harm would it do?

A wave crashed against the rock dock, and sea spray stung her face. She couldn't just stand there. She had to either go back into the secret room or . . .

Just like that, she found herself on the slab of slippery rock, barely registering the moment when her legs propelled her forward and made her decision seemingly without consulting her brain. She twisted her head to where the secret door should be, but behind her she saw nothing but open water. That was okay; she remembered where Ricky had stood on the dock to find the door again. She could do that too.

Near the mouth of the cave, she hesitated. Were the illuminated bats standing guard? But when the biggest wave yet crashed on the dock and the water rushed toward her, she sprinted inside.

"*Freesia?* Is that really you?"

Eyes adjusting to the darkness, Freesia followed the voice beyond the domed room and into the alcove, where she found Taser relaxing in the teardrop-shaped spa, his face glowing green from the reflected phosphorescence.

"Taser! Oh my Todd. I'd heard you'd gone to the military academy!"

He grinned. "Even soldiers need pampering now and then."

"I've been utterly worried about you. The last time I saw you here, you seemed . . . squiggy. In a destroyed-brain kind of way."

"I was having a bad day. Everyone has bad days. Come! Join me for a soak."

"I'd adore that, but I'm not exactly dressed for it." Freesia looked down and gasped when she saw that she was no longer wearing her silver dress and glass slippers but a one-piece swimsuit and sandals.

"Towels are over there." He pointed to a pile against the wall.

She took a fluffy white towel, placed it near the edge of the spa, and slipped into the silky warmth.

Taser looked so much healthier than the last time she saw him. His hair had grown in, his face was clean-shaven, and his skin was tanned, clean, and free of cuts and bruises. But it wasn't just his body that looked healthy. He seemed to exude a new self-confidence that she hoped came from somewhere other than the new mix of medications Ricky had mentioned.

She took a deep breath. "I am so glad to see you looking well, Taser. But I need to warn you about Todd Piloski. He sold most of Agalinas to Ricky's father, but he kept the interior for himself. The military academy could be dangerous."

Taser slipped under the water for a moment, then popped up with his hair newly slicked back. "Ricky's father will ruin Bubble World. I'd much rather be in Todd Piloski's school."

"But it's not really a school, Taser. The military academy is just an excuse for Piloski to develop war games."

"Piloski is a genius. I'd trust him with my life."

"Taser! Have you ever even met Piloski? Because I have. He may be clever, but he's cruel and manipulative and—"

She stopped. And stared. The boy across the spa leaned against the edge with his eyes closed and a big smile on his face.

Taser almost never smiled. But it wasn't just that. While Taser had doubts about whether or not Agalinas was real, he'd never mentioned Todd Piloski to her—because he didn't know who Todd Piloski was. The boy in the spa looked like Taser. He sounded like Taser. But he was someone else entirely.

"It's you. Isn't it." She hardly recognized her flat voice. Had Todd altered her appearance again? She examined her arms, her hands, her knees. No: she was still Freesia.

His eyes popped open. His grin grew even wider. "Francine. The last time you got kicked out of Bubble World, it was because I heard what you said in the cave. Ergo, I knew about the cave. Ergo, you should have stayed away from the cave. As your eternally charming little sister would say, *duh*."

"So you've just been holed up here, hoping I'd show up?"

"Oh, please," Todd said. "Do you not understand how this works at all? I stuck Taser's avatar in the spa and set the cave patch to alert me if there was any activity. You interrupted a really intense game of Words with Strangers. But don't let that bother you."

"I thought Taser was at your military academy."

"He is. In a new-and-improved body. You wouldn't

recognize him, he's so buff and square-jawed. Oh—and he changed his name. To Darth. I'm not even kidding."

"I'm leaving." She hauled herself out of the spa and wrapped herself in the fluffy towel. She'd gone maybe three steps when her flesh began to sting. "Argh!" She chucked the towel on the ground. Tiny red ants ran in circles on her arm. Shrieking, she flicked them off.

"Oh, I should have mentioned," Todd said. "I saw some fire ants near the pile of towels. You should be careful. They bite."

"You are evil!"

He grinned. "You're just saying that."

"Don't hurt Taser, Todd. I mean it."

"Oh, please. Taser is fine. With all the antianxiety drugs they're pumping into him, he could fall off the edge of the world and not break a sweat. Looks like you could use some of those meds yourself. Maybe Ricky has some happy juice in his secret room?"

"You know about Ricky's room?"

"Of course I know about the room. I know all. I see all. Why does that surprise you? And I'll get Bubble World back someday. Just wait."

He held up an arm and snapped his fingers. Immediately, a swarm of glowing bats swooped toward her. Freesia turned and ran.

The sea had grown even wilder, but she ran to the very edge of the slippery dock, chanting, "The bats can't hurt me because they're not real. The waves can't knock me down, because I'm in my bubblepod."

She held her hands up against the angry air, and a door appeared. She pushed, and just like that, she was back in Ricky's not-so-secret room.

● ● ●

"*There* you are!" Jelissa pushed her way through the crowd of swimsuit-clad newbies.

Freesia, still jittery, hugged her bestie and forced a smile. "You look de-vicious."

Jelissa tossed her shiny red hair, which she'd curled into perfect corkscrews. "We both do. Which is more than I can say for any of these other fashion-backward dolts."

Jelissa's dress was made of apple green silk and trimmed with crystal beads. Freesia was back in her silver sheath and glass slippers; the one-piece tank suit had disappeared along with the cave.

"Come." Jelissa grabbed her hand and tugged her through the crowd till they found Cabo, Ferdinand, and Dare on the edge of the pink marble ballroom. A Chase Bennett cover band played on a temporary stage in the middle of the vast room, but no one was dancing.

The three boys all had their heads bowed toward their PESTs. "What are they doing?" Freesia asked.

"They are transfixed by an electronic hamster game," Jelissa told her. "It is utterly un-utter."

"Got ya both!" Dare said, waving his tablet like a victory flag.

"Dash it!" Cabo and Ferdinand said at once.

The three boys looked up.

Dare said, "Freesia. Hey."

"Dare. Hey."

"Haven't seen you in a while."

"That's because . . . the thing is . . ." It didn't matter that she didn't know what to say. Dare had already started another hamster game.

"This party is borrifying," Jelissa whispered. "And don't tell Ricky, but I liked his old house better."

"Me too," Freesia said. "Though the unicorn stable is utterly magical. Do you want to see it?"

"Of course!"

Jingle, jingle, jingle.

Everyone froze.

"I think those are the wind chimes," Freesia said. "That means we have to go home."

"But it's so early!" Cabo and Ferdinand said at once, still clutching their PESTs.

Around them, newbies headed for the doors.

"We don't want to get in trouble," Dare said.

Jelissa scowled. "All I can say is that they'd better have extra-scrummy snacks in our new classes. Because so far I don't adore this new program, not one itty bit."

41

F reesia was deep in a dream about blue slushies and blooming cacti when she heard the music.

It's another day.
On the island we say, Hey,
Hey, oh. Hey, oh. Hey, oh.
Don't wanna see you frown,
Girl, turn it upside down.
Hey, oh. Yeah, turn it upside down.
Girl.
Hey.

Chase Bennett? Was maybe not as much of an artistic genius as she had once supposed. Then again, only silence would sound good this early in the morning. Six o'clock was no time to be awake.

Their song complete, Ashley and Jennifer, the peacocks, wandered back out to the balcony, hopped up on the railing, and fanned out their magnificent tails.

the sumummy appeared in the doorway holding a translucent white china cup. "It's Shanghai Moon Green Tea with hibiscus flowers and honey! Nothing like Shanghai Moon to start your day in a Zen-fully delicious way!"

"No coffee? Okay. I mean—thank you, Mummy." Freesia took the cup and yawned. "I'll have my pancakes in here, please."

"Your tofu scramble with millet toast is in the kitchen."

Freesia almost asked if she could eat something else instead, but then she realized it didn't matter. In Bright Planet, everything tasted the same.

"No dawdling," Mother said. "Your physics class starts in an hour." She turned and left the room.

"*Please. Check. Your. PEST. For. Important. Information.*" On her night table, her tablet flashed pink. She picked it up and read the screen.

Welcome to morning, FREESIA SUMMERS! Here is your PEP schedule for today.

Report to the Island Beach Club at 7 A.M. From there, you will proceed to the Rotunda for an interactive physics demonstration. Wear school uniform (navy top, khaki bottom, white sneakers) and bring a *positive attitude*!

With something less than a positive attitude, Freesia chucked the PEST back on her night table and slurped down her green tea. There was no time for a shower, so she yanked on a navy polo and khaki slacks and spent a little extra time curling her hair and applying makeup—though really, with a face and body like this, she looked de-vicious no matter what she did or didn't do.

On her way down to breakfast, she halted outside Angel's closed door. Had she ever been in that room? She couldn't remember.

She knocked. And knocked. And—

"I heard you the first time. Geez!" Angel, in a ruffled nightie, flung open the door and stalked back to a giant circular bed covered with a bright pink satin spread. She climbed up and sat cross-legged in the middle.

"I didn't think you'd be up so early," Freesia said.

Angel smiled because it was all she could do. "It's not early. It's four-thirty in the afternoon. Your time is all messed up there. You've been gone four days."

"But—"

"There's a bubblepod in my room."

Freesia scanned the space. She saw a dollhouse, a wicker basket full of Barbies, and a floor-to-ceiling mirror with a bal-let barre. "I don't see it."

"Not here," Angel said. "In my real room. In Phoenix. Duh!" She smiled.

Freesia began to shiver. "I don't understand."

"Mom and Dad say I've left them no choice. They're sending me to Bright Planet."

Freesia shook her head. "Tell them you don't want to go."

"I did! And they don't care. They say look what it's done for Francine—how happy she is. How confident. After living in both worlds, you chose the virtual one. So they think it must be better."

"It's not—" Freesia stopped herself. Even with all the changes, Agalinas was her home. She belonged here. "It's not for everyone. It's probably better if you stay at Tumble-weed."

"You need to talk to them, Francine!" A smile remained plastered on Angel's face, but it sounded like she was crying. "You don't know what you look like, lying there in your pod, mumbling and sweating and laughing at nothing. It's like having a zombie in the next room. I don't want that to happen to me!"

A strange sensation prickled along Freesia's spine. "Are you in my room now?"

"I don't like to go in there."

"But can you take your laptop over to my bubblepod? Tell me what I look like right now?"

Angel smiled. And smiled. And smiled. "Okay."

She didn't move from the bed.

"Are you there yet?" Freesia asked.

"No."

"Now?"

"Patience!"

"Sorry! I just—"

"Okay, I'm here. Right outside your pod."

331

In the fancy cake house in Avalonia, prepubescent Angel remained cross-legged on her circular bed.

"And?" Freesia asked.

"You're standing in front of your recliner. Your posture's not so good. And there's drool on your chin."

"How's my hair?"

"Flat and matted on one side, sticking up on the other."

"Oh my Todd." Freesia touched her glossy locks.

"But your hair isn't the problem," Angel said. "It's your eyes. They're so dead. You can't let that happen to me, Francine."

● ● ●

Mummy stood at the stove, spooning a white-yellow mess onto a plate.

"I need to talk to Mother," Freesia said.

"Would you like another cup of Shanghai Moon Green tea with hibiscus flowers and honey?"

"No. Thank you. I would like to talk to Mother, please. Or Father. *Now.*"

"You'd better hurry if you're going to make it to your inter-active physics demonstration on time!" Mummy placed a slice of grainy bread on the plate and put it on the table. And then she began to hum.

42

hree newbies, two girls and a boy, all dressed in navy tops and khaki bottoms, made it to the zipline before her.

At the edge of the platform, a pretty brunette peered at the drop below. "What happens at the bottom? Will I crash into something?"

Freesia piped in. "Oh, no. About halfway down, warm sea winds will rise up and slow you down. And then, at the very end, the line will angle up, and you'll eventually stop. Just put your feet down and take off your harness."

The three newbies examined her. "How long have you been on the island?"

"Three and a half years."

Their eyes widened. "You are so lucky," said the other girl, a blonde who bore a remarkable resemblance to the brunette. "This place is awesome."

"Awesome," the boy echoed.

Freesia smiled. *Everything will be okay, Angel,* she thought. *Life is better here. People are better here. You'll see.*

"How long have you been here?" she asked the blonde.

The girl blinked her jade eyes. "I have no idea."

At last, Freesia got her turn on the zipline. As always, the bottom dropped out of her stomach when she first jumped, and she laughed at the sight of the houses and the boats, all looking like toys below her. It wasn't until she had passed the town that it registered: there was a roller coaster encircling the Rotunda!

From the zipline, she hurried past the beach club bar to the pink sand, where maybe a dozen students in school uniforms sipped cappuccinos and nibbled on scones.

"Decaf," Jelissa told her, holding up her cup. "And the scones are multigrain. But they're surprisingly scrummy."

"Did you see the roller coaster?" Freesia asked.

"It's for our physics lesson!" Jelissa said. "We're going to learn about energy and speed and mass and . . . other physics-y things, and then we're going to ride the roller coaster and they'll record our speed."

"Vicious!"

"I know! It's even better than eating Korean tacos in cross-cultural immersion class."

"It's almost worth wearing these odious uniforms." Freesia plucked at her polo shirt.

Jelissa giggled. "I thought about wearing red platform stilettos with my uniform. Just to see what they'd say." The boxy cut of the blue polo shirt hid Jelissa's curves, and her khaki shorts, like Freesia's, were much too long for someone so young. They weren't supposed to wear jewelry with their uniforms, but the edge of a gold chain, hidden under Jelissa's polo shirt, glinted in the sunshine.

Freesia looped her arm in her friend's elbow and guided her closer to the water. "At least we don't have to watch the newbies parading around in bikinis," she whispered.

At the water's edge, the girls tugged off their white sneakers and walked on cold, hard sand until the sea scurried up to lick their toes.

"Is it just me," Jelissa said. "Or do the newbies all look alike?"

"It's not just you."

Something flashed in the shallow water. Freesia reached into the bubbly sea and pulled out a perfect white sand dollar.

Jelissa peered at the shell. "It's good luck if you keep it, but if you throw it back, you get to make a wish."

Freesia thought for a moment. "Now that I'm here, I've got everything I want." She slipped the white disk into her pocket.

Jelissa peered out at the horizon. When she spoke, her voice was unusually subdued. "One day when you were gone, I found a sand dollar on the beach, and I wished as hard as I could that you'd come back."

Tears glittered in Jelissa's cornflower blue eyes. Even though it wasn't her fault that she'd left, Freesia's heart ached at having caused Jelissa pain.

Freesia took the sand dollar out of her pocket and laid it on her palm. "I wish our teachers would realize that uniforms are un-utter and they'd let us wear our own clothes."

Jelissa threw back her head and laughed. Freesia chucked

the sand dollar over the water like a tiny Frisbee. It skipped three times over the surface and then disappeared into the blue.

● ● ●

Ricky didn't make it to the beach in time to hear their physics instructor, Mr. Einstein, explain something called relativity. (Not that it mattered; Freesia was maybe forty seconds into his confusing lecture before she figured out how to play the hamster game on her PEST.) But just as they were pairing off for roller coaster rides on the plaza outside the Rotunda, Ricky showed up, the last remains of a jelly doughnut in his hand.

"Ricky, you ride the roller coaster with Freesia," Jelissa suggested. "I'll cozy up next to Ferdinand."

Ricky popped the last bit of doughnut into his mouth and licked sugar off his fingers. "What about Cabo?"

Jelissa peered across the plaza, where Cabo was fizzing with three newbies. "Cabo has no taste. Where is Ferdinand, anyway? I saw him earlier."

Ricky gazed up at the twisty rails. "I've never much liked amusement park rides."

"You rode a flying unicorn yesterday," Freesia reminded him. "This isn't half as frightening."

Ricky shook his head and spoke quickly. "But I control the unicorn. And there are no sharp turns or sudden drops."

"Don't be a fraidy," Freesia said. "I'll hold your hand. Even if it is a little sticky from the doughnut."

Ricky's mouth quivered. "The last time I went on a roller coaster, I—"

He stopped speaking and froze. Just stood there on the plaza, utterly still, utterly expressionless, his eyes as big and wide and dead as sand dollars.

"Ricky? Ricky!"

"What's wrong with him?" Jelissa asked.

"I don't know. This happened the other day. I think he loses consciousness." She put her hands on his arms. "*Ricky?*"

Just like that, he was back—breathless and frightened, but back.

Freesia took both of his hands and squeezed them. She took several long breaths, wishing as she did so that she could give some of her air to Ricky. Finally, she spoke. "You have to leave."

He shook his head. "I'll sit on a bench. You two go on the ride."

"*No.* I mean you have to leave this place. You need to get out of your house, out of your room. You need to exercise. To save yourself."

"I am out of my room." He kept his voice even.

"You know what I mean. Ricky, I don't want you to leave. But I'm so afraid that if you stay, you'll—"

"The line's moving," Jelissa said. "Come on, Free. You sure you're okay, Ricky?"

"Positive."

Defeated, Freesia gave Ricky's hands a final squeeze and followed Jelissa onto the roller coaster, where they scored the first row of the second car.

"Just to warn you, roller coasters make me scream," Jelissa said.

Freesia, still worried about Ricky, forced a smile. "I'll just scream louder, then."

As if reading her mind, Jelissa said, "I've never seen Ricky look so odd. Do you think he was playing a trick on us?"

"No. I wish he were." Freesia tried to spot Ricky through the crowd, but now that she was sitting, it was impossible to see over the sea of heads.

Soon, the open car began its steep, jerking climb to the top of the Rotunda. With each moment, more of the town and harbor came into view. At the beach club, a marine biology class set off in kayaks to explore the coastline. On Front Street, a geometry class measured cobblestones. Outside one of the yellow learning center buildings, a small group of students held their arms up high and swayed from side to side. Freesia hadn't the vaguest idea what they were doing or learning, but she was pretty sure the class was more fun than a single period she'd ever spent at Tumbleweed High.

As they neared the top, Freesia's pulse quickened. Time to stop looking down. Next to her, Jelissa craned her neck to see the view, the edge of her gold chain glinting in the light.

The roller coaster made a creaking noise. Freesia's palms grew moist. "What necklace are you wearing, Jelly?" Accessories distracted Freesia like nothing else.

"What, this?" Jelissa looped a finger under the chain. "It's our bestie necklace." She pulled out the pendant. It was the right half of a heart, with two letters engraved on it: *ST*.

Just like that, Freesia forgot about the roller coaster and

how high it was going and how far and fast it would drop. "When did you get that?"

"We've had them for as long as I can remember. You know that. Oh, no—all your clothes were gone when you came back. Does that mean your bestie necklace is gone, too?"

A lead ball settled in Freesia's chest, right where her own broken heart pendant would have rested. "I still have the necklace. It's in my closet. In my house." She took a deep breath. And then she said it. "In Phoenix."

Just then, they reached the top of the roller coaster, the paradise that was Agalinas spreading out all around them. And then they dropped. Around and around, down and down they went. Jelissa held her arms up and screamed. Freesia screamed too, but not because the roller coaster frightened her.

The roller coaster wasn't real. Nothing was. Not even Jelissa.

When they reached the bottom, Jelissa saw her tearstained face.

"Oh my Todd, Free? What's wrong?" She grabbed her friend's hands. Her half-heart necklace swung from side to side like a pendulum. Like a piece of a machine.

Freesia looked at Jelissa's clear blue eyes, her curly red hair, her apple cheeks. Why hadn't she recognized her before?

"You're my Insta-friend!" Freesia's voice cracked.

"I don't know what you're talking about." Jelissa's eyes glistened. "I am your bestie. Now and always."

"Yes. Because my parents paid to have you created. To make you into the friend I wanted, the friend I'd lost."

The roller coaster car stopped, and giddy students spilled onto the plaza. Freesia pushed her way through the crowd. She had to find Ricky.

"Freesia! Wait!"

At the sound of Jelissa's distressed voice, Freesia halted. When Jelissa caught up, she was breathing hard and just barely holding back a sob. "Without you, I am nothing," she said.

"I know. That's the problem."

They found Ricky sitting on a bench, drinking something pink out of a very large cup.

"You look better!" Jelissa said, all traces of sadness gone.

"I feel better." He began to smile, but when he saw Freesia's expression, his eyes widened.

"Jelissa is not from Canada," Freesia said.

Ricky's head dropped. "I know."

"Why didn't you tell me?"

"I was afraid it would matter to you."

"It does."

Head still down, he nodded.

"I'm going home," Freesia said.

"No!" Ricky and Jelissa shouted at once.

"Come with me, Ricky. I'll visit you as much as I can. And we can video chat and text and e-mail and—"

"I hate that world." He crossed his arms over his chest.

"What world are you talking about?" Jelissa asked.

"The only one," Freesia said.

"It's odious there," Ricky said.

"In some ways, yes. But at least they have Pop-Tarts. And my sister, Angel, needs me."

"I need you more," Ricky said.

"Me too," Jelissa added.

"Ricky, you can leave this place. I know it's hard, but it's not safe to stay. You have to think of your health. Besides, Todd Piloski is still here, and he's still determined to ruin everything." She looked at the sky. "And I don't care who hears me say it!"

"I'm not leaving Agalinas ever again," Ricky said, his voice barely a whisper.

"Can I go with you?" Jelissa asked.

Freesia bit her lip. "In a way you're already there."

"So this is good-bye?" Ricky looked so lost, so hurt.

"Unless you change your mind."

"I won't," he said, and she knew he was telling the truth.

She took one last look at the diamond-sparkled blue water, the lush green hillsides, the fancy-cake houses—and her two best friends. And then she clapped her hands three times.

"There's no place like home."

43

*S*he groped around in the darkness till she found the cold metal tray, the stainless steel cup, one half-eaten nutrition bar, and another not yet touched. The recliner was still warm from her virtual roller coaster ride. It was oddly comforting, touching things and knowing what they really were, not just what they seemed to be.

She found the handle and let herself out, crossing to the bedroom doorway. The light from the hall made her eyes ache. She stood, blinking, until everything was clear.

Angel's door was closed. She pushed it open, and there it was: Angel's bubblepod. It was a bit smaller than Freesia's, also more oval than round (which made it easier to squeeze in among the bedroom furniture). But the recliner was the same, and the stainless steel table was so new and un-scratched that it shone like a mirror. (Angel's windows had not yet received their blackout treatment.)

"Francine?" Mother stood in the doorway. "I received an automated message from Bright Planet. It said you'd acti-vated the emergency exit system."

Freesia nodded.

"So it wasn't an error."

Freesia shook her head.

"Did something go wrong? Because I've been moderating the Bright Planet message boards, and parental satisfaction is measuring in the high nineties. I assumed the students were enjoying it as well."

"They are. It's just me. I don't need it anymore. And also . . ." It was hard for her to explain exactly what she was feeling. "I don't want to live in a world without Pop-Tarts."

Mother wandered into the room and put a hand on the Plexiglas wall. "Angel's bubblepod arrived yesterday. She'll be disappointed that you won't be there to greet her."

"You can't send her to Agalinas," Freesia said. "She doesn't want to go."

"She's left us no choice." Mother's voice sounded tired. "I'm too afraid of what will happen if she stays here. She snuck out a couple of nights ago, did she tell you that?"

"No."

Mother nodded. "Didn't come home till after midnight. Wouldn't tell us where she'd been. I almost called the police, I was so scared. At least if she's here"—she gave the bubble-pod an affectionate pat—"we'll always know where she is."

"I'll watch out for her," Freesia said. "At home, at school— I won't let anything happen. Father can watch her at school, too."

Mother shook her head. "Only till the end of the year. Father got a new job. Starting in June, he'll be the sheriff at Western World. It calls itself a living history museum, but it's really a theme park. Father's already started growing a handle-bar mustache and wearing cowboy boots. They'll do terrible things to his feet, I just know it."

Father had found a way to live in an earlier time after all.

"I'll watch Angel extra carefully, then. I promise. *Please*, Mother."

Mother thought for a long time and finally nodded. "We'll give it a month. If you can keep her out of trouble that long . . . then we'll give it another month."

Freesia sighed with relief. "It's a deal."

"Okay, then. I'm glad to have you back with us." Mother held out her arms.

Freesia was so shocked, she almost didn't know what to do. But when she saw the suggestion of hurt flicker in her mother's eyes, she stepped forward and accepted the embrace. It was strange. But nice. In a strange way.

"Right." Mother patted Freesia's back to signal the end of the embrace. "I need to get back to the boards, but your father and Angel should be home in an hour or so. We're out of Pop-Tarts, but there are some new cookies in the pantry. Also some chocolates, I think."

Going downstairs, Freesia held tight to the banister. Just a few days in the bubblepod had been enough to set back her coordination. The kitchen was just as stark and colorless as always, but when she opened the pantry, her mouth began to water. On the top shelf, between a stale bag of tortilla chips and an unopened box of granola bites, she uncovered the chocolates.

She couldn't keep eating this way. If she was going to stay

in the real world—and she was—she had to take better care of her body. She would ask her mother to add fruits and vegetables to her shopping list app. Maybe she and Angel could even learn to cook together.

But today, there were chocolates. She took the gold box over to the counter and opened it. A few were missing, but there were still plenty left. A brown rectangle was most likely caramel. A round one could be either marshmallow or a fruit cream.

Farther down the counter, something pink caught her eye: her cellphone. She picked it up and powered it on. To her surprise, she had a text message waiting from Adam.

I don't know if you'll ever read this. Or where you are. But I miss you.

Freesia stared at the words for a long time before punching in her response.

No reason to miss me. I've been here all along. I just didn't realize that until now.

She hit Send and placed the phone back on the counter. Then she plucked the round chocolate from the box and popped it into her mouth.

She closed her eyes and chewed.

Acknowledgments

Thanks to:

Kate Farrell, brilliant editor and reliable muse, for knowing precisely when to nudge me and when to stand back; for seeing the direction this story should take long before I did; and for always, always believing in Freesia's world.

Everyone at Holt for their enthusiasm, creativity, and attention to detail. And for this cover. I really love this cover.

Steph Rostan, the best agent I (or anyone) could hope for, and to the tremendously smart and nice team at Levine Greenberg.

Jean and Mike Lee for providing translations (as well as an ongoing education in Korean food).

My husband, Andrew, for believing in me, bringing me coffee, and forcing my books on strangers; my daughter and style icon, Lucy; and my son, Philip, who, at the age of three or so, dreamed up an island called Agalinas (which had far more explosions than mine).

My mother for sharing her love of books, laughter, and the *New York Times*; and my father, greatly missed, who appreciated a good sunset better than anyone I've ever known.